firefly

WHAT MAKES US MIGHTY

WHAT MAKES US MIGHTY

firefly

BY M. K. ENGLAND

TITAN BOOKS

Firefly: What Makes Us Mighty
Hardback edition ISBN: 9781789098358
Paperback edition ISBN: 9781789098365
E-book edition ISBN: 9781789098419

Published by Titan Books
A division of Titan Publishing Group Ltd
144 Southwark Street, London, SE1 0UP.

First paperback edition: June 2023
1 3 5 7 9 10 8 6 4 2

A CIP catalogue record for this title is available from the British Library.

Printed and bound in Great Britain by CPI Group Ltd, Croydon, CR0 4YY.

To everyone fighting their own revolution, or suffering in silence until their moment comes. You are mighty.

(And, of course, for my best Browncoats: Dave and Lisen.)

AUTHOR'S NOTE

The events of this novel take place during
the *Firefly* TV series, before the episode "Heart of Gold."

1

The atmosphere aboard *Serenity* had seldom been more tense and full of murderous intent than it was on the eve of their arrival at Kerry.

It was nothing to do with the job. Pretty straightforward, that. Pick up some sealed cargo from a black-market broker. Drop it off to some guy who calls himself a duke. Get the second half of their payment. Dust off, get back in the black with pockets looking a little more shiny. True, the duke was an Alliance type—at least, in the sense that the Alliance left him alone to play at ruling his little empire—but his money spent the same. Captain Malcolm Reynolds didn't *love* taking on any sort of work that might benefit Alliance folk, but a captain had to take jobs as they came, even when it meant rubbing elbows with those friendly to the enemy (still the enemy, *always* the enemy). They weren't working directly *for* the Alliance, and they were staying far away from the Core, so there was a line there.

Somewhere.

A line that moved depending on how empty the crew's bellies were and how many parts were currently falling off the ship.

So thankfully, no, there was no problem with the imminent

delivery of their cargo. There was, however, a murder about to be committed. A murder between crew members. Fratricide, one could call it, considering how cozy and family-like the crew had become, and with all the associated complexities and irritations.

Unsurprisingly, Jayne Cobb was the would-be perpetrator of violence upon Simon Tam's delicate personage.

"You rotten, no good *hún dàn*!" he shouted across the dining table, his face turning an alarming shade of vermilion. "I oughta strangle the life outta you with that fancy little tie of yours."

Simon Tam's eyes went wide, immediately flicking over to Mal and Zoë as if to ask, "Are you going to protect me from this madman?" Help was decidedly not coming from either corner, considering the amusement both seemed to be enjoying at Simon's expense. As much as they appreciated having a brilliant doctor around, they equally appreciated witnessing his delicate, well-bred feathers ruffled at every opportunity. Their smirks told Simon he was most definitely on his own in the ongoing war against Jayne's itchy trigger finger. He looked to Shepherd Book for one last plea, and the good Shepherd took pity, as his kind was wont to do.

"Now, Jayne—" he began in his soothing diplomatic voice, but Jayne cut him off.

"Don't you start with me, preacher man. I ain't feeling so holy at the moment."

Book held up his hands and shrugged at Simon, returning his gaze to his cards.

"Come on, Jayne," Kaylee said, ever the peacemaker. "It's a game. You're supposed to try to win. Simon's just playing by the rules. Ain't his fault he's smarter'n all of us."

She beamed at Simon, who lit up with a half-dazed grin under her attention, then promptly looked away with flushed cheeks.

"Hey, now, I take umbrage at that claim," Wash said, sliding his game piece six spaces forward, overtaking both Simon and Jayne in one move. He looked to his wife and waggled his eyebrows. "Your husband is not only a master pilot, but a veritable king of strategy and deception."

"Wiley as a fox, my man is," Zoë deadpanned. She played a series of cards on the table in front of her, pointedly ignored the sputters of disbelief as she sailed past all three of them to win the game, then served up a cool smile.

And that was the last straw for Jayne.

"You got straight-up swindled, Kaylee. This ruttin' game is broken. Waste of our gorram hard-earned credits!" Jayne said, scooping up his game piece and chucking it across the galley. It bounced off the long-serving counter with an anemic sort of ping, then tinkled gently to the ground somewhere behind it. Jayne, not satisfied that his ire had been sufficiently expressed, pushed back from the dining table and stood, his pistol already half drawn.

"No discharging of firearms on my boat 'less there's a life in danger," Mal said from his vantage point in the doorway to the forward hall. "Leastaways not while we're underway."

"Oh, there's a life in danger, all right," Jayne groused, but holstered his weapon all the same.

Good thing, too. As much as Mal would freely admit he enjoyed flexing his captainly authority at times, it could, on occasion, be a mite alienating to the rest of the crew. Being as they were about to put down and deliver to a brand-new client who paid well and had the potential to bring in future coin, Mal was of a mind to keep things light and easy aboard *Serenity*. Make a good first impression on the "duke" and his people.

Seemed the others hadn't quite had their fill of teasing Jayne, though.

"I dunno, Jayne," Kaylee said, leaning back in her chair and beaming cheerfully over at the now victorious Zoë. "I sorta feel like I'm getting my money's worth of entertainment from our new game."

"Did you know Kaylee was a secret psychopath?" Jayne asked, looking around to the others at the table. "Honestly, I'm not that surprised. Always was too cheerful by half. Ain't natural. There's a darkness lurking beneath, you mark me."

Kaylee rolled her eyes. "It was the only nine-player game that merchant on Dyton had and I wanted something we could all play together! Course, River's having an off day, which is *fine*—"

"Meaning she's talking to herself in her bunk," Jayne muttered. "Least she's stopped shrieking for the time being."

"*And*," Kaylee continued, glaring, "Inara and the cap'n ain't playing—"

"'Cause Mommy and Daddy got more important things to do than play your silly little games," Wash said in a terrible impression of Mal's Shadow-born drawl.

"'Cause Inara's busy preparing for her next client, and the captain is a boring old stick-in-the-mud," Kaylee corrected him as she rose from the table, swinging past Mal's position to drop a no-hard-feelings kiss on his cheek on her way to get a drink.

Mal shrugged. "Someone on this boat ought to have a sensible head on their shoulders."

"Damn shame it didn't work out that way, sir," Zoë said, collecting all the game pieces and returning them to the box. The others stood and helped pack away the game, snickering. All except Jayne, who grumbled and went in search of a snack instead.

Inara swept into the room from the direction of her shuttle, dressed in her finest. She'd foregone her usual palette of warm reds for a stunning jewel-tone blue sleeveless gown accented with gold lacework around the neckline and bodice. A golden sash was cinched around her waist, providing completely unnecessary accentuation to her figure. A sapphire sparkled at the hollow of her throat, and thin bangles tinkled musically on her wrists. She was a vision, as always, and Mal's mouth went dry at the sight of her, his heart pounding so loud he thought the whole crew might hear.

He wished she were dressed so lovely for *him*. Hell, she didn't even need to get all fancied up. She was lovely no matter what she wore. It was the deep brown of her intelligent eyes, the wry humor in the curve of her lips, the sharp wit and serene nature that filled up every room she inhabited right to the brim. Mal had spent time enough looking at his feelings for her from the corner of his eye, keeping a careful watch but never approaching, never *really* acknowledging outright. And yet, they were there, and they reared up in the worst possible ways and times.

Like jealousy.

Like now.

"Well, well," his mouth said without input from his brain. "Aren't you lookin' mighty shined up! I'm sure this client of yours will count you worth every one of his pennies. Which lucky gentleman has engaged your services this time?"

Inara blinked in that sweet "I'd love to stab you" sort of way and smiled. "The duke's top general. She is a formidable woman of learning and refined tastes, well respected by her troops. I look forward to spending the next few days with her."

Kaylee, starry-eyed as always at the glamorous life of a Companion, hopped onto the edge of the table and kicked her feet. "What were you doing to get ready to meet with her? Just finding the right clothes that'll be to her liking, or…?"

Inara's knife-edged lips softened as she turned from Mal to Kaylee. "I prefer to meditate before meeting with a new client whenever possible, to align my energy with theirs and consider their needs."

"I got needs," Jayne interjected with a smirk.

Kaylee and Inara's faces fell into disgusted scowls.

"Gross," Inara said simply.

"Yeah, no one wants to hear about your *needs*," Kaylee added.

A tone sounded, indicating *Serenity*'s proximity to their destination and drawing everyone's attention.

"Ah, my mistress calls," Wash said, then glanced at Zoë, anticipating a reprimand.

"Oh, please, by all means," she said, gesturing for him to go. "Attend to your other woman."

Wash pressed a kiss to her cheek. "Thank you for not killing me."

"I've got other uses for you yet," she replied.

Wash stepped away from the table and squeezed past Mal to head to the bridge and take manual control of *Serenity*. Mal turned to Kaylee, who was quietly scooting closer to Simon as they sorted cards into the game box together.

"Kaylee, do us all a favor and keep an eye out in the engine room as we're making our approach. Make sure that pressure regulator don't go exploding on us during our descent, *dǒng ma*?"

"I can stare at it all you like, Cap'n, but it ain't gonna stop it from explodin' if it really wants to," Kaylee said, handing her stack of cards to Simon. "Darn thing's held together with spit 'n' prayers at this point."

She pressed her lips together and glanced back at Simon, cheeks glowing. "I mean, not that it's *my* spit holding it together. Won't catch me spitting. I more just—"

"Shiny. Hop to it," Mal said, just as much to save Kaylee from herself as it was to save his own ears from her fluster. She snapped her mouth shut and scurried off in the direction of the engine room, pulling the strap of her coveralls back over her shoulder where she'd let it slip down. That done, Mal turned back to Inara and forced a smile.

"Well then," he said. "Let's get ready to meet His Grace and marvel at his very fine robes."

Inara rolled her eyes and returned to her shuttle to prepare for landing. Mal watched her go, studying the way the light shifted and slid over the midnight black of her curls. Mesmerizing, it was. He shook himself, casting a quick glance to see if anyone had noticed; Zoë had, of course, but held her tongue as always. Never a better first mate in all the 'verse.

"Hurry it up, folks, and get yourselves strapped for landing," Mal said, turning to head to the bridge. "We got ourselves some pockets in need of filling.

2

The planet Kerry filled half of *Serenity*'s forward viewport, a yellow-orange ball of rock with vast continents and relatively small glittering golden oceans. On the bridge, Mal had taken up his post behind Wash as they made their approach, angling for the largest landmass in the northern hemisphere. Wash's toy dinosaurs sat atop his console, silhouetted against the planet like a reptilian procession marching through the desert.

"You been here before?" Mal asked Wash, moving to take his seat in the captain's chair.

Wash hummed an uncertain sound. "Eh, once or twice, long time ago. Ain't done much on the planet itself. Did a few drops on Madcap, Kerry's moon, back when I was a runner for PonyMacro."

"Don't look like much."

"Not the loveliest hunk of dust in the 'verse, I'll give you that. Orange skies, if I remember. Kinda creepy, some quirk of the atmosphere and the spectrum of their sunlight. But they got a whole mess of people living there, so must be some kind of redeeming qualities."

"All the same, maybe we best keep our time on the surface short," Mal said, leaning back in his chair as Zoë walked onto the bridge. "Everyone secure?"

"Yes, sir," she answered. "Ain't we sticking around until Inara's appointment is up? Thought she said three days."

"Three days it is. Don't mean we gotta sit around in a dustbowl the whole time, though. Seems a mite cozier up here in orbit." He gazed out at the planet, growing ever closer and filling more of the viewport. "Orange skies. T'ain't natural. Makes you wonder if something went wrong with the terraforming, only no one wants to say."

"Planets look all kinda ways round the 'verse. Don't necessarily mean they're duds," Zoë said.

"Don't necessarily mean they ain't, either," Mal said. "We'll see what we see when we make landfall. Could be it's pretty as a peach down there and I'll happily eat my own words and enjoy their hospitality. But, knowing our luck, I'm gonna guess we'll be bunking down spaceside tonight."

"I do so love your cheerful outlook on life, Captain," Wash said, leaning back to exchange an amused glance with Zoë. Mal pretended not to notice, instead pulling up information on the world they were about to visit. He'd done his basic due diligence already, but a deeper look never hurt.

Kerry was a Border planet in the Georgia system, fourth planet out from the yellow sun Huang Long. Many of the pivotal moments in Mal's life had taken place in the Georgia system, though under the light of its other star, Murphy: his birth on the now uninhabitable ghost planet of Shadow, and the crushing defeat at Serenity Valley on Hera that broke his faith and changed the course of his life, among other things.

He'd never had cause to visit Kerry, though, and no jobs had taken *Serenity* there. It had about the same population as its neighbor Boros, but spread out over a planet that was half the size, dry as a bone, and—its best feature—much less heavily patrolled by the Alliance.

What it lacked in actual feds monitoring the grounds and skies it made up for in self-styled nobility sucking up to the Alliance from afar. The world's four continents were overseen by four people who, at some point in the planet's almost two-hundred-year history, had decided to call themselves dukes and duchesses. The whole practice got under Mal's skin. Didn't sit right, people giving themselves fancy titles just to parade around acting better than everyone else. But he had done business with such folks before, and recently at that. The job for Sir Warwick Harrow on Persephone would not be one he'd forget anytime soon, most especially because they had yet to get the smell of cattle dung fully gone from *Serenity*'s cargo hold despite months of deep cleaning. Also, the stabbing bit that had preceded the cattle deal. Quite memorable. Harrow himself had come through for Mal, fancy title and sash aside. Business was business, even if some folks seemed to speak a different language about it.

The ground whizzed by beneath *Serenity*'s belly as Wash guided her in, giving them an opportunity to get a better look at the world. It was beautiful, in a way. Sure, the orange skies were creepy, but the world was also home to wide open fields of yellow-gold grasses grazed on by beasts of all sorts. Five hundred and fifty million people seemed like a lot, but when you spread them out across large landmasses instead of huddling them together in cities, it became quickly apparent just how many acres could be between folk. Some of the other continents had parts approaching city-like, but this duke apparently preferred to keep his holding rural. Sure, there were some small clusters, villages and the like, but by and large the people of the main continent, Killarney, needed a mighty fine set of binocs to see their neighbors.

But then, there were the duke's grounds. They were visible from kilometers away, a bright point even within the golden countryside. White-walled buildings dotted the landscape, a few particularly tall ones towering over the rest, all ringed by the thin meandering line of a white wall. The grid pattern of crop fields was visible on the north side of the compound, right near what looked like a brand-new water tower. The closer they got, the more detail came into focus: fountains, pools, gardens, sculptures, sporting fields, a horse track, and so much more. *Serenity* flew low and slow over the long wall surrounding the duke's personal holdings, directed by beacon toward a private landing pad ringed by blinking guide lights.

"Whoa," Wash breathed, never once faltering in his control of the ship even as his eyes boggled at the sights before them.

"Yeah," Mal agreed.

Zoë laid a hand on Wash's shoulder and squeezed.

"Thinkin' you might wanna reconsider shore leave plans, sir. I'm gonna need my husband to bring me a very nice whiskey at that fancy pool over there."

Wash looked up from his piloting duties just long enough to cast an adoring look at his wife.

"Will you be wearing a skimpy bathing suit in this scenario? I'll buy you one. I would *love* to buy you one."

"Depends. Can I buy you a skimpy bathing suit too?"

"I vote no," Mal cut in. "Do I get a say in this?"

"No," Wash and Zoë said in perfect unison.

Mal shrugged and studied the view over the console in an effort to rid himself of the mental image of Hoban Washburne in a skimpy bathing suit. Zoë was right to be impressed; the duke's grounds brimmed with luxury, but an understated sort. Not overwrought, or overly gilded, but simply fine in quality and amenities. The buildings were constructed from small bricks of a polished white stone that reflected the sunlight in a way that made each one glow against the backdrop of the orange skies. They'd flown over an old abandoned quarry on their way down, and Mal would bet that was where it had all come from.

The largest building, likely the duke's personal residence and place of business, towered over the rest, but not ridiculously so. Other smaller but no less finely constructed buildings were connected to the main structure by well-maintained paths made from a different type of stone, one with veins of pink, orange, and gray woven throughout. The buildings had no external identifiers, but Mal could figure out a few from context: a barracks for the duke's defense forces, a garage and maintenance shop, a hospital, and a stable Mal would bet was full of very expensive horses. Everything in the compound spoke of high maintenance standards and a great deal of care.

As Mal and Zoë disembarked to coordinate their arrival and transfer of cargo, Mal had to admit that the people seemed happy, too. They'd never gone a day without a shower in fresh water or a set of clean clothes, by all appearances, which was certainly not something Mal could say for himself. Beyond that, though, the men who came to receive them seemed in genuine good spirits. They wore big grins, and jostled each other and joked as they approached. More than anything, Mal noted the lack of stress around the eyes, that pinched, slightly wary look that most on the Border worlds (and especially on the Rim) wore even in the best of times. Existence in the 'verse was hard for all but the very rich and the very Alliance. These people, though, seemed… happy.

"Captain Malcolm Reynolds, I presume! Welcome to the Kenmare estate," the foreman boomed as the ground crew neared.

"Sure 'nuff," Mal said, then gestured to his right. "And my first mate, Zoë Washburne. Pleased to make your acquaintance, Mr.…?"

"Barnhart," the man said, extending a hand to Mal and Zoë each in succession. "But most round here just call me Chief."

Mal pasted a congenial smile on his face. Easy going so far. No warning bells from his gut. Could be the job would actually go off as intended, hitch-free and profit-full.

"Well, Chief, I've got a hold full of sealed mystery crates for Duke Farranfore here. I assume you know there wheres and whats for 'em?"

"Surely do, Captain Reynolds. If you'll permit my men aboard, we'll have them out of your way in a jiff," Chief said.

"By all means," Mal agreed. "Though there is the matter of the second half of our payment. We'll be out of your hair quick and easy once all's said and done."

"Well, now, don't be scattering before you have a chance to enjoy our fair home! The money guy up at the duke's place has your payment," he said, pointing a thumb over his shoulder in the direction of the palace. "I can have one of my guys escort you there. It's only about a ten-minute walk. His Grace has also invited your entire crew to an audience with him. He always rolls out the best food and drink for his guests, so if I were you, I'd go for it."

Mal had a brief flashback to getting stabbed at Atherton Wing's estate after the shindig on Persephone and winced. Kenmare had an altogether different feel to it, but that didn't mean Mal wanted to get quite that cozy. He exchanged a look with Zoë, who shrugged as if to say, "Do we have a choice?"

Mal sighed. An audience with a fancible noble type didn't exactly sound like his idea of a good time, but he supposed he could manage to bite his tongue long enough to make nice with the man. Wouldn't do to burn a new bridge that might bring them more work in the future. Besides, Zoë and Wash seemed to have their hearts set on a little R&R planetside, and while Mal's feet got itchy standing on solid ground too long, he had to acknowledge that not all of his crew shared his affliction to quite the same degree. They were owed some shore leave, and he needed to provide if he could. The audience would be a good test, and if Mal smelled anything rotten, then they'd grab some space and wait out their three days in orbit.

Decision made, Mal hooked his thumbs in his gun belt and nodded. "We'll accept. There are nine of us total, though our resident Companion has taken a client and may already be gone by then."

"On the contrary," Inara's voice said from behind him, "I've just spoken to my client and I've arranged to meet with her at the audience. I would be delighted to join you all. Please thank His Grace for the invitation."

She swept down the ramp and paused at Mal's side, giving a courteous greeting to Chief and his crew. Chief, momentarily struck silent at the sheer *presence* Inara exuded, could only nod and gesture to one of his crew to deliver the message.

"Well then," he said once he recovered. "Let's get to work, shall we?"

3

Kaylee was mighty glad for the opportunity she'd had on Persephone, rubbing elbows with the rich and fancy. It prepared her at least somewhat for the experience of entering the duke's palace. There were no floating chandeliers or cheese fondue, but there were plenty of hints as to the duke's wealth just the same. Delicate paper scrolls with hand-painted artwork, plush woven rugs, vast floor-to-ceiling windows, and artfully arranged fresh flowers all spoke to incredible amounts of spare platinum, and all without a scrap of overused precious metals or cluttered possessions.

The people, too, exuded the same sort of refined, moneyed air. Servants were simply and cleanly dressed, and the hum of guests and their conversations filled every room and hall. The duke played host to a constant stream of local nobility, it seemed, which made Kaylee all the more curious that he'd give his time to a crew like *Serenity*'s. It wasn't exactly their kinda scene.

It was nice all the same, though, being off the ship in a new place. Kaylee often ended up staying aboard *Serenity* when they made landfall, using the time to tune her up and conduct necessary maintenance. She loved going into town whenever her duties allowed, though, and this place had much more offer than a brothel for Jayne and a bar for Mal to pick a fight in.

All in all, she was grateful she'd taken the time to wash her face, change into some clean coveralls, and throw her cerulean blue cropped jacket over the top. It wasn't quite the same level of armor as her frilly pink and white ball gown would have been, but that dress hadn't done squat when it came to the noble ladies of Persephone. There was no reason to believe the people here would treat her any differently. Besides, it was more about how the dress made Kaylee feel, and *that* she could summon up from within herself perfectly fine without it.

Simon, on the other hand, seemed to fit right into this place, even dressed down as he was in an attempt to blend in more with the crew. Her heart ached at the thought; it only emphasized how different they were, how he belonged to a different world than she did. Sometimes things between them seemed *so close*, like they were right on the edge of something new… and other times, like now, the gulf seemed so vast that it'd never be crossed in a million years.

Then he looked up, caught her eye, and smiled.

Well, maybe not a *million* years.

Her cheeks flushed, she looked away as they reached a set of large double doors, and those at the head of the group paused. A brief conversation, and the doors parted before them, revealing a vast throne room. Well-dressed people were clustered around the room: men enjoying drinks and boisterous conversation at a long, polished wooden table; ladies in long-sleeved dresses gathered at easels around a magnificent picture window, applying paint to canvases in delicate strokes while they sipped wine and chatted in low voices; a troupe of dancers performing an intricate, flowing routine for seemingly no audience; and even more besides. Mal and Zoë led the way toward the front, where an ornate throne sat upon a low dais, plush and purple-cushioned and exuding power.

It was also empty.

Her eyes were drawn to a handsome, pale-skinned man in a fine black suit who sat on the step at the edge of the dais, his head bent in conversation with what looked like a gardener or groundskeeper, nodding as the man spoke to him in a low voice. They exchanged a few more words, then the two men stood and shook hands. The handsome man—the duke, Kaylee now realized—turned to receive their group, and a big grin broke out on his face.

"Captain Reynolds and crew, I presume!" the duke said with his arms spread wide. His voice was broad and friendly with only a tinge of the formal accent common on the core worlds. "Welcome to my ridiculous home! It's a bit much, isn't it?"

"It's a fine place," Mal said without skipping a beat, exercising some of the self-control that often seemed to escape him when faced with nobles and the like. Kaylee was impressed. He even managed to not sound sarcastic.

"We appreciate your hospitality and the work, Your Grace," Zoë added, which Mal *should* have said but probably couldn't bring himself to. Zoë hated the Alliance and the people who paid into their system just as much or more than Mal, but she also didn't have quite his same level of stubborn pride.

The duke flicked a glance over to Zoë, then looked right back to Mal. "Captain Reynolds, will you introduce me to your crew, please? I must admit, I have something of a pent-up wanderlust and often daydream of what it would be like to sail among the stars."

Mal, taken aback, took a second to collect himself, and Kaylee thought she knew why. Normally these noble types didn't care much for the average grunts like themselves. She felt a little thrill—this powerful man was going to hear her name and notice her. She shouldn't care about the approval or regard of a person like him, but she couldn't help it; there was something so glamorous about the kind of life people like him led.

"Well, uh, yes, of course. Uh, Your Grace," Mal stumbled, then reasserted himself. "Well, this is Zoë Washburne, first mate. Hoban Washburne, pilot."

"Ah, the pilot," the duke interjected. "It must be pure magic to fly a ship through the black from planet to planet. You must be quite a pilot to have such an important responsibility entrusted to you by your captain."

"Thank you, Your Grace," Wash said, managing to sound both stiff and sarcastic at the same time.

"Oh, please, drop that 'Your Grace' stuff, all of you. My grandfather was the one who decided we should all be called 'Duke Farranfore of Killarney' and it's honestly ridiculous. I keep it only because of tradition, and because the other minor nobles here cling so desperately to their ranks. No offense, you lot!"

The other assembled nobles laughed good-naturedly and raised their drinks in salute. The duke waved in acknowledgment.

"Please, just call me Tarmon. Now, on with the rest! Who are these fine people?"

Mal cleared his throat and gestured down the line. "Jayne Cobb, public relations."

The duke barked a laugh. "That's certainly one term for it. I know a security man when I see one. Certain you know your way around a weapon or two."

Jayne opened his mouth to reply, but Mal wisely cut in before anything horrific could emerge. "He's mighty useful in his way. Next up, Inara Serra, registered Companion and our unofficial ambassador. Kaywinnet Lee Frye, ship's mechanic."

Kaylee put on her best smile, expecting some kind of brief acknowledgment. But the duke's eyes passed right over her, on down the line, and she deflated.

"This here is Doctor Scott, our shipboard medic," Mal continued, "and his cousin and apprentice, Ocean."

Anyone who didn't know the captain would probably never notice the slight pause in his voice as he struggled to come up with an alias for River. Kaylee heard it, though, and it took quite some willpower to keep her snicker at bay.

"A bona fide doctor on board a shipping vessel! You must get in scrapes fairly often to warrant such a qualified crew member," the duke said, raising his eyebrows at Simon.

Simon, flustered as ever when there was dishonesty afoot, opened and closed his mouth twice before he managed to speak. "Well, I… like to travel. Wanted to see… unusual places. I'm fortunate to not have too much urgent care required of me aboard."

Well, at least he recovered by the end.

The duke laughed again, jolly as ever. "Too right, my boy, too right. And finally?"

"And finally," Mal said, with some reluctance, "Shepherd Book."

"Fascinating," the duke said, moving to shake the

Shepherd's hand. "Truly fascinating to see a preacher traveling with a crew such as this. You all must be a godly bunch!"

Mal's self-control had apparently reached the beginnings of his limit, because he couldn't help but snort. Kaylee shot him a dirty look, but Book recovered with grace, as always.

"The Lord's creation is vast and strange, and I've taken it upon myself to see as much as I can, bringing the Word to thems that's receptive along the way."

The duke's expression softened a bit. "Ah, quite diplomatic wording there, Shepherd. Well, let me assure you, you are most welcome here among my court, and you'll find many eager for a fresh perspective on the word of God. Our own Pastor Michael is a sweet man, but some here are a bit… well. I don't want to be unkind. He's been our pastor for nigh-on forty years and he's like family."

Kaylee's lips twisted in amusement, but she held her tongue. Her preacher back home in Tankerton had been an old fossil like that. Some elders were wise and gentle, guiding the younger generations with care and generosity of spirit. Others were cantankerous and bitter, determined to use the rough nature of life on the Border worlds as an excuse to enforce their more puritanical views. The New Virginia province on Kowlonshi was not as rough and resource poor as some parts, especially in a coastal city like Tankerton, but the church her mother's family had been attending for generations was one of the more conservative ones that would have preferred to see Kaylee in a dress instead of coveralls. Reading between the lines, she could imagine they might have a similar situation here.

"A fresh perspective," Book said with a kind smile. "I'd love to meet with your pastor. If he's amenable, then perhaps I'll see about giving a guest sermon during our stay in orbit."

"In orbit?" The duke looked taken aback for a moment, then shook his head with a laugh. "Oh, no, no, no, please, Captain Reynolds, you and your crew *must* avail yourselves of my hospitality, I insist! How long will you be staying?"

Mal waved a hand to Inara, who performed a half curtsy.

"A client has engaged our resident Companion's services for the next three days, so we'll be in the area for at least that long. If you don't mind us taking up your berthing, we can certainly keep *Serenity* parked and stay groundside. Are there lodgings available?"

"Of course, Captain, you and your crew must stay and enjoy my guest house. There is a whole wing free at the moment, as the Viscount of Shoreward and his family have just departed. Free of charge, of course, and your food and drink will likewise be provided when you dine there. Though, of course, I would encourage you to spend some of the credits I'm paying you back into our coffers and support some of the fine businesses within our walls," he said with a laugh. He waved over a stiffly dressed staffer, who appeared with a pouch of platinum. Mal took it and pocketed it smoothly, playing it cool, as if they hadn't already spent through the first half of the payment just keeping the boat in the air.

The duke held out his hand for Mal to shake once more, patting their clasped hands with his free one. "You are my personal guests. Please, enjoy! Speak with my friends gathered here. Explore the grounds at your leisure. And perhaps we can discuss more work for *Serenity* if something should come up in the meantime."

The duke gestured to a servant, a girl in a plain dress who had been so perfectly still in the corner Kaylee hadn't noticed her. The girl scurried out of the room so quickly and quietly it was like she'd never been there. Presumably she was off to make arrangements for the very fancy stay they were about to have.

Kaylee felt a little thrill of excitement. It wasn't often—or ever, really—that the crew of *Serenity* got to enjoy a little luxury. Her gaze drifted over to the men sipping drinks at the table, then over to the ladies painting before the window. At the shindig on Persephone, she'd eventually found her stride talking vehicle engines with a group of gentlemen who had hung on her every word. It had felt awful nice, being the center of their attention and having the chance to show off her knowledge. But it wasn't what she craved. She got to be an expert mechanic all day, every day. It was only when she spent quiet time hanging out with Inara that she could really embrace the parts of her that loved traditionally feminine things.

With that thought in her head, she set her sights on the painting ladies and their fine dresses. If they didn't welcome her, then oh well. Kaylee knew her own worth. She wouldn't let it get her down.

4

Zoë pursed her lips, watching the servant girl scurry out of the throne room to tend to their lodging arrangements. Things were going a little *too* smooth, and that didn't hold with tradition. Was it just that which had her on edge, or had they missed something?

The duke had turned to receive a staff member with a question, signaling the end of their meeting, so the group immediately converged around Mal, excited as a litter of pups.

"We free to go, then, Cap'n?" Kaylee asked.

Mal withdrew the pouch of platinum from the pocket of his duster and hefted it. "I imagine you'll be wanting your share of the haul first, yes? Let's find ourselves a table where we can sit and do this like civilized folk."

Mal led the group away from the dais and toward an empty table at the back of the room where they could divvy up their funds out of sight of their employer. Zoë lowered herself into a chair next to Mal, and most of the rest of the crew filled in the rest of the seats. Jayne elbowed in next to Zoë without bothering to sit, his hand held out and fingers crooked.

"Make it snappy, Mal, there's free drink flowing and I'm getting me a pour."

"Now, hold your horses there, Jayne. That drink ain't goin' nowhere. You'll get your fair share."

The double doors at the back of the room creaked open as Mal counted out the currency, and everyone turned to look as a butler announced the new arrivals:

"Her Grace Jīn Mèngyáo the Duchess of Killarney, and General Li Xiùyīng!"

Two women walked in side by side, arms linked at the elbow and deep in conversation, seemingly oblivious to the attention suddenly directed their way. Oblivious, or simply above it, perhaps. It was clear which woman was which simply by dress and manner. The duchess wore the finest gown of all the ladies they'd seen so far. The rich purple silk of her dress flowed down her body, the light slipping over it like the calm waters of a spring creek. Metallic gold edging around the neckline and sleeves contrasted beautifully with the medium olive tone of her skin. Her black hair was swept up in an intricate braided bun that left her elegant neck bare but for a simple gold necklace. She practically glided across the floor, her every motion careful and poised.

The general, on the other hand, wore a crisp military uniform in slate gray, though her black hair was twisted in a similar braided bun style. Her olive skin was a shade or two lighter than the duchess's, and her epaulets and the rank insignia over her left breast matched the duchess's gold accents. She had permitted herself a single personal embellishment: a plain purple braided cord around her wrist, revealed only when the bend of her arm pulled the sleeve of her uniform jacket up by an inch. She was solidly built, beautiful and commanding, and Zoë recognized a kindred spirit in her. A warrior who moved with purpose and coiled power.

As they approached the front, the duke turned to them and held out his arms to his wife. The duchess released the general's arm and went to him, pressing a kiss to his cheek.

"Mèngyáo," he said, squeezing her hands and escorting her and the general over to their table. "This is Captain Reynolds and his crew. They've just brought us another delivery. I've invited them to stay with us for a few days."

Mèngyáo turned and gave them a lukewarm smile. Her deep brown eyes darted appraisingly over each one of them, sharp and intelligent, taking in the details. She lingered on their weapons for a moment, then turned back to her husband.

"Sounds like fun. Shall we arrange a welcome dinner tonight?"

The duke beamed at his wife. "A splendid idea. You're the best hostess on Kerry, my love."

He turned to the crew, one hand at the small of his wife's back. "You'll join us, I hope?"

"We'll be there," Mal said, casting a quick glance around the group to convey that it was, in fact, required attendance and they *would* all be there. Zoë imagined he was seeing an opportunity to cozy up to the duke and get more work. If they could have their hold full when they left Kerry, it would save the extra step of having to head back to one of their familiar ports and ask around for leads on a job.

And yet… something had the hairs at the back of Zoë's neck prickling. Nothing she could put her finger on, but her gut was setting off alarm bells.

The duke and duchess walked away side by side, heads bent in conversation, apparently dismissing them. A soldier had approached the general and saluted, clearly checking in with a question. The general listened attentively as her man spoke, then gave brief instructions and a dismissal. The soldier saluted once more and rushed off with a look of purpose and confidence. Zoë knew the bearing of a good leader, one whose people respected them and followed them gladly. The general clearly was such a leader, and it gave Zoë a slight bit of ease to know it.

With her escorting duties apparently done and no further surprise reports, the general turned toward the assembled crew of *Serenity*. Her eyes locked onto Inara, whose face bloomed with a smile.

"General Li. Such a pleasure to finally meet you in person."

She strode forward and took the general's outstretched hand in both of hers, performing a perfect curtsey over it. The general, despite her solidly professional exterior, seemed almost flustered by Inara's greeting. Her cheeks were lightly flushed when she returned the gesture.

"Please, just call me Xiùyīng. It's an honor to have you here."

When the general seemed lost for further words, Inara swooped in with all her genuine kindness and social grace.

"Are you available to give me a tour of the grounds? I would love to see some more of the palace before I set up for our welcoming tea ceremony."

"Oh, of course, yes! Please, right this way. I'll need to check in with some of my people before I go on leave for the weekend, but I'd be delighted to have you accompany me," the general said, offering her arm. Inara took it and nodded to

Mal and the others as she was escorted away from their table. The general received the salutes of her troops on the way out, talking quietly with Inara as she went.

Mal's jaw tightened, but he didn't say anything as he watched her walk away. He never did. That man was as emotionally constipated as a dog at a cheese festival. Instead, he averted his gaze and finished doling out the platinum until everyone had their fair share.

"Now, don't go getting crazy here," Mal said. "Good behavior. We play our cards right, might be more work in this for us. No fights. No drinking yourself to the point of embarrassment. No waving weapons about."

"Why are you only looking at me?" Jayne said, arms held wide to protest his innocence.

Mal held his frank stare, completely locked on Jayne, for one more beat, letting his silence speak for itself. Zoë did the same when Jayne looked to her instead, trying to pull a "Dad said no, ask Mom" routine, which had never in the history of their crew worked. Jayne dropped his arms and squirmed in discomfort.

"Well, whatever. Ruining all our fun. Kaylee's right, you are a stick-in-the-mud."

Zoë rolled her eyes. She'd likely have to spend her time keeping an eye on Jayne instead of attempting to relax in this place. Seemed far too easy to give offense and start a ruckus.

"Yes, not getting into a bar brawl in a palace is such an inconvenience," Simon said dryly. He turned to his left to say something to his sister… but she'd slunk away at some point, quiet and sly as a fox. Concern instantly creased his face.

"River?" he said, his voice already threading with panic.

"Ocean, Dr. Scott," Mal murmured. But he, too, spun to look for her, likely concerned she was already damaging their chances at more work.

And that was a good possibility, considering River's present company. She had walked right up to the duchess and was leaning in to peer closely at her eyes.

"You're a lioness," River said, swaying gently, then stepped back. "Good. I don't need your teeth, but I'll stick close in case you need mine."

Simon rushed forward, taking River gently by the arm. "I'm so sorry, Your Grace. My… cousin, she's not well."

The duchess waved a hand dismissively, her expression warming. "Not at all. I've not been paid such a nice compliment in some time. In fact… I have a sense that you love music. Is that true?"

"The movement of the stars is universal and its song is ever present. All places and times, *entrechat*, every planet and star in a constant *rond de jambe* until the end."

The duchess didn't bat an eye at this seeming non sequitur, instead giving River a warm, welcoming smile. "You know, I bet the dancers would adore you. They're all so talented, and they love to meet new people. What's your name? I'll introduce you."

Zoë held her breath but needn't have worried.

"Ocean," River said. "Vast, full of knowledge. And sharks."

Duchess Mèngyáo laughed a gentle laugh. "Too right. Come, Ocean. Let's dance."

Simon watched them depart, chatting happily as they made their way over to the dancers, and his shoulders sagged. In relief or in disappointment, Zoë wasn't sure. He returned to Kaylee's side at the table, but she wasn't paying him any attention, either.

"Good to go *now*, Cap'n?" she asked, already edging her way toward the painting ladies by the windows. "It looks like they've got trays of fruit tarts over there!"

Mal waved her on. "You keep a level head about you, though, little Kaylee. Don't go letting them very fancy ladies disrespect you."

"Don't you worry, Cap'n," Kaylee said with a wink. "I know better now who's worth a wag and who ain't."

And with that, she all but skipped off, ready to make friends… or at least eat some fancy desserts.

Simon watched her go, looking lost.

"Oh, come on now, Doc, you look like someone kicked your puppy," Mal said with a slap on Simon's shoulder. Simon flinched away.

"I'm just… used to needing to look after River, is all."

Zoë darted a quick glance around the room, then lowered her voice. "Second reminder, Dr. Scott. Never know who could be overhearin'. Even in private."

"He's just jealous that Kaylee and *Ocean* are both off paying attention to other people," Jayne said with a laugh. "Why don't you go find yourself a corner and read a schoolbook or whatever it is uptight prissy pantses like you do for fun."

"Right," Simon said. His gaze lingered on Mal for a moment, like he might receive orders or another option, but Mal only shrugged as if to say, "I got nothing." With that, Simon drifted away from the group, snagged a drink off a passing tray, and walked right up to a group of fine-looking gentlemen. Probably his type of crowd: moneyed, educated, and fancy talking. Zoë didn't think Jayne was too far off the mark, honestly, but she didn't find any pleasure in needling the person who would need to stitch her head back on if she stuck her neck out too far. He was an okay sort, beneath all the fuss.

"I'm off as well," Shepherd Book said. "I'd like to go meet the pastor here and check in at the local abbey, see some of the world outside the walls."

"You be careful out there, Shepherd," Zoë said, pursing her lips. "Ain't no telling what things are like outside this compound. You want an escort?"

"Wait, now—" Wash began beside her, but Book spoke up before he could voice his protest.

"I'm quite capable of looking after myself, thank you, but I appreciate your concern." And that was the truth. For whatever reason, Book was more capable of defending himself than any simple preacher had right to be.

"Well, you give a shout if you get outside the walls and find things ain't so shiny as you might hope," Mal said, giving Book a nod as he hefted his satchel and turned to leave.

That left just Mal, Zoë, Wash, and Jayne.

Jayne took one look around the remaining group and shook his head.

"Why the hell am I still here?"

And he left, grabbing a drink in each hand on his way out the door, evidently going in search of less stuffy company. Company he could pay by the hour, in all likelihood.

Zoë scanned the room, looking for the source of her unease. Everything seemed normal, or normal enough for these high-society types. But all the same, Zoë shook her head, looking to Mal.

"I don't like it, sir," she said. "Something's not right."

"Nooo, no, no, no, hey," Wash said, drawing her gaze,

his eyes pleading. "We're finally someplace nice with a bit of coin in our pockets. Can we please just do the skimpy bathing suits and whiskey plan we talked about earlier? For both of us, of course, because I believe in gender equality and all. Let's just this one time not look for trouble in every corner, okay?"

Zoë's heart tugged at her husband's words and the pinched look at the corners of his eyes. They didn't get much time together off the ship, having new experiences or just relaxing and enjoying each other's company. But that didn't mean she could let it go. She was a protector, a soldier, and that meant if the people she loved might be in danger, she had to be on her guard.

"I don't think I can do that," she replied with reluctance. "Don't you feel it? Something is off."

Mal shook his head.

"I'm with Wash on this one," Mal said.

Wash reared back in surprise, eyes wide. "You are?"

He nodded. "I am, and no need to go looking so shocked. Despite what Kaylee and Jayne say, I do, in fact, like to have a little fun now and then."

"Yes, sir, but your idea of fun typically involves punching some fool at an Alliance-friendly bar, not…" She trailed off and looked around the room significantly. "Not rubbing elbows with these types."

"Free booze and food for three days sounds like a mighty good time to me," Mal countered. "Quite a convincing argument. Keeps morale up. And if it brings us more work, then all the better."

He swept his gaze around the room, then returned his eyes to her. "If this were the Core, that'd be one thing. We wouldn't be here in the first place. Out here on the Border, with these folks playing at nobility, and not a fed in sight? I think we can enjoy a little R&R. Decision's made. We're staying."

"There, see that?" Wash said, turning on the puppy dog eyes. "Your captain has given the order. Let's lighten up and enjoy a little vacay. Please, let me whisk you away to that very sparkly pool we saw on the way where I will feed you grapes from a pillow like the goddess you are."

Zoë wavered, scanning the room one last time for any hint of what had her so on edge. Nothing unusual struck her, though. Maybe it was just the simple fact of being around so many Alliance-friendly folks. A minor predator in a den of lions.

River had called the duchess a lioness. She was never wrong when it came to her hunches or intuition or mind-reading, whatever it was. It was just a matter of deciphering the coded language she spoke. In this instance, Zoë had nothing to go on except for River's apparent ease with the duchess. Surely if she were a danger, that wouldn't be the case.

Right?

Zoë sighed and looked to her husband, whose face was earnest and pleading. He needed a break. *They* needed a break, needed time to focus on each other as a couple instead of always being pilot and first mate.

Some time to roll around in a nice, comfortable bed in a room that that didn't perpetually smell of engine grease and share a wall with Jayne Cobb, even.

Well. A woman had needs, after all.

"Fine," she said with a sigh and grabbed Wash's hand. "Take me to a fancy bed and relax me."

"I live to serve," Wash said with a grin, waving at Mal over his shoulder as Zoë dragged him away.

5

Shepherd Derrial Book took a deep breath of fresh air through his nose as he made his way toward the outer wall of the compound. He did so love a bit of solitude. It wasn't that he lacked an appreciation for life with the crew of *Serenity*, and he had his cramped passenger dorm for privacy whenever he desired it. They weren't designed for long-term habitation, though, so he preferred to stay in the ship's common areas whenever possible. That meant he crossed paths with the other crew members quite often, whether he was in the mood for company or not.

Even after all his years traveling the stars on ships of various kinds, he had never gotten wholly used to being confined inside a metal can floating through the blackness of space. No sky, no vegetation but for the occasional houseplant or hydroponic crops, and no horizon to fix your gaze upon. He sat in contemplation before the view of the wide-open 'verse often, whenever the cabin fever started to get the better of him, and wondered: was there something built into humanity, into their brains and blood and bones, that yearned for those things? For clouds above, no matter the color of the sky, and for the crunch of dirt under boot?

It certainly felt that way, whenever they made landfall and had the opportunity to walk planetside. It was like a spiritual sigh, a release of tension unconsciously held in the shoulders. Book never felt more *human* than he did with his feet on solid ground and his head uncovered by metal or mortar.

That said, Kerry *was* one of the more unsettling worlds he'd visited in his time. The orange sky was the culprit, he believed. Something about it felt ominous or unnatural. As he drew in another long breath, though, his vague disquiet eased a bit. The air was sweet and clean, free of industrial smog or any hint of terraforming chemicals run amok. The weather was pleasant, sunny and warm. Nothing at all to be nervous about.

Well, nothing to do with the planet, at least. Book did have some small concern for the spiritual state of the flock tended to by the Farranfore family preacher, Pastor Michael. He'd met with the man, though only briefly, as that was all either of them could tolerate of each other. Book prided himself on his ability to have a respectful conversation with anyone, regardless of belief. When that respect didn't go both ways, however, there was only so much one could do. The man turned out to be exactly as the duke had politely implied—a dull dinosaur with outdated ideas who easily took offense. Needless to say, Book's offer of a guest sermon had not been well received. He'd happily gone in search of better sights and conversations.

The walls surrounding the duke's estate were at least twenty feet tall, maybe more, and made of a similar quarried stone to the walkways connecting the various structures. Gates of varying sizes were set into the walls at regular intervals, and while Book had initially let his feet carry him automatically toward the main double gates, he'd diverted to one of the smaller single gates once he'd drawn nearer. One got a better, truer impression of a place slightly off the beaten path.

As he approached, a guard posted at the gate came to attention, looking him up and down.

"You planning to go into town, preacher?" the woman asked, her expression skeptical.

"I am. Been in space a while and feel the need to walk among people."

"Plenty of people in here," she replied. "I don't necessarily recommend Dunloe as a sightseeing destination."

Book shrugged in acknowledgment. "Perhaps. But I hear there's an abbey, and I'd like to go be among my brethren for a spell. You know anything about the ones in charge?"

The guard's face twisted into an expression of mild disgust. "They're a different sort out there. The abbess chooses not to associate with us, and the feeling's mutual. If you're set on meeting her, though, then you go right on ahead. Just keep a close watch on your coin and valuables while you make the walk."

"I will do, and I appreciate your concern. May I pass?"

The guard shrugged and opened the gate, waving him through. "Have fun, I guess. Don't say I didn't warn you."

Book mustered one last pleasant smile for the woman and strode through the gate, taking in the landscape as he put distance between himself and the compound. The path to town was marked with a signpost, informing him that Dunloe was 0.75 kilometers away. And so, Book set off, admiring the golden waving grasses and orange rocky formations along the way.

He was just starting to get an appreciation for Kerry as a destination when the town came into view.

There wasn't a gleaming white stone in sight. Whatever quarried stone materials they'd used to build the duke's compound, still shining in the afternoon sun behind him, they clearly hadn't spared any for the common folks. The buildings were sturdy enough, built of wood and brick and scrap, but there was an air of unkemptness to the whole town, like no one had made time to perform basic maintenance in quite a while. He encountered very few people on his way to the abbey, which was near the edge of town closest to the duke's estate and easily found by its single cross-topped tower... and the long line of people stretching from the front entrance.

The abbey was a simple, modest brick building that stood out from the rest of town both with the height of its steeple and the obvious care that went into maintaining its gardens. The building was ringed by well-kept plots of herbaceous plants, and a grid of raised beds also peeked around the side of the building, lush with cages of climbing tomatoes, feathery-topped carrots, trailing squash vines, and more. It reminded Book of the last abbey he'd lived at, where he'd so enjoyed tending to the gardens. Most especially the strawberries. He had a sense of what the queue might be for but walked up to the end to verify just in case.

"Good afternoon," he said to the last man in line. The man had a small child strapped to his chest, the girl's cheek pressed to his shirt as she napped. Book couldn't help but marvel at her sweet face, innocent and calm in sleep. The man lifted a protective hand to her back as he nodded a greeting to Book, cautious. When he didn't speak, Book tried again.

"Is this line for food assistance?" he asked, hoping the question would not give offense.

The man nodded again, and this time, he replied in a low voice so as not to wake the child.

"What need has a preacher for food assistance?"

Book smiled. "No need of the food, just a need to help out where I can. Is there another entrance where I could offer my services to the abbess?"

At that, the man finally seemed to relax a fraction.

"Around the left side, near the gardens," the man said, pointing. "I'm sure they'll be happy to see you. They do their best, but there's a lot of us and a bare handful o' them."

Book held up a hand in farewell. "Perhaps I'll see you inside, then. Thank you for your help."

Book made his way around to the side entrance, which was propped open with a loose brick. The door opened directly into a large walk-in pantry with wall-to-wall shelves stocked with cans, jars, tins, and boxes of foodstuffs. Another propped-open door led straight into the kitchen, where three people in the garb of the clergy bustled around at a frantic pace. An older woman a few years Book's senior staggered under the weight of a box full of potatoes, and Book rushed forward to steady the box, catching it as it nearly went tumbling.

"Who the hell are you?" the woman snapped, jerking back with the box of potatoes.

Book blinked in surprise at her harsh tone and language. "Uh. Book. Shepherd Derrial Book. In town for a spell and thought I'd check out the local abbey. Saw the line out front and thought maybe you could use another set of hands."

The woman looked him up and down, then thrust the box of potatoes into his arms.

"Well, then. There's another scale in the far cabinet on the left. Weigh out three-pound portions and bag 'em up. We've got a lot of mouths to feed."

Book's spine straightened automatically in response to her authoritative tone, muscle memory from another lifetime. He'd bet anything that this woman was the abbess.

Well, then. He had his orders.

Book set to work in silence, letting himself sink into the quiet rhythm of the repetitive task. There was another box of potatoes, and another, and the process became almost meditative. Weigh, bag, tie, pass it off. Weigh, bag, tie, pass it off. His hands worked in concert with the others, letting their familiar blessings wash over him as they handed off food to each person in need.

"You take care now, Seanny. Make sure your daddy eats some of those beets, they'll help with his blood pressure. Peace be with you, child."

"Five in the household, yes? Here you are, then. I pray for your health and well-being."

"You've got an extra mouth to feed this week, right, Clint? A cousin in from Tullig? Here, I can't do much, but hopefully some extra rice will help you stretch your meals. Go with God, my friend."

"Now, since your wife is pregnant, I made sure to slip an extra satchel of beans in there. She'll be needing the extra iron. God bless you and keep you both."

At one point, the woman turned to Book, glancing at the remaining stock of potatoes. "Make the next three bags five pounds each, please. Our farming families will need the extra energy for the harvest."

Book had no time to acknowledge the request before she was back to her well-choreographed dance of packing food and passing it off to the parishioners she clearly knew well. It took nearly two hours to get through the rest of the line, and by the end Book was sweating and rubbing at the sore joints of his hands. Once the last person had left, the woman finally turned to Book and gave him an appraising look.

"Thank you for the help, Shepherd Book," she said. "Can I offer you a cup of tea while you tell me why you're here?"

Book smiled, both amused at her blunt manner and already anticipating the warm steam and comforting scent.

"That would be lovely, thank you."

She waved him over to a small dining table and he took a seat, waving to the other two kitchen helpers as they disappeared to give them privacy. Suspicion confirmed—most definitely the abbess. She busied herself at the kettle, throwing Book a significant look that said, "Well? Get on with it."

He got on with it.

"Thank you for having me, and for the opportunity to jump in and help earlier. It's been a fair few months, near on a year, since I last stayed at an abbey for any length of time. It's always a delight to put my hands to good work."

"Where was your last posting?" she asked, measuring out tea leaves and pouring the water.

"Southdown Abbey on Persephone," Book replied.

"White Sun system, eh? Bit different from Kerry."

Book hesitated over his answer, sensing a test in her seemingly innocuous comment.

"Not so different, depending on the part you make your home in. There's Persephone City, which could easily sit on Londinium or Sihnon… and then there's Eavesdown, where the Southdown Abbey resides. I spent some years there, tending the gardens and feeding the hungry. And there were a great many hungry."

The abbess served him his tea in silence and sat down across from him with a mug of her own, so he continued, offering up a little something for her to grasp onto.

"I imagine it's much the same here. I don't suppose life in Dunloe is all that similar to life inside the duke's walls," he said.

Her lips twisted in response, and she sat her mug down hard enough that it clunked heavily on the table. "So you've seen the inside of the duke's little world there, have you?"

"I have," he said cautiously, sensing a minefield beneath those words. "I travel with a shipping crew who recently delivered some supplies to the duke. I don't participate in their dealings much, just travel the 'verse with them and bring the word of God to anyone who welcomes it. It's a strange life, and it's a mite more exciting than I'd like at times, but it's been good to walk in the world and witness the truth of people's lives and livelihoods."

The abbess gave him a long, searching look, then nodded. "Well then. You can call me Mother Serrano. And if what you say is true, then I hope you'll join us for this evening's soup-kitchen service. We'll expect almost as many people, and an extra set of hands would be a blessing indeed. You can see firsthand what the towns under the duke's stewardship are really like outside of the fantasy land he and the other nobles have built inside their walls."

"I'd be delighted to join you, Mother Serrano," he said. "You said towns, plural? Does the duke oversee more than just the land immediately around his compound?"

The abbess's lips pressed into a line. "Duke Farranfore is responsible for the entire continent of Killarney and all one hundred and thirty-two townships and villages within it, along with all the farming, mining, and forestry we do here. Killarney may have the lowest population of Kerry's dukedoms, but we produce the lion's share of what the planet needs to survive."

Mother Serrano hesitated, as if she had more to say but couldn't decide if she should… then sipped her tea instead, gaze drifting out the window.

Shepherd Book curled his hands around his own mug of tea and breathed in deep, taking in the warm vapors and soothing mint scent. He was glad he'd come. He'd be missing the duke's fancy welcome dinner, it seemed, but he'd send word back to the crew. He'd rather be at the abbey, spending his time in service, than enjoying the fruits of ill-gotten gains anyway. And the more he heard from the abbess, the deeper his suspicion grew that there was more to Kerry than first met the eye.

There was a truth to be uncovered, and Shepherd Book meant to find it.

6

Inara hummed quietly to herself as she arranged the pieces for the welcoming tea ceremony. The general's home was clean and minimalist and warm and inviting all at the same time, filled with natural wooden pieces and simple white porcelain. A few candles were strategically placed along the south wall for best energy flow, and more candles floated in a glass bowl in the center of the dining table, whose bottom was lined with pebbles and flecks of metal. Inara lit the incense, filling the air with the warm woody and floral scent of sandalwood and plum blossom, a perfect match for her surroundings and one of her personal favorites. She had a sense it would be one of Xiùyīng's as well.

A client's home said a lot about who they were, and it carried a lot of their personal energy. Sometimes, such as in this case, it was a boon. Other times, Inara wished she'd set the appointment for her shuttle instead. This day, and with this client, she was content and filled with the joyful purpose that sometimes came with her work. When the environment was right, and one had all the physical and mental tools needed to perform good work, what might under some circumstances be labor became a fulfilling spiritual effort.

It helped to have a truly wonderful client, of course.

Xiùyīng hovered in the doorway between the dining room and kitchen, the sleeves of her silky button-down shirt rolled up to her elbows, her hands in her pockets. The general was a fit woman in excellent fighting shape, as would be expected of a soldier, and she was strikingly beautiful as well. High cheekbones, expressive dark brown eyes, and strong features made her a truly arresting sight.

But it was her manners and soft nature that had ultimately sealed the deal for Inara, that had made her accept Xiùyīng as a client with real anticipation. For a warrior, Xiùyīng had a gentle heart, and Inara looked forward to becoming better acquainted with the spirit of such a woman over the next few days.

"Is it okay for me to be here?" Xiùyīng asked, leaning against the door jamb. "I can leave, if the tea ceremony is supposed to be prepared without gawking witnesses."

Inara smiled, a genuine laugh startling out of her. "No, please, gawk away. You can be as involved or uninvolved as you like."

Xiùyīng relaxed and tucked back a piece of flyaway black hair, bolstered by Inara's laughter. "Good, that's good. I'm a bit of an over-preparer when I'm nervous, so I've bought rather a lot of fresh local spring water and a brand-new kettle to boil it. I've been looking forward to the tea ceremony bit."

She paused, then shrugged and laughed at herself. "I mean, I've been looking forward to all of it, of course. The physical aspects, I mean. Probably a bit weird to be fixated on the tea."

"Not at all," Inara assured her. "This is your time, and I want the whole experience to be worthy. Though I've no doubt the physical aspects will be memorable indeed."

Xiùyīng blushed deeply, grinning down at the floor, and Inara found herself thoroughly charmed. A little harmless flirting to set the stage for their days together, and the results were promising indeed.

"What is it about the tea ceremony that has you so intrigued?" Inara asked, deescalating the tension a bit to let Xiùyīng off the hook. Sure enough, the woman relaxed a fraction and was able to meet Inara's eyes again.

"I'm just fascinated by traditions that stretch back to Earth-That-Was. I know it must have changed over the years, probably a lot. But even having common elements, knowing my ancestors did something similar… it's interesting, to me. Speaks to something in my soul."

"That's beautifully put," Inara said. "I feel the same way. My own ancestors had somewhat different traditions surrounding tea, from what I understand, but as a Buddhist and a Companion, I've been raised with these tea ceremonies and they feel very much a part of me. I'm grateful to be able to share this with you. I hope your ancestors won't mind it coming from me."

"I wouldn't presume to speak for them," Xiùyīng said. "But I'm glad for it regardless. Shall I boil some water for us?"

"Please."

Xiùyīng disappeared back into the kitchen for a moment to tend to the water, and through the doorway Inara glimpsed an enormous kitchen that wouldn't look out of place in a restaurant, large enough for a full staff to prepare a feast for twenty guests. A moment later, Xiùyīng reappeared with a freshly boiled kettle, which Inara took with a grateful nod. Noticing the direction of Inara's gaze, Xiùyīng glanced back over her shoulder at her kitchen, then rolled her eyes.

"It's a bit much, isn't it?" she said. "The house came with the title. Trust me, it's not what I would have chosen for myself. It goes unused a frightful amount of the time."

"It's lovely, though I did think it was a bit of a mismatch for you," Inara said diplomatically. "Thank you for putting the effort into finding quality water for this. It makes all the difference."

"That's what I read. I love a good cup of tea, but I'd never paid all that much attention."

"Well, I hope you'll enjoy this experience. Maybe it'll even affect how you make your morning tea in the future."

Inara had one last look over the tea set to ensure everything was in place. One wide-bottomed pot and two cups, a matching set made of earthy brown clay, sat atop a long, polished wooden box. The top was patterned with wide slats, leaving room to drain the spilled water as the cups and pot were washed. Below, the dark wood of the box was carved with intricate blossoms and branches. A small clay turtle lay at the top corner of the place setting, facing toward Inara. Finally, Inara picked up the boiled kettle.

"Are you ready to begin?" she asked.

Xiùyīng nodded. "Am I allowed to talk? Or is this more of a… meditative thing?"

"It can be either, as you choose. The Companion greeting ceremony is the official beginning to our time together. Some like to simply chat so we can get to know each other, some choose to meditate or enjoy a moment of stillness, and others like to discuss hopes or expectations for our time together.

No matter what you decide, I'm glad to be here with you. As much as I have chosen you from the pool of potential clients, you have chosen me as well, and I'm honored to share this experience with you."

Inara bowed over the tea set, then began. She carefully measured tea leaves from a tin into the pot and poured the water into it, then picked up the pot and tipped the contents into each cup, letting the stream of water splash freely over the sides, drenching the entire cup both outside and in. She then set down the pot, picked up the first cup, and poured its contents over the pot, repeating the process with the second cup. As they watched, the pot slowly absorbed the liquid remaining on its surface.

"It's like the pot is drinking the water," Xiùyīng whispered over the gentle sounds of water dripping through the wooden slats.

"Exactly," Inara said. "The clay is designed to become seasoned, to absorb the flavors of the tea over time. Eventually, tea made from a seasoned pot will have its own unique flavor. I only ever make oolong tea with this pot."

Inara took up the kettle again and refilled the pot with more water, her movements practiced and graceful. She loved the greeting ceremony. Loved ritual in general, really. It made her feel connected to the universe, even when the universe did its best to bring chaos. The universe… or certain people within it, at any rate.

But now was not the time for such things. Now was the time for a calm mind and open heart, ready to receive Xiùyīng and meet whatever needs she was bringing to their time together. Inara looked up and met Xiùyīng's gaze as she lifted the pot in one hand, the tip of her thumb holding the lid.

"The first pour is to wake up the tea leaves and wash the cups and pot," she said. "This pour is our first cup of tea that we'll share."

Xiùyīng's eyebrows went up. "That's all the time it takes to steep?"

"That's all," Inara said. "There are other methods of brewing tea, but in this style we use more leaves and brew for only ten seconds. We'll use the same leaves a few times, and the flavor will change with each infusion."

With that, Inara began the pour, letting a stream of light brown liquid splash down into and over the cups from chin height, moving between the two in an elongated oval pattern.

"Why do you pour it between both cups like that?" Xiùyīng asked, then winced and sat back. "I'm sorry, this must feel like an interrogation."

"No, not at all!" Inara insisted. "I love that you're taking such an interest. I truly enjoy this ceremony, and it makes me happy to share it with someone who appreciates it."

When both cups were full, she poured the last dribbles of tea over the clay turtle, then set the pot back down.

"The tea is stronger at the bottom of the pot where the leaves are," Inara said, carefully lifting one of the cups and offering it to Xiùyīng. "Some choose to pour the tea into a separate decanter first so the tea will mix there and give an even pour to each person. I prefer this method."

"It is a bit more theatrical," Xiùyīng said, bringing the cup to her nose and letting her eyes flutter shut as she took in its scent. Inara did the same, enjoying the familiar toasted rice notes of her favorite oolong.

"Well, I can be accused of enjoying some theatrics, I

suppose," Inara said with a coy smile. She raised her cup to her lips and sipped slowly, letting the flavor burst over her tongue. Beautiful.

Xiùyīng opened her eyes after her first sip and blinked in surprise.

"Wow. Either these tea leaves are amazing or the whole experience is magically enhancing the flavor. I feel like all my senses are fully awake."

"Why not a bit of both?" Inara said. "That is part of the purpose of this ritual as it relates to a Companion's work. Every aspect of our time together will be enhanced if you are open and receptive."

Xiùyīng stared down into her tea for a long moment. Inara took another slow sip, patiently waiting for whatever needed saying. Eventually, Xiùyīng stood and took the kettle to reboil it, then appeared a minute later looking determined.

"I've invited you here for multiple reasons," she said.

Inara took the kettle from her and set about preparing the second infusion of the tea leaves.

"I'd love to hear them, if you're willing to share," Inara said. "Open communication and clear expectations are the best way to make sure this is a good experience for us both."

Xiùyīng nodded, but her jaw seemed wired shut with doubt once more. Inara poured the next cups of tea, giving Xiùyīng a moment of space, then set the tea pot down and stood. She moved around the table and sat down directly next to Xiùyīng, meeting her gaze head on.

"Another important aspect of the greeting ceremony is to establish first consent." Inara reached for Xiùyīng's hand, stopping just short of touching. "May I touch you?"

Xiùyīng's breath caught. "Yes."

Inara took her hand gently in both of hers and lifted it to her lips, pressing a kiss to the smooth skin there.

"Thank you," she said. "We'll reestablish consent constantly as we go, but this first trust means a lot."

She looked down at their hands, then back up at Xiùyīng through her lashes. "Will you tell me why you brought me here? What you hope to gain from this time?"

Xiùyīng, despite her flushed cheeks, straightened and seemed to gather a bit of confidence back, a bit more of the authority she so easily wielded in the throne room.

"Well, part of it is very straightforward. My job is stressful and demanding, and most of the people I interact with every day are my subordinates. And, in the case of my second-in-command, just a generally horrible person placed there specifically to make my life as difficult as possible."

"So, not an option for stress release," Inara said with a wry grin.

"Colonel Blenner?" Xiùyīng blurted, her eyes going wide. Then she laughed. "Oh, God. No, definitely not, the man's a nightmare. The duke prefers not to deal with me, so he's installed a lackey to do his bidding. I'm sure the colonel is wreaking havoc in my absence, but that's a problem for later. I refuse to spend my first vacation in an embarrassingly long time thinking about his meddling."

The mirth crinkling the corners of Xiùyīng's eyes fell away as she returned to the topic at hand.

"There's also the small matter of me being rather… hung up on one particular person. It's never going to happen for a whole host of reasons, but have you ever just… had that one person who won't get out of your head no matter how much you know it's not good for them to be there?"

Inara's mind bolted from the question like a skittish horse.

"I know exactly what you mean," she said, hoping that would be enough to move the conversation along.

Xiùyīng grimaced, apparently reacting to something she saw in Inara's face. "Yeah. So, in a sense, I'm somewhat hoping this will be like a dividing line for me. I'm paid well in my position, have always had the money to do this, but I've let my feelings hold me back. This weekend is when I finally let go, move on from her, and enjoy a little stress relief in the process."

She downed the last of her tea and placed the cup gingerly on the table. Her eyes, when they met Inara's, were suddenly serious.

"I do have a confession to make, though. There is one final reason I requested your presence here."

Inara drew back slightly, cautious, but through years of training managed to master her reaction. The hairs on the back of her neck stood up in warning.

"And what reason is that?" she managed to ask in an even tone.

Xiùyīng straightened up in her chair, her shoulders back, suddenly the general again. No more of the blushing, somewhat shy woman, nervous but ready for an intimate weekend. Her expression was solemn and determined as she spoke.

"I brought you here because Companions are bound to keep client confidentiality, and I am invoking that bond now."

She paused, took a breath, and pressed on.

"I need your help. You... and the crew of *Serenity*."

7

They'd only been on Kerry for half a standard day, but Mal was already thinking he needed to worm his way into a regular shipping deal with Duke Farranfore. The perks at the Kenmare estate were just way too good to pass up.

He could get used to the fine accommodations—he'd taken an actual nap, sleep of the dead, on his very nice fluffy pillows in the guest cottage. In his own private room, no less. He had a private bunk on *Serenity*, of course, but you couldn't walk more than two feet without banging your shins, and on the very rare occasion that they paid for lodgings planetside, they usually had to double up to afford it. And that, more often than not, meant bunking with Jayne. No one should be forced to endure such hardship. Mal now knew things about Jayne he desperately wished he'd never had cause to know.

The food and drink were an unexpected and almost intolerable luxury, too. His body wasn't used to rich foods— the amount of textured protein they ate aboard *Serenity* was too horrific to quantify—and just the afternoon snack that had been passed around on trays by servants in crisp suits had been enough to set his tastebuds to dancing and his intestines to burbling. Getting older was no pretty feat, and his newfound propensity for heartburn was a gift he could certainly do without. He doubted cheerful Kaylee or baby-faced Simon were battling with such ills, and he indulged in a spot of well-earned bitterness about it before diving right back into more food he'd likely regret later.

The duke had certainly delivered on his promise of a dinner party "in their honor," though Mal highly doubted the man needed much excuse. If it led to him and his crew getting to eat a fine meal and enjoy some fancy (and free) libations, then Mal could certainly forgive the duke his thin excuses and indulge happily.

Three long tables in the palace dining hall sat twenty people each, and Mal was surprised to see the dancers from earlier and several staff members present among the diners. For a lordly type to include the hired help in such an affair spoke well of the duke. Perhaps he wasn't a complete stuck-up Alliance puppet after all. Inara and her client, the general, sat at the duke's right hand, while his wife the duchess sat to his left. Mal was surprised to find himself seated in a place of honor near the head of the table… right next to Inara. The look she gave him when he sat down was cool, though she did manage to cover up her mild irritation masterfully. No doubt she expected him to embarrass her or cause problems with her client. He would do no such thing, of course. He knew how to be a gentleman. Maybe not as fanciful as some present, but he could make do.

"Your Grace," Mal said as he took his seat. "Thank you for arranging this lovely meal, and please accept my apologies for the state of my crew's dress. We don't find ourselves with cause for finery often."

"Or ever," Inara muttered under her breath, and Mal smiled pleasantly at her. Ha. She had broken first, cast the first stone. He would enjoy this bit of high horsing.

"Not at all, Captain Reynolds!" the duke said, waving away his apology. "And stop with that 'Your Grace' business, I said. Just call me Tarmon."

"Then I hope you'll call me Mal, as well," Mal said.

"Of course, of course," the duke said. "Now, let's see, is your whole crew here?"

Mal looked down the length of the table to survey. Zoë and Wash sat across the table from him, with Zoë at the duchess's side. Kaylee came next, then River, who chattered to one of the dancers in the seat next to her. Jayne sat next to Mal, and then Simon next to him. That left...

"All but one, it seems. Shepherd Book went into town to visit the local abbey and hasn't returned. Not too surprising, if I'm honest. He might spend the whole evening there. Sometimes he has enough of us heathens and needs to recharge his godliness overnight."

The duke's mouth hardened slightly, and he rolled his eyes. "Yes, well, let's hope he doesn't absorb too much of what they're serving there. The abbess in town is... hm. How to put it. Let's say... a bit of a roadblock. I've tried to make inroads with the people of Dunloe, but she blocks me at every turn. I just want to help. I don't like to see people hungry just outside my walls. She riles them up, though, gets them so defensive, makes it impossible to find allies out there. She just doesn't want her control threatened. She has them totally reliant on her for food and medicine."

The duke sighed. "I hate it, but I can't force them to get on board with my plans. I give them their freedom, and they can do with it as they like. Even if it kills them."

Inara frowned. "I'm sorry to hear the people suffer so. It's a shame that one person can exert so much negative influence on a community. Can she not be replaced?"

The duchess's expression went stony, her mouth downturned and hard, but the duke only looked resigned. "I'm afraid it's not so simple. Church politics are what they are. I will continue to try to work with the people, but I don't have much hope."

A bell dinged from a side room and servants came bustling out with the first course of the meal, a collection of tiny bite-sized pastries with unfamiliar roasted vegetables and cheeses. The duke lit up, clapping his hands briskly.

"Enough of that dour subject. Let us dig in! Our chef is the finest on all of Kerry, and he incorporates local ingredients in the most creative and delicious ways."

The duchess, taking her cue, spoke up in a light and almost musical voice.

"The pastry is made with butter from farrow's milk, one of the few creatures native to Kerry that was preserved during terraforming. The vegetables are fairn, like an onion but sweeter, and caramelized keets, which are like carrots but have an earthier flavor more like a beet. Please, enjoy."

Mal looked across the table to share a raised-eyebrow look with Zoë, only to find her watching the duchess sidelong, her face unreadable. With a shrug, Mal snagged one of the tiny pastry cup things and turned instead to Kaylee, who could always be counted on to get excited about food.

Sure enough, Kaylee's eyes were practically rolling back into her head as she bit into the flaky, buttery pastry. Across the table, Simon watched with wide eyes and slightly parted lips at the nearly explicit sounds and sight of Kaylee enjoying good food. Downright comical, it was.

"That little bit of fancy meeting with your liking, there, Kaylee?" Mal said, a little too loud so it would startle Simon. Sure enough, Simon nearly jumped out of his skin and flushed deep red, which Mal found quite hilarious. He aimed an innocent look at Simon, then turned back to Kaylee, who wiped a tiny golden flake from the corner of her mouth.

"Oh, Cap'n," she said, then leaned over the table to aim her next comment at the duke. "This thing right here is heaven all wrapped up in butter and hot cheese. Your chef should be mighty proud."

Then she slapped a hand over her mouth and shrunk back into herself. "I'm so sorry, Your Grace, probably no one's s'posed to talk to you but the cap'n."

The duke gave a hearty laugh and waved a hand, turning back to Mal. "I'm glad your crew are enjoying their time with us. I always invite admiration for the pleasures of our court."

Kaylee grinned in relief but leaned back in her chair and sat up straighter all the same.

"I can't wait to see what course is up next," she said, snagging another pastry. "You should bring us places like this more often, Cap'n."

"Speaking of that," the duke said, grabbing Mal's attention back from Kaylee once again. "I hope you don't mind if we talk a bit of business over dinner?"

"Not at all," Mal said. He'd actually been hoping for and somewhat expecting it. Why else would a fancy gentleman invite a ship's crew to a dinner party? The job that got them here had paid quite well, compared to most. For all his reservations about brushing up too close to Alliance folk, this man struck him more as Alliance *sanctioned* rather than Alliance *loyal*. He'd seen the type often enough in the Border worlds: happy to pay lip service to the Alliance and their regulations, but much more concerned with building their own little empires. He still didn't love it, but he loved his ship falling out of the sky for lack of fuel and parts even less.

"I'd love to learn more about the business you do, Mal," the duke asked as servants swept away the remainder of the first course. "What kinds of cargo do you typically haul?"

"Oh, just about anything, so long as it poses no danger to my crew or vessel. Or at least, no danger t'ain't commensurate with the pay we're offered," he amended, thinking of the ill-fated job they'd taken from Badger involving the transport of some HTX-20 explosives, colloquially known as "Satan's Snowflakes" and typically used in mining operations. In hindsight, Mal should have left Badger hanging on that offer.

"We've hauled everything from foodstuffs and medicine to weapons and cattle," Zoë added. "Not at the same time, though, and not sure I'd love a repeat of the cattle job."

The duke hummed with interest and turned back to Mal. "Anything you don't haul?"

Mal shrugged. "Only hard line is human beings. The only people on my boat are crew and paying passengers. We don't participate in trafficking. In general, I just go with my gut. It says a cargo ain't worth the trouble it'll bring, I turn down the job. If I take a job, it'll get done. I keep things fair and square."

Next to Mal, Jayne gave a rude snort, but the duke thankfully seemed not to notice. Sure, there'd been a time or two when the nature of a job had become clear partway through and they'd needed to back out. Most notably, the time they'd taken a train job from Adelai Niska only to discover they were stealing medicine from those who desperately needed it. Going back on the deal had brought a whole world of hurt and complications down on them, but needs must and all that. It had been the right thing to do, no matter what Jayne thought. So long as Duke Farranfore was on the up and up with his jobs, then there'd be no problem.

"That's good to hear, Mal," the duke said. "I'm glad you're open to a variety of cargo. It's so troublesome to deal with shipping companies. So much hassle, red tape, regulations, tariffs, blah blah blah. Working directly with a private crew is much simpler. Besides, I like to support small businesses."

"And we do so love to be supported," Mal said. "We certainly ask a lot fewer questions. Not a scrap of paperwork in sight."

The duke laughed heartily in response. "Well, I do like that. I think I've got another job for you and your crew, Mal. Hopefully I'll have some more details for you tomorrow. In the meantime, I'd love to hear some tales of your adventures out in the 'verse! I love my home here, but I must admit to some curiosity about the worlds beyond our own. Please, regale us all with the story of your most exciting job."

The faintest huff of a sigh came from Inara at Mal's right, but she kept her back largely turned to him, focusing instead on her client. As she should, he supposed. She was being paid, after all.

Mal wracked his brain for a suitably entertaining yet clean story and found himself struggling. An awful lot of their work of late had been of the illegal sort, thefts and the like, and he didn't quite have the duke's measure well enough to trust him with such information. Perhaps he could sanitize one of their capers, make it sound like shipping work.

"Ooh, tell 'em about the time you accidentally got married," Kaylee said.

"Or about the time Jayne was a folk hero," Wash chimed in. "I still can't believe that actually happened. Did it happen? Was it a fever dream?"

"It was unfortunately real, and burned into our hearts and minds forever," Zoë said, her curving lips hidden behind her wine glass.

"Or there was the time you got stabbed," Inara added. Her tone was light and humorous, but Mal thought he read a touch of warning there.

Well. That sounded like a challenge. And nothing made Mal Reynolds more itchy to do a thing than a challenge.

Especially one from Inara.

"Well, there was this one time on Persephone..."

8

Zoë awoke the next morning unable to enjoy the gloriously comfortable bed, on account of the brutal hangover she was suffering. Last night at dinner, that gut feeling of "something's off" had refused to leave her, even as Mal made nice with the duke and seemingly secured them more well-paying work. So, she'd drunk it away, with the encouragement of her dear, sweet husband, who she was possibly going to murder now.

Zoë did not often indulge heavily, but every time she did, Wash was certain to be at the center of her drinking escapades. He had a way of cutting right through her defenses, getting her to relax and laugh a little. Or a lot. It was impossible not to laugh when in the company of Hoban Washburne. It was one of the things she loved most about him, the way he made life just that little bit lighter. They didn't get to spend much time off the ship, so when they did, Zoë tried her best to ease up and let him in. She made him work for it a little bit, of course; that was half the fun for both of them. He enjoyed throwing all kinds of humor and hijinks at her to find the cracks in her armor, to discover what would make her open up again and again. But she didn't want to waste their precious little time together stonewalling his attempts to draw her out.

So, she drank. And drank. And drank. She let Wash pour glass after glass and feed her the bite-sized desserts that never seemed to stop coming on shiny silver trays. Things got hazy after dessert, but she had a vague recollection of losing her boots, jumping in a fountain alongside some fancy ladies, finding her boots and someone else's, and laughing a lot. Wash was there the whole time, goading her into more and more ridiculosity and holding her arm as they stumbled back to the guest cottage together for a moderately successful drunken tumble. All in all, it had been a fantastic night.

All in all, it was shaping up to be a horrific morning.

Zoë peeled herself out of bed, unsure which was more urgent: the need to pee, or the need to brush the dead animal feeling out of her mouth. She settled for the toilet first, then twisted her hair up under a shower cap and brushed her teeth while showering as her time in the military had taught her. Her shower was not military efficient, though; since exiting the army, she'd luxuriated in long showers, one of her few indulgences in an otherwise practical and regimented life. And in a shower like this, with water pressure like this, with a hangover like this... Zoë let the water beat down on her back and zoned out.

Wash was still asleep when she finally emerged, damp and warm and moderately more alive. He showed no sign of imminent wakefulness, so she decided to let him sleep off their adventures and instead went in search of the greasiest meal on Kerry. After leaving a note, she closed the door with a quiet click and turned to find Mal and Jayne in the hallway, both looking rather worse for wear.

"Food," Mal grunted.

"Hair of the dog," Jayne added, which made Zoë's stomach lurch unpleasantly. She turned to Mal and nodded, but gently, so as not to disturb the angry crabs that had taken up residence inside her skull.

"Food, yes," she said, then turned to Jayne. "You, just… no."

They walked to the kitchen on the bottom floor in that soft-stepping silence shared by all hungover people. A full hot breakfast of eggs, meats, steamed buns, fruits, rice porridge, and sweet breads sat under warming lights, and Zoë's stomach gave an audible growl. Mal and Jayne didn't comment, only grabbed plates and loaded up. Once they all three were sat down and had gotten a decent pad of grease in their bellies, Mal sat back to pick at his bread.

"Was thinking of going into town this morning," he said. "Couple things we need for the ship, some parts and such. Plus, we got some time to kill, and a walk in the daylight might go far toward bringing us back to the living again."

"Yes, sir," Zoë agreed. "I admit to being curious about the town and its folk after what Duke Farranfore was telling us last night. Give me something for this headache and I'll come with. Jayne, you joining?"

Jayne gave a grunt. "Suppose so. Feeling a bit cooped up at the moment. Might as well soak up a little daylight afore we're trapped in that tin can again."

Mal bristled. "Hey, that tin can is our home and livelihood, and I'll not hear her disparaged so."

He said it with a humorous sort of tone, but Zoë spotted it

for truth. *Serenity* was as much a member of the crew as any one of them, and she had won Mal's heart fully on the day he bought her. Love at first sight, it was.

Jayne grumbled something under his breath involving the words "obsession" and "*lè sè*", which Mal charitably let go.

Zoë loaded up a plate of food and ran it back upstairs, leaving it on Wash's nightstand along with a note that she was heading into town, then crept back out without waking him. Knowing him, he'd probably sleep until they returned anyway. She met Mal and Jayne back out in front of the guest house and they made their way through the duke's estate, taking it at a leisurely pace. Even so, they slowed as they crossed into the town limits, all three unconsciously feeling the unsettling current in the air.

The town was smaller than Zoë had thought it would be, being so close to one of the primary settlements on the world. It was a familiar setup they'd seen around the 'verse: one central main street, a few businesses and other buildings on a side street or two, a few houses for those who worked in town but didn't live in the same building as their business, then nothing but lots of farmland in between distantly spaces homes farther out. Barely big enough to call itself a town, in truth. The fields of golden wheat waved in the warm breeze, seemingly healthy and growing well, but many of the other crops seemed to be struggling, stunted and with an unhealthy pallor. Zoë was no farmer, but even she could tell that something was wrong.

"Seem a mite quiet to you?" Mal asked, stopping once they'd reached the first businesses of Main Street.

Zoë pursed her lips. "Was just thinking the same thing, sir."

"Where's all the people?" Jayne asked. "I was hoping we might find a whorehouse or a bar."

"Of course you were," Mal said with an eyeroll. "Well, let's explore, shall we? Perhaps this town has hidden jewels just waiting for—"

"You lookin' to buy?" a high voice cried out, startling them all. Zoë spun around, hand on her gun out of instinct, then lowered it when a dirty-faced little girl came running out of the shop next to them. "We got goods, parts and supplies, best prices you'll find!"

Mal and Zoë looked at one another and shrugged, then followed the girl inside. They were looking for parts and supplies, after all. When they stepped through the doorway, though, Zoë's expectations came crashing down.

The shelves inside the ramshackle building were nearly bare. A few sad tins of beans sat on a low dusty shelf, and a bin of unrecognizable mechanical bits dominated the center of the room. A few other items here and there, but nothing that could reasonably be called a shop inventory. The lights were off, which Zoë expected was to save on generator fuel, and the sunlight streaming through the cracks in the walls illuminated the whirling dust motes floating throughout the room.

"You finding anything you like?" the girl asked. "Can give you a real good price."

Mal had barely opened his mouth to reply when the girl rushed to add: "And we got a mule out back, got four good tires on it! Could sell those to you, if you help me lift 'em. I can take 'em off myself, though," she said, beaming with pride.

Even Jayne was starting to look troubled. "Where're your parents at, girl?"

"In the fields," she said. "Been havin' lotta problems with critters getting into the crops, all running down from the hills ta get away from the mining. My dads are having ta do a lot of replanting. And the first crop of cucumbers failed, on account of the Kerry Rust, so they gotta rip it out and burn it, and—"

Zoë cut the girl off before they could get the entire history of the farm's woes. "Ain't you got schoolin' to be doing instead of running this shop?"

There were, in theory, mandatory courses on the Cortex for all children in the 'verse who weren't enrolled in a traditional school. The idea was that every child would have access to a free education, no matter their circumstances. As always, reality differed from ideal. The farther out from the Core worlds one got, the shakier Cortex access became. The ability to afford the equipment needed to access the Cortex was another issue. And then, of course, there were circumstances such as these.

"No, ma'am. They closed the schools on account of the cost and the need for farm work. I run the shop and make dinner while my dads work in the field. When it's raining too hard, they bake me treats and read me stories instead, though!"

"I thought Kerry didn't have much in the way of rain," Mal said with a frown.

The girl's shoulders sagged. "It don't. Daddy always says he prays for rain every day so we can be together. I wish it rained more."

Mal turned away, but Zoë caught a glimpse of his face before he could hide it—something like anger, or frustration. Zoë spoke up so he wouldn't have to, and saved him the fight with Jayne he would have provoked.

"Some of the tires on the mule bike are looking mighty worn, sir. Could do with a spare or two in case one of 'em blows."

Jayne's brows furrowed. "Didn't the mule bike get wrecked on Niska's—"

Zoë elbowed him hard in the ribs and Jayne shut right up.

Mal shot her an unreadable look, then turned back to the girl. "You sure you can part with those tires? Don't wanna be leaving you without something your daddies need for that farm o' yours."

The girl shook her head so hard Zoë was concerned it might pop right off her neck.

"No, no, promise, I got permission! We need the money more'n we need a working grounder. Ain't got no gas in it anyways."

Mal nodded, silent for a moment, then waved a hand at the girl. "Well, then. Let's get those tires off and get you paid."

It was the work of about ten minutes to get the tires removed and stacked behind the counter for them to pick up on their way back to the duke's estate. They left the shop, and the now very happy girl, Jayne grumbling the whole way.

"Don't see why we need to spend our hard-earned credits on tires for a mule bike we don't even have anymore," he said for the third time. Mal swung around to face him.

"I'm fixing to buy us a new one, soon as this job's done. Say something about it again and I'll be buying it out of your cut."

And, with that nipped in the bud, the trio made their way farther down Main Street to see if the town had anything else to offer.

The answer was… no, it did not.

Every shop they went to told the same story. Scrawny, hungry-looking kids working the counters, bare shelves, and adults out working in the fields trying to squeeze a decent harvest out of Kerry's dusty orange soil. They returned to the first store to collect their tires, then made for the edge of town, passing near the abbey along the way.

"Well, I'm seeing what the duke meant about people going hungry outside his walls," Zoë murmured, scanning the horizon for any glimpse of hope—either for the people of Dunloe or for their supply stores.

"Makes you wonder what's truly going on between the duke and that abbess," Mal said, frowning as he looked back toward the abbey. "Might be it's time for us to drop in and pay a visit to Shepherd Book. He hasn't checked in since letting us know he'd be spending the night there, and I wasn't really concerned about that until just now."

"You saying we gotta go to church?" Jayne said.

"Don't worry, you can stay outside. Wouldn't want you to burst into flames."

Zoë hummed in amusement. "Not sure Jayne's the only one we should be worrying about in that regard, sir."

"Okay, okay, enough commentary, let's just pop our heads in and be done with—"

An explosion drowned out the last of his words.

9

Jayne hit the dirt on pure instinct, diving behind a scrubby bush and leaving the mule tire he'd been carrying lying in the middle of the road. He pushed himself up into a crouch and drew his weapon, a LeMat percussion revolver, peeking around the side of the bush to evaluate the situation.

Mal, who had been closest to the blast, picked himself up out of the road and kept low, scrambling to Jayne's side. Zoë was stationed across the street, her Mare's Leg lever-action rifle at the ready as she sighted down the barrel in the direction of the explosion.

"*Shén shèng de gāo wán*, what the hell was that?" Mal swore as he slid down beside Jayne, drawing his weapon.

"Dunno," Jayne grunted back. "Can't see through all the gorram dust's been kicked up. Thought I caught movement up the road. You hurt?"

"Aw, so sweet that you care."

"I care that you can gorram shoot and be useful, considering the bombs an' all," Jayne shot back. Sure, Mal and the others were a bit like family-ish by now, despite his best efforts, but that didn't mean they had to be all soft and mushy-like about it.

"That weren't no bomb," Mal said, returning to seriousness. "That was a rocket. At least two of 'em, by my reckon."

Jayne hummed an acknowledgment. Mal would know, he supposed. Jayne hadn't fought in the war—didn't want nothing to do with it, even now—but Mal and Zoë had both been fighting for the Independents until the bitter end, and he knew it had made them both who they were in ways he would never understand. Didn't care to understand, truly. But what mattered in this scenario was that while Jayne had plenty of knowledge of firearms and hand-to-hand weaponry, Mal knew his weapons of war and could identify them by sight and sound.

"So, what's that mean, then? Does it matter?"

"Matters loads. Means different delivery methods. A rocket could have been fired from a good vantage point anywhere around here. We need to keep an eye out. Who knows where the *niú shi* could be if—"

The report of gunfire cut Mal off, and Jayne peered through a gap in the bushes to try to find the location of the combatants. Just up the road, barely fifty yards from the abbey, a group of uniformed soldiers from the duke's estate were huddled behind bullet-proof shields. But apparently the assault had come from a trench dug a quarter-mile off the road, filled with plainclothes fighters wielding all manner of weapons, their faces mostly obscured by masks or bandanas.

Zoë, seeing that the attention was focused elsewhere, used the opportunity to dash across the road, keeping low. When she landed beside Jayne, she looked immediately to Mal.

"Remember when I said something wasn't right, sir?"

Mal scowled. "None of that. What could you see from over there?"

Zoë shrugged. "Not much more'n you, I imagine, sir. Two sides, one squad of about twelve from the duke's forces, and the other side, no identifying symbols. They're just folk. They were the aggressors, fired them rockets. One right into the squad as they came into firing range of that ridge over there," she said, pointing past the boundaries of town to a rocky outcropping. "The other one was aimed straight at the wall of the compound, for all the good it did 'em."

Jayne leaned out for a peek and saw that there was, in fact, a scorched and crumbled area of the huge wall surrounding the duke's estate. The rocket had done almost no real damage, though. The white stone was apparently a facade, and all the weapon had managed to do was reveal the real wall underneath, which seemed to be made of solid steel.

"Your assessment of their combat abilities?" Mal asked.

"Enthusiastic but disorganized, sir. The fighting should be over momentarily. The duke's forces are better armed and better trained. The plainclothes folk got the superior numbers by a lot, more than triple far as I can see. But unless they have a lot more rockets up their sleeve that they haven't fired for some reason, then they're fixing to lose badly."

Then the whistle of another large projectile broke through the sound of the fighting, followed by another, and another. Jayne, Mal, and Zoë all hit the dirt behind the bush as four more explosions drowned out the gunfire.

"You were saying?" Jayne shouted over the renewed fighting.

"I said *unless they have more rockets*," Zoë said, gesturing to the new strike points on the wall. Once again, the rockets hadn't done anything more than cosmetic damage.

When two more whistles sounded, Jayne couldn't help

it—he had to see. He poked his head out just enough to see both rockets go sailing *over* the wall this time. Right toward the part of the compound where *Serenity* was parked. Jayne paled, a mental image of the ship, his home, going up in flames superimposing itself over the scene. His eyes went wide.

"Mal—"

Then two bright explosions burst in the sky over the wall like fireworks. Countermeasures. Jayne slumped back behind the bush in relief.

"That was way too ruttin' close," Jayne said. "Did you see that?"

"With my own two eyes," Mal said. "Zoë, any casualties you could see when you were over there?"

"One dead and one wounded on the duke's side, from my vantage point, but visibility was poor and I suspect things are a mite different now."

Jayne felt the frustration building inside him like a bottle of ale that got shook up hard. These two, always on with their war stuff. The war had been over for a long time, and their side lost. Sometimes it felt like Mal and Zoë always had one foot back in those times, though, like they were still living it even when the rest of the 'verse had moved on.

"Okay, can we quit playing soldier for a second? None of this has anything to do with us," Jayne said. "Please don't tell me you're thinking of getting involved in that… whatever's going on. Ain't our business, and I'm not about to go get my head blown off for no reason and no coin. I'd think you wouldn't want your precious ship blown up neither."

"You can untwist your underthings there, Jayne," Mal said. "You're right that it ain't got nothing to do with us. That said, if we're gonna be doing more work for this duke fella, mightn't be a bad idea to keep an eye on any unrest. 'Specially any that might be a threat to *Serenity*. *Dŏng ma*?"

"You're thinking we go back and talk to the duke, get his take on the situation?" Zoë asked in that flat, businesslike way of hers.

"I'm thinking," Mal said, "his reaction will tell us a lot. Also wouldn't mind hearing his take on why this town is so…"

"Bleak?" Zoë suggested.

"Depressing as hell," Jayne amended. Even at its worst, life growing up on Sycorax was never this bad. Sure, it was rustic, but he had a good enough life. They had what they needed. These people were barely surviving.

"Exactly so. I'm thinking things ain't quite as shiny round here as the good duke would have us think," Mal said. "I've got some questions I mean to have answered."

"Bet the Shepherd has a right nice view of this fight from where he's at," Jayne said, and Mal slapped him on the arm.

"You're a genius, Jayne."

"I am?" Jayne asked.

"He is?" Zoë added, disbelieving. Jayne scowled at her. Mal ignored them both, instead pulling out his handheld comm and speaking into it, keeping his voice low.

"Shepherd Book, you read?"

A crackle, a beat of silence, then a reply came back.

"Captain Reynolds. You aren't involved in this violence happening outside the compound, are you?" Shepherd Book replied.

"Surely not, but we happened to be walking back from

town when it sprang up. You and the folks there at the abbey okay? No damage from that blast?"

"No, and thank God for it. We're a mite shook up, but that's all."

"Jayne here thought you might have a good eagle eye on the fighting over there. Anything you can tell us about what's going on? Does the abbess know anything about this?"

Jayne puffed up a bit at the recognition, then tamped down the reaction. He wouldn't let Mal see him looking like a dog who'd been told he's a good boy.

"Let me get over to a window and take a peek. One moment."

"You be careful, Shepherd. Don't be getting shot up on our account," Mal replied.

The line was quiet for a moment, and when he returned, Shepherd Book's voice was lower, quiet, like he was trying not to be overheard.

"No one here at the abbey will say a word, most especially the abbess. She's a distrustful sort with little to say to the likes of me. They all started getting a mite shifty and nervous about an hour ago. When I asked them about the fighting, no one would answer my questions. I can't tell if they're scared, or if something else is going on."

A pause, then his voice returned, a bit louder.

"It looks like the duke's forces have just about eliminated all the other combatants. There are many dead on the opposing side, and the rest seem about to flee. I believe we'll have quite a lot of work to do here, once this is all over."

"You planning to stay a while longer, then?" Mal asked.

"If they'll have me, then yes, I'd like to stay and help." His voice lowered once more. "And to see if I can learn any more about what's happening here."

"Okay then. Stay safe. Thanks for the intel. Let us know if you learn more."

Mal shut off the comm without waiting for a reply. The fighting died down a moment later, and silence fell once again over the bleak, depressing-as-hell little town. Mal held up a hand to forestall any movement when Jayne shifted uncomfortably, itchy to be getting back on the road.

"Let's give it a minute, make sure no one's got any last tricks up their sleeve."

Jayne grumbled, plopping back down into the dirt while Mal and Zoë looked for who knows what.

"That's it," Mal said.

"Med evac, most likely, sir."

"For the duke's forces?"

"Seems that way."

Jayne snapped. Again.

"Will you cut that out and tell me what the hell's going on?"

The whiny roar of a small-engine craft came not a second later, providing his answer. Jayne poked his head out to see a small shuttle in solid white with a red cross painted on the side coming in for a slow, careful landing near where the duke's forces had staged their resistance. Two people leaped out, quickly followed by two more who brought out a stretcher.

"Should be clear now, sir," Zoë said. "If the bird could land, zone must not be considered hot anymore."

"Agreed. Let's grab our tires and get a move on. We paid good money for them, ain't about to let them rot in the middle of the road."

Jayne, thankful to finally be on the move again, came out

from behind the bush slowly with his pistol still drawn, crouching down to grab the tire without ever letting the gun's muzzle waver.

"Guns away, Jayne," Mal said.

"Like hell," Jayne replied without missing a beat. He wasn't about to walk through an area where people'd been trying to blow each other up mere moments ago without being visibly armed and at the ready. No one got the drop on Jayne Cobb. Well, not usually.

Mal tensed in that way he did every time someone disobeyed one of his orders. Jayne loved getting that reaction out of him. Did it intentionally, more often than not. He wasn't one of Mal's little soldiers to order around, and the crew of *Serenity* didn't give Jayne near enough respect, all things considered. He had to take it where he could.

"It's in your best interest, Jayne," Mal finally said, once he mastered his automatic reaction. "Them's that were the aggressors weren't wearing any colors or symbols I could see. We walk toward those fine Alliance-funded troops with weapons drawn in the aftermath of a firefight, they're like as not to shoot first and ask questions of our bleeding corpses."

Jayne absolutely hated it when Mal was right. With a grumble and a string of curses, he holstered his pistol and readjusted his grip on the tire.

"Let's get a move on, then. This thing's ruttin' heavy," he said.

But Jayne did not remove his hand from the butt of his weapon the whole time. Couldn't hurt to be prepared. Could hurt very much not to be. With a smug smirk, he noticed that Mal and Zoë did the same.

Maybe Jayne knew a thing or two after all.

10

Mal had expected the duke's compound to be in a state of locked-down readiness, reacting to the threat just outside the walls. And certainly, the guards at and around the gates were on alert, eying his crew's weapons as they waved them through. The streets were quieter than usual, but there were enough people still cheerfully out and about on their business for Mal to feel almost annoyed about it. Was this sort of upheaval so regular that people didn't care, or did the duke's propaganda machine keep them feeling safe enough that it didn't even register?

They dropped off the tires by the ship and made their way straight for the palace, and specifically the duke's receiving room, which seemed to be the daily hangout space for all the nobility living in the compound. It was their best chance of catching the duke for a quick friendly chat.

As they passed through the courtyard outside the palace, a chorus of cheers went up, and Jayne's face broke into a grin. Mal braced. That was rarely a good thing.

"Hey, fellas! You pourin'?" Jayne called to a group of the duke's troops clustered outside the compound's drinking establishment for the less fancy folk.

"If you got more stories, we sure are!" a young woman with military short hair and a bright smile called out.

Jayne swung around to look at Mal, his expression plaintive.

"You don't need me to talk to that blue blood in there, right? So, I'm gonna…"

He trailed off, edging away with his thumb indicating his new drinking buddies.

Mal nodded. "Don't get too off your face, though, hear? There's trouble afoot, and we might need to move at a moment's notice. I know this ain't your specialty, but moderation, yes?"

"I can hold my drink, Mal, get off my back."

"You surely can. It's drinks I'm a mite concerned about," Mal said, emphasizing the plural.

"Fine, fine," Jayne said, already walking away.

Mal pondered for a moment as Jayne was warmly welcomed by the group and immediately handed a very large mug of ale.

"I think he means to disregard my keen advice."

"Wouldn't doubt it, sir," Zoë agreed.

"We're gonna have to peel his face off that table if we decide to leave early."

"Thinking so. Is leaving early on the table?"

Mal shrugged. "Might be, if this unrest intensifies. I wouldn't have said so if the fight stayed small, but those last two rockets heading over the wall have me feeling a little twitchy. Don't wanna give up our shot at more work or deprive the crew of their creature comforts if I don't have to, but safety first and all that."

Zoë raised her eyebrows and leveled a look at Mal. "Right, because you aren't enjoying the creature comforts at all. Wash and I heard you running that shower for near on forty-five minutes, then snoring the house down after. Sir."

"A man can enjoy some leisure when it's well earned."

Zoë turned away, her lips quirked. "Indeed."

"Such a shame we have to have this audience with His Grace without Jayne's refined presence next to us, though," Mal said, deflecting to a new topic as they entered the palace.

"Probably for the best anyway, sir. Not wise to have Jayne mouthing off to important people as he sometimes does."

"You wouldn't be referring to that time he called Badger a 'puddle of piss,' would you?"

"I would, sir."

"Well, that's hardly a comparison. I wouldn't give Badger the label of 'important people.'"

"He sure would for himself."

Mal snickered. "Yeah, well, that's between a man and his mirror. I ain't giving him the courtesy."

They walked into the duke's receiving room and were greeted by a nearly identical sight to when they first arrived. Nobles milling, people snacking and sipping, dancers dancing, the usual delights of the court, and with the duke and duchess seated at the head of the room overseeing it all. Today, though, Mal recognized a few familiar faces among them. River stood with her head bent close to one of the dancers, apparently locked in close conversation. Then, as one, they both stepped back and executed a series of flawless steps in perfect unison. River beamed, for once seeming light and unburdened by pain.

Dance, it seemed, helped her push beyond her constant struggle, the memories and pain from what had been done to her. Perhaps, Mal thought, he should talk to Simon about finding a space aboard *Serenity* for River to practice her dance on the regular. Could be it would help stabilize her a bit. And, of course, a less volatile River would be a boon to the crew, who had to put up with her constant shrieking, occasional knife-wielding, and general creepiness of manner.

Mal knew, in the corner of his mind, that none of it was River's fault and he should perhaps show a bit more empathy for the girl. (The voice of that thought sounded a lot like Inara, actually.) But when there was danger to his crew, and unpredictable danger at that, Mal struggled to feel anything more than tense and wary. River and the other dancer finished their short demonstrations and struck a pose, then burst into giggles.

Well. He'd see about that dancing space, at any rate.

As before, a group of ladies sat to one side near large picture windows, though this time they appeared to be sketching instead of painting. Kaylee sat with them, chattering away happily—and, to Mal's surprise, being chatted right back to. She seemed to have found a degree of welcome among the ladies of the court, far unlike what she'd experienced on Persephone. It was good, that. Sometimes with enough long days in space and not enough parts to work on *Serenity* beyond basic maintenance, a tiny bit of the shine started to wear off Kaylee's sunny disposition. Things like this seemed to help her recharge: meeting new people, seeing new places, even going down to a junkyard to haggle over prices and gape at shiny new tech. Whenever they did decide to leave Kerry, it would be with a more cheerful and renewed Kaywinnet Lee Frye.

God help them all.

"Malcolm Reynolds!" the duke's voice boomed out. "Just the man I wanted to see! Come on up here, my friend."

Mal, a bit taken aback by the strong welcome, glanced over to catch a skeptical Zoë's expression. Seemed she hadn't given up her dislike of the duke just yet, then. She wouldn't say anything that would jeopardize the work, though, so he approached the duke with a hand extended.

"Duke Farranfore, a pleasure to see you again today."

The duke shook his hand enthusiastically, his wife the duchess smiling blandly beside him. "I trust the accommodations were to your liking? I heard several of your crewmates had a very enjoyable time last night after our little dinner party."

Next to him, Zoë shifted uncomfortably and looked fixedly at a tapestry on the far wall. Mal wondered what kind of hilarity he had missed. At some point, he'd grabbed a spare bottle of something—he still wasn't sure what, exactly—and retreated to his room to escape the vision of Inara and General Li flirting, teasing, and laughing together, right up until they left the party hand in hand. Mal had downed most of the bottle and passed out on the very comfortable bed, happily unconscious.

"The drink was delicious and the beds were comfortable, so you can be sure a good time was had by all," he said, pushing down the slight wave of nausea the memory of his hangover brought on. "You said you wanted to see me?"

The duke clapped his hands with a laugh. "Yes, yes, to business! We discussed last night the possibility of another cargo job for you and your crew. Are you still amenable?"

"Sure am. Always nice when one job can flow right into the next. What's the cargo?"

The duke leaped from his chair and turned to hold a hand out to his wife, drawing her along after him as he stepped down off the raised dais. He sat down on the edge of the dais steps and waved for Mal and Zoë to sit at a nearby table. Mal expected the duchess to join them, considering her attire, but she sat herself down at the duke's side despite her fine gown, and he took her hand.

"It'll be a similar arrangement to last time," the duke said, back to business. "It'll be sealed cargo that you'll go pick up from Silverhold. There's a little flexibility in the timing, so you could even stay there for a day to enjoy some shore leave if you and your crew would like. The market in Silver City is rather famous for its cutting-edge technological gadgets, and you could enjoy some of the beautiful vistas that haven't yet been turned into mines. I'm working to arrange some light cargo for your trip out there, too, so the trip can be profitable for you both there *and* back. I know it's a bit of an ask for you to fly such a distance with an empty hold just to retrieve my shipment. No promises, but you have my word I'll do my best. What do you say?"

Mal blinked, taken aback. He wasn't used to anyone else thinking of the economics of running a ship, much less giving a damn. He was right that every trip *Serenity* made without cargo in her belly cost them hard-earned money, and they had to be wise about such travel, most especially between systems.

But then there was the sealed cargo.

He hadn't loved taking on mystery cargo in the first place. He had no interest in anyone else's business, but he still preferred to know what he was hauling. With no idea what was inside be could be carting around something potentially harmful to the crew. Or something horrible, like human organs harvested from unwilling contributors, or corpses. But the initial job had come to them from a trusted middleman who had assured him there was nothing poisonous, volatile, or offensive to his sensibilities. They'd been in need of food, fuel, and parts, and their coffers were running dangerously low, as they often did.

So the question was, could the duke be trusted enough for Mal to take on another such job from him?

"What kind of payment are we talking?" Mal asked. Crucial details.

The duke smiled, apparently appreciative of his business acumen. "Same fee as before, half up front and half on your return, to fund your travel needs and make sure you have a little fun spending money for your arrival. And, to sweeten the pot, if I'm not able to secure any cargo to fund your journey out there, I'll increase the pay by an extra fifteen percent. Sound fair?"

Mal pursed his lips in thought. It was the fairest deal anyone had offered them in a long time, actually. He was so used to having to negotiate for every little thing, to scrape and cajole just to ensure they would make a profit on a job. He'd be stupid to turn this down, especially when the first job for the duke had gone so smoothly. Mal didn't want to end up too deep in the pocket of this guy, no matter how easygoing and removed from direct Alliance involvement he seemed, but developing a regular business contact would be fine. Right?

Zoë's warning words echoed in his mind, though: *Something ain't right, sir.*

Normally he trusted Zoë's gut nearly as much as he trusted his own. But in this instance, the risk-to-reward was well in their favor, and Mal wasn't getting any particular bad feelings about the duke. And the crew *would* likely appreciate a day in that fancy high-tech market.

"One thing to settle before I agree," Mal said. "We were nearly caught up in a bit of unrest on the way over here. Some gunfire, your troops against some plainclothes aggressors. A couple rockets even made it over the wall, though your forces handled them before they could land. What's the story there?"

The duke frowned, but he didn't seem angry. More like... deeply disappointed, maybe. Troubled. The duchess, on the other hand, seemed much more concerned, her mouth and eyes tightening with some deep emotion.

"I'm sorry if you were put in any danger by that situation," the duke said, sincere as could be. "I will admit that we have a small ongoing problem with a group of insurgents trying to unseat me. They popped up for a while, then went away for long enough that I'd thought the problem dealt with. I recently started hearing rumors that they may be active again, so I've been preparing for that eventuality. Today was the first we've seen them in quite some time."

Zoë shifted next to him but didn't speak. He could hear loud and clear what she wanted to say, anyway. A repeat of her warning. The duchess shook her head silently, looking frustrated, but she didn't speak, so Mal pressed the duke further.

"What's their cause? Why are they trying to remove you?"

The duke heaved a heavy sigh. "I truly don't know. They haven't attempted to deliver any terms, only come at us with violence. I have to assume it has to do with the conditions in town—I'm not a fool, Mal, I know you've seen what it's like and how that must reflect on me. I only hope you can believe me when I say I've truly made efforts to improve things there, to share some of the abundance we enjoy here on my grounds. I've cut taxes to almost nothing to ensure families can scrape by, but the abbess and the other local leadership won't have anything to do with me. I believe it might be an old conflict that began with my predecessor, an uncle we all hated, but until they're willing to come to the negotiating table I'll never know."

"That's unfortunate," Mal said, assessing the duke's facial expression and body language. He seemed, for better or worse, to be completely sincere. Mal honestly didn't believe the man was lying. He couldn't reconcile it with Zoë's warning, though. And it didn't seem to be reason enough to put down an opportunity for easy, guaranteed work that would take them somewhere nice for a change.

"One last thing," Mal said. "Do you believe this unrest is likely to continue during our stay? We're scheduled to be here for at least two more nights, on account of our resident Companion's services being engaged for such time."

The duchess gave Mal a warning look and a slight nod, clearly much more troubled by the attack than her husband. The duke only shrugged helplessly.

"I honestly have no idea," he said. "I wish I could tell you otherwise, but as I said, we haven't dealt with this in some time. I suspect not, but I'd be disingenuous if I didn't admit the possibility."

Mal nodded, appreciating the man's honesty. "Well then, Duke Farranfore, if it won't offend you, then I may consider rounding up a few of my crew members and sending *Serenity* into orbit to wait out our stay. I don't want our ship to present a tempting target. She would, of course, return if you ended up finding cargo for us to haul out to Silverhold."

The duke's shoulders slumped a bit, looked crestfallen. "I understand. Your ship is your entire livelihood. I am sad that some of your crew will be leaving us, though! We've so enjoyed having them around. Your doctor friend is even helping out in our infirmary, tending to those injured in that attack. Very kind of him. You do pick your people wisely, Mal."

Mal hadn't exactly picked Simon, so to speak, or his sister. Truth be told, he wouldn't have picked them out of a lineup of two. But, for better or worse, they were part of the crew now, and therefore under Mal's purview.

"Thank you. He's come in handy a time or two. He can probably stay, if he's willing, though we'll likely need to pull a few of our less combat-experienced crew members. Just as a precaution, of course."

"Of course," the duke said. The duchess pursed her lips and looked away, silent.

"Well then, I suppose we'll be on our way to make arrangements," Mal said. "Pleasure doing business."

"Indeed," the duke said, going in for another firm, friendly handshake.

As they turned to leave, Mal glanced down at his communicator to see a new message from Inara waiting for him. He waited until they stepped out of the palace and into the Kerry's golden sunshine to look at it.

It was short and to the point, and it sent a tinge of warning up Mal's spine.

Be careful.

11

Mal marveled that Zoë managed to hold her tongue all the way out of the duke's palace, down the walkway to the guest cottage, and up the stairs to their suite of rooms. As soon as they barged through the door to Zoë and Wash's shared room, though, Zoë rounded on him.

"I don't like it, sir," she said. "Something ain't felt right the whole time, and this is not a step in a comforting sort of direction."

"Um, hello," Wash said, standing in front of the door to the en suite bathroom with a towel held in front of his crotch. "Welcome to our bedroom, wherein people do naked-type things that typically invite a courtesy knock before entering, you know what I mean?"

Zoë strode over to Wash and pressed a kiss to his cheek, patting his belly affectionately.

"This is a pants-wearing kinda situation, sweetie," she said. "I know you don't hear this from me often, but you might wanna get some clothes on."

"Think I might just do that," he said, grabbing a handful from a drawer and slinking back into the bathroom, walking backward so as not to show Mal his bare backside. That done, Zoë snapped right back to the topic at hand.

"I know you seem to be the duke's new best friend, sir, and I won't deny that the work is welcome and needed—" she began, but Mal interrupted.

"We ain't braiding each other's hair and skipping through meadows, here. He's offering good work for good pay and he's treated us well while we've been here. He's still an Alliance man, and I don't doubt he's got black marks on his record, but we're running a business here. We do a job, we get paid. That's it."

"Ooh, is the captain being all authoritative-like again?" Wash said, coming out of the bathroom as he buttoned up his loud floral shirt.

"He is the captain," Zoë said with the air of someone who had said the same words a thousand times.

Wash sighed and stopped at her side, arms folded. "I know, I know. So, what, have you broken up with the duke? Is this something to do with that explosion that woke me up?"

"It is," Mal said. "'Fraid I gotta ask you to cut your cozy stay short and take *Serenity* skyward. Thinking maybe you take Kaylee, River, and Book and head to Madcap, see if you can't find a better source for the supplies and parts we need. The town was a total bust."

"We did get mule tires," Zoë interjected.

"Did we even need mule tires?" Wash wondered aloud. "Wait, first, what's going on? Is it really so bad as to miss out on the free wine and amazing showers?"

"Bad enough, hon," Zoë said. "There are insurgents attacking the compound, and they may attack again. If they damage *Serenity*, we'll be in a whole heap of trouble."

"Yeah, you're right," Wash said. "Then we'd be stuck here, forced to endure days of fluffy beds and gourmet-cooked food while we made repairs. The horror!"

"Yeah, assuming *Serenity* was in fit state to repair," Mal shot back. Wash's humor had a tendency to grate at times, most especially when he was doing his whole manly "I have to stand up to the captain" thing. He thought they'd worked most of that out during their cheery stay with Adelai Niska, enjoying his particular brand of torturous hospitality. Apparently not enough to wipe it out altogether, though.

"This ain't a request," Mal snapped, then forcibly reined it in. "You have until midday to get the bird in the air. Like it or not, your wife there says her gut's jangling alarm bells. I'm not feeling it, but we've been through enough for me to know I should trust it. You should know the same, being her husband and all."

"He's right, sweetie," Zoë said, rubbing a soothing hand up and down Wash's arm. "I get it's a raw deal for you, but I'll feel a lot better knowing you're safe on Madcap."

"Eh, safe and Madcap ain't exactly two words I'd put together. You've never had to run from the smugglers that hang out up there, just waiting to take out humble courier pilots and their cargo of rich-people vacation supplies."

Zoë gave a consoling nod. "I know you've had some bad times there, but I'm sure you can find yourself a little nook to tuck *Serenity* away. Better than being here while people are shooting rockets over the walls."

"Yeah, easy for you to say," Wash grumbled. "You'll be wallowing around in this bed all by yourself, eating cheese off a platter and sipping fancy champagne. Or getting drunk and jumping into fountains without me there to enjoy it."

"Say what now?" Mal asked, intrigued.

"Absolutely nothing, sir," Zoë said, cool as ever. She grabbed Wash's duffel bag from underneath the bed and threw it on top. "Time to do something that doesn't involve your mouth talking, honey."

"Well, you should have said that in the first place," he replied, coming forward to wrap his arms around her waist, ignoring the bag. "Bye, Mal. I've got some business to take care of before my midday deadline."

The dismissal rankled, but not so much as it once had. He averted his eyes to the ceiling and raised a hand in farewell, then fled the scene, pulling the door shut behind him. He briefly thought about returning to his room, but considering Wash and Zoë had been able to hear him snoring the night before, he feared what he might hear now. Instead, he left the guest cottage, snagging a piece of fresh fruit from a bowl in the dining room on the way out, and made for one of the duke's many lush gardens.

He chose a garden that featured few trees but many low flowering plants so the sightlines around him were clear. Didn't want anyone dropping eaves, no matter how banal the upcoming conversations would be. He sat on a stone bench next to a low shrub covered in blood-red blossoms and took out his communicator.

First up, Kaylee. He told her what was what and asked her to round up River and head back to the ship by midday, same as Wash. Her disappointment was palpable, but he couldn't let that get to him. He had make sure his people and his ship were safe first, and ensure their happiness second. When those things conflicted, the choice was obvious.

Next up, he checked in with Simon and, as he'd predicted, the doctor chose to stay and continue to help where he was able. The struggle was evident in his voice; he always wanted to be where River was, and it took a lot to pry him from her side. His duty as a doctor was the only thing that swayed him most times, and with the threat of possible further violence on the horizon, he couldn't, in good conscience, leave the planet just yet.

Just as well. If anyone of *Serenity*'s crew were injured planetside, he'd rather they all be stitched up by a doctor he trusted.

Trusted? Well, *knew*, at any rate. Maybe trusted.

Mal briefly notified Jayne of the plan—he'd be staying planetside, of course. Wherever there was imminent violence, there Jayne Cobb would be. Jayne had done his share of bellyaching when Mal ordered him to sober up just in case, his slightly slurred voice belying his protests that he was "totally fine, Mal, I'm good to go!"

Mal didn't need to see him to know he was very much not good to go. He could only hope Jayne would follow orders… that, and go check on him within the hour. He had anything other than water in his glass, there'd be hell to pay.

Finally, Mal contacted the last person on his list: Shepherd Book, still at the abbey as far as Mal knew. When he answered, Book spoke in that same lowered tone as earlier.

"Captain Reynolds. Have you learned any more about the situation here?"

"A bit," Mal said, and filled him in on the scant details the duke had provided. "It sounds like bunk, but I know when a man's lying, Shepherd, and he was being completely up front.

Not sure what to make of that. You learn anything new from your priestly types?"

"Almost nothing," Book said, voice heavy with regret. "Not for lack of trying, though I can't push too hard without risking getting asked to leave. We are treating the few who survived the retaliation by the duke's forces, though none are awake and able to speak yet."

Mal sighed. "Ah, well, it doesn't much matter. I'm sending *Serenity* off planet with you, Wash, Kaylee, and Ocean aboard. With all this potential for bloodshed, we need to protect *Serenity*, and I'd feel better knowing all our noncombatants were out of the line of fire."

"I'm no stranger to dangerous situations, Captain. I'll be staying behind to help the poor and wounded here. The abbey folks're providing critical aid, and they're severely understaffed. I'm needed."

"I don't doubt you are, Shepherd. All the same, I think you'd be better off on the ship. We may need to make a quick getaway if things go too far south, and I don't wanna be waiting on you to come back from your little prayer camp retreat."

Mal winced, knowing he'd gone a step too far and likely sabotaged his own argument. He couldn't help it. Shepherd Book and his religiosity put him on edge like little else in the 'verse.

"I wasn't asking permission, Captain Reynolds. I was informing you of my plans," Book said, his voice firm. "Unless *Serenity* is leaving the planet for good, then I'm staying behind. That is my final decision. If that means my time with *Serenity* comes to an end here, then so be it. There is still work to be done here, and I'm the one to do it. I can provide you with information from the abbey, should any eventually come my way. And should you have need of me if a fight breaks out, I'll be here."

Mal clenched his jaw shut to hold in his frustration, then sighed.

"You are weirdly useful in a fight for a holy man, I'll give you that," he said, wondering for the umpteenth time about the shepherd's murky past. Questioning had won naught but vague statements and wise-sounding but empty platitudes. At this point in their relationship, Mal just accepted that Book would always be a mystery... but a mystery that surprised you in helpful ways when you least expected it.

"Only when necessary," Book amended. "But yes. You can count on me."

"I'll be in touch," Mal said, then cut the connection.

And that was everyone.

Well, all but one.

Inara wasn't technically part of his crew. All the same, as she was his tenant, it was only courteous to inform her of *Serenity*'s movements and availability, no?

And so finally, against his better judgment, he broke one of Inara's many rules. No calling while she was on a job. Still, she had sent him that vague warning, so there was always a chance. He could always say he was just following up on the message, that she had contacted him first.

But there was no answer.

Mal stared down at the comm in his hand, turning it over and over, trying his best to master the basketful of snakes writhing in his belly.

She would be fine. Inara was a formidable woman, well capable of defending herself. And she was in the company of the duke's general to boot, an accomplished warrior in her own right, if the stories held true.

But all the same, her warning wouldn't leave his head.

Be careful.

12

Kaylee was enjoying a leisurely brunch with the ladies of the court, complete with bubbly drinks and everything, when the call from Mal came through.

"Kaylee, you there?"

Kaylee's expression, which had been lit up with the joy of good conversation, immediately fell. An unplanned call from the captain was rarely a good thing.

"Here, Cap'n, what's up?" she said, taking a few steps away from the group for a bit of privacy.

"'Fraid I'm gonna have to break up your fancy lady party. Wash is taking *Serenity* to Madcap, and I need you aboard."

Kaylee sighed. She'd been halfway expecting it—these little vacations never did go as smooth as they ought.

"On account of the explosions and such?" she asked, dismayed.

"Just so," Mal replied. "Liftoff at midday. Can you find River and bring her with you?"

"Will do, Cap'n. Do you think they do champagne to go? Or those little cheese pastries?"

"I'm sure you can shove a few in your pockets. Assuming they haven't got you all dressed in their frills."

Kaylee looked down at herself and sighed again. She had actually borrowed a dress from one of the ladies for today, a jewel-tone green dress that hugged her curves before flaring out at the waist and looked amazing with her hair. She adored it and felt even more confident and beautiful than she had at the shindig on Persephone. She'd been hoping Simon would catch a glimpse of her in it, maybe finally get things moving between them. Ah well. She'd enjoyed the dress her own self, and she didn't need him to see it to know she looked hot as all heck.

The joke was on Mal, though. The dress had pockets.

"I'll be there midday with River alongside, Cap'n. Stay safe out there."

"You too, Kaylee."

Kaylee shoved the communicator back into her pocket and returned to the group of ladies—her new friends—and sat back down. Her dejection must have shown on her face, because the lady who had lent her the dress, Oganya, leaned over and put a warm brown hand on her shoulder.

"Kaywinnet, are you well? You look as though you've received some troubling news."

"I have, at that," Kaylee said. "You went to all the trouble to lend me this amazing dress, and now turns out that I gotta leave early. Captain wants *Serenity* off planet because of the violence an' all that."

The other ladies all cooed their protests, their faces showing sincere sadness.

"No, you must stay!"

"We'll miss you so much!"

"Can't you stay just a little longer?"

Kaylee's heart gave a pang. For once she'd felt like she'd been making actual friends, people she might keep in touch with. Needed more than a day and a half to get to that point, though. It was fun while it lasted, at least.

"I get it, I guess. Without *Serenity*, we got no work, and it's our duty to protect her. Still… it's been awful nice spending time with you all. Thanks for, you know, including me. Even though—"

"Even though nothing, Kaywinnet. You are a delight, and interesting company to boot, and we are crushed to see you go," Oganya assured her, expression fierce.

Kaylee's heart warmed, and she performed a little curtsey like they'd taught her.

"Well, thank you, ladies. It's been a delight. I love my job and *Serenity* and the others to pieces, but sometimes it's really nice to just hang out with a group of awesome women and talk about something other than how broken the ship is," she said, full sincere.

Several of the ladies stood to give hugs or clasp hands, until Oganya patted her shoulder.

"Come on, you probably want your other clothes back. Can't imagine that thing would be very practical for working on a ship, though you're welcome to keep it. It looks far better on you than it does me," Oganya said.

"Oh, no, I couldn't possibly," Kaylee said, though she really, really could. She loved this dress even more than her pink and white one. But it wouldn't be right, and she didn't have much storage room for frivolous things she'd never get to use anyway. "Thank you so much for letting me borrow it, though. It felt real nice."

Oganya, as part of a local noble family close to the duke, lived in a manor house within the estate, though their family land holdings were elsewhere on the continent of Killarney. They returned to her room at the manor, making light conversation as Kaylee slipped out of the dress with much regret. The smooth, shimmering material slipped over her hands as she handed it back to Oganya.

"Thank you again. You done a real kindness. If there's ever anything I can do…" Kaylee began, then trailed off. "Well, I guess anything in the next hour or so, 'cuz after that I'll be gone."

Oganya shifted uncomfortably and looked away, running her fingers nervously over the fabric of the dress.

"There's… one other thing I wanted to ask you, actually."

She clammed up for a moment, seeming to debate with herself over whether to actually say anything. Then her face hardened, and she pushed on.

"I have an old shuttle I've been trying to get running. I've researched and done a lot of work myself, but I'm afraid I'm just not experienced enough. No one to teach me, you know, so I have to learn from the Cortex. Please don't tell anyone. It's… a secret."

Kaylee's face lit up.

"Oh, that's so great! I love that you're learning mechanical stuff. Do you want me to take a look at your shuttle? Please say yes, I'd love to help."

Oganya looked infinitely relieved.

"Yes, please, Kaywinnet. That would be wonderful. But truly… I can't emphasize enough how important it is that no one knows. If I show you where it is, can you keep it to yourself?"

"Of course," Kaylee said, her voice softening. "Would you get in a lot of trouble if your mama knew you were getting your hands greasy doing something like that? My mama was like that. Kinda traditional, you know."

"It's… something like that," Oganya said, cagey as all heck. Kaylee let it go. Her gut wasn't calling danger, and she understood better than most about how some people didn't want womenfolk working on machines. It was an honor to help another woman with a project like this. Kaylee gestured to the door with a flourish.

"Lead the way, my lady," she said, pretending to curtsey again. "I can't wait to see this shuttle of yours."

Kaylee expected to be led somewhere far away, maybe even outside the walls of the compound. Mal wouldn't have liked it, what with the brimming violence and all, and truth be told she wouldn't have liked it either. But instead, Oganya led her to the next manor over, a more modest but still very fancy dwelling with a large garage at the back of the house. Oganya withdrew a key card from her dress pocket (all her dresses had pockets, she proclaimed) and pressed it to a scanner next to a small door leading into the garage. She took one last look around to make sure no one was watching, then slipped inside, beckoning for Kaylee to follow.

"Whose house is this?" Kaylee asked, keeping her voice low.

Oganya hesitated for a moment, then spoke.

"It's General Li's house. Xiùyīng. Her family has been close with my family for years, so she's like an older sister. She's always kind of looked out for me."

That tracked with what little Kaylee had heard about the general. The garage was the tidiest she'd ever seen, and she'd worked in quite a few. The walls were lined with meticulously organized tools hung on peg boards. Two vehicles sat side by side. One was a relatively new and seemingly untouched two-seater Hummingbird-class skimmer, beautiful and shiny with clean lines and a very sexy engine that Kaylee knew made for a fun ride. The other was… not that. It was visibly aged, though not so old as to be obsolete, and definitely needed a wash and shine. It was a solid workhorse of a shuttle, only large enough to get four people from origin to destination with no creature comforts. Or space to move. Or even a toilet, Kaylee thought.

"I know it's rough," Oganya rushed to assure her. "I don't need much. Might not even need to fly it more than once. But if I do need it, I'll need it to just work immediately, not give me any trouble."

"Sounds like you're aiming for a quick getaway," Kaylee said, turning to study Oganya a little closer, considering. "Why would you wanna go anywhere when things are so nice here? Is it the violence that's got you shaking? Or is someone threatening you?"

Oganya opened her mouth as if to protest, then clamped it shut again and shook her head.

"I've already said more than I should. Suffice to say, I may need to make a quick getaway, as you say, and this shuttle is my only option. I promise I have not harmed anyone. I'm not running from the law or anything. But things here… aren't always what they seem. And that's the last I'll say of it."

With that, she pressed her lips together as if physically

restraining herself from telling Kaylee more. Kaylee frowned, but nodded.

"Okay, well… I hope you know that if you're ever in trouble and *Serenity* is around, you can give me a call. I'll do what I can to help. Starting with this beauty!" Kaylee said, walking toward the shabbier of the two shuttles with her arms held open as if for a hug. "All she needs is a little shine, a little tuning, and she'll sing real pretty for you, no doubt. Let's see what you've been working on!"

Oganya brought over a small carrier full of tools from a workbench against the wall and handed Kaylee the one that matched the bolts on the engine housing.

"I hope you won't judge my efforts too harshly," Oganya said, twisting her hands with nerves. "I'm still learning, and I've done my best, but…"

"Don't you worry 'bout a thing," Kaylee said, popping the housing off and sticking her nose right up in the guts of the shuttle. "I'm mighty impressed that you've worked on it at all. Now let's see here…"

Kaylee stuck her hand deep inside to flip a latch, which let her pull aside another panel and see deeper.

"Is this compressor rebuilt?"

Oganya's voice became even more distressed.

"Yes, and I'm sure it's not right, the diagram was so confusing, but I—"

"Hey, hey, whoa now, who said anything was wrong?" Kaylee asked, withdrawing enough to look back over her shoulder. "I could only tell because some of the parts were newer and the wires had been stripped and soldered. It's good work. You should be proud of yourself."

Oganya blinked as Kaylee turned back to the engine, running her fingers over each part, willing it to tell her what was wrong.

"Do you have an inkling of what might still be broke?" Kaylee asked.

"I… I thought that something didn't look right with the readouts coming from the drive feed, but I couldn't tell you what. Everything else looked fine to me, but I obviously don't know what I'm looking at, so don't take my word for it."

"I am gonna take your word for it," Kaylee said, brushing a little grease off the part in question. "Because you're right. And this ain't a common problem, so I wouldn't expect you to notice. If we remove this part…"

Kaylee fished in the box for a different tool, then set to work doing just that. When it popped free, Kaylee held it out for Oganya to see.

"I didn't even know it could be removed. It had that 'do not touch' label on it, and no visible fasteners, so I thought—"

"You thought exactly what those no-good swindlers who manufactured the thing wanted you to think. They want you to bring it in to them to get fixed and pay them a boatload of money, but really…"

She flipped the part over in her hand and used the tip of a flathead screwdriver to pry a tiny cover off, then held it up for Oganya to inspect.

"Fuses?" she said, puzzled. "That's all it is?"

"Darn things blow all the time on these Endeavor-class shuttles. Think they do it on purpose, you ask me. And you'd never know they were there if you paid attention to their silly little warning labels. You got any replacements around?"

Oganya rushed over to a workbench and dug through with

no seeming care for the grime on her hands, then said, "Aha!" and came running back.

"Careful not to touch your dress," Kaylee said, accepting the replacement fuses. "Won't keep your secret for long if you walk out of here greasy."

Oganya flushed and looked down to inspect herself, holding her hands a few inches away from her sides.

"You're right, sorry, I forgot. I normally change clothes when I come in here. I keep a spare set in the cabinet."

"Smart," Kaylee said. She popped out the old fuses and tossed them to Oganya, who brought them close to her face to study the blackened casings while Kaylee put the new ones in. She had the part re-installed barely a moment later, then closed the whole thing back up and wiped her hands on her coveralls.

"Well? Wanna fire her up, see if she sings?"

Oganya grinned and climbed into the cockpit, dress tangling around her legs, with Kaylee right behind her. It wasn't the most pleasant sort of place to be, but Oganya beamed at it like it was her pride and joy as she settled herself in the pilot's seat. She flicked a few switches and then, with a flourish, hit the ignition.

The shuttle rumbled to life, and Oganya turned to Kaylee with a grateful smile.

"Thank you so much! I can't tell you how much this means to me," Oganya said. She reached over to grab Kaylee's hand and squeezed. "You are a treasure, Kaywinnet Lee Frye, and don't you forget it."

"Awww, no, you are," Kaylee said, awkward but pleased. "Happy to help, honest. And you remember what I said about needing help, okay?"

"I will," Oganya said. "I'm gonna stay here for a while, make sure she keeps running okay, but you go on ahead. I hope we'll see each other again before you leave Kerry for good. Take care, Kaywinnet. Be careful. And just… remember that this shuttle is here. Just in case. You have my wave code."

The warning struck Kaylee as odd, but she nodded anyway.

"Make sure you open the exhaust vents if you're gonna keep her running in the garage. Can't have you asphyxiating yourself!"

With that, Kaylee waggled her fingers in farewell and slipped out of the garage, looking both ways for any witnesses first. The last thing she wanted was to get Oganya in trouble. Her heart hurt for the girl, both for her having to hide her mechanical talent and for whatever had her so spooked she was hiding a shuttle in the first place.

Whatever it was, it probably meant that Mal was right to send *Serenity* off the planet, no matter how much Kaylee wanted to stay.

Time to go find River and get a move on.

13

River's mind never felt so quiet as when she was dancing. There was something about it that was completely different from any other form of physical and mental activity. Her body and mind hummed in alignment, her awareness pulled perfectly taut between brain, arm, leg, core. She flexed and moved and swayed and twirled, recreating every complicated step her new friends taught her. And though she still struggled at times to speak in ways they could understand, they communicated all the same.

The band's song built in intensity, crescendoing and speeding and taking River's heart and feet right along with it. She and her new friend Ari whirled around each other, complicated footwork in perfect time, and the joy of it was so pure River felt like shouting to the stars. When the song came to a rousing finish, with her and Ari in matching finishing poses, the applause was thunderous. The whole of the duke's receiving room had paused to watch them, even the servants. Even the duke himself, though he didn't matter. The duchess—she mattered. River performed a little curtsey in their direction—but it was only for the duchess.

Ari grabbed her hand and drew her to a small seating area where the dancers could stretch and rest between performances. There was water and wine, fruits and pastries, soft breads and fresh whipped honey butter. And below it all, a plush rug with velvet pillows for them to rest on as their muscles sang with the exertion. Ari passed her a glass of cool water, knowing by now she would not drink the wine, and snagged a flaky, buttery bread thing that seemed to be half air. A croissant, River thought they were called.

Her early life on Osiris felt so distant most times, but once in a while, a memory would trigger—a pleasant one, not one to flinch from—and she would remember a small detail. The scent of the sweet jasmine her mother always requested the gardeners plant. The fine leather chair in her father's study, soft and worn in. She wasn't supposed to be in there, but he was never mad when she was. And Simon, always Simon, there in every memory as the best big brother one could possibly have.

He still was that. Always would be. Though he did need so much protecting and looking after.

"Dancing with you is a gift, Ocean," Ari said as they picked at their croissant. "I know I've said it a hundred times by now, but I'll say it a hundred more. I've had more fun this past day than in a long time."

"Dancing is a gift for me, too," River said. "Makes things quiet. Easier. Math can do it sometimes, too. Physics. Equations have their own sort of rhythm and flow."

Ari's eyes lit up in surprise and delight. They looked around, then leaned in closer and lowered their voice.

"I'm actually studying mathematics. At night, after the

dancers are free to go. Don't tell anyone though, okay? I'm... not supposed to."

River cocked her head and studied her friend closer. She'd been so excited to find a dancer who could keep up with her that she hadn't bothered to look farther beneath the surface. She looked now, peering this way and that, meeting Ari's eyes. And she saw.

"Ah," River said. "You're a lion too. I see. I should have known. You shine so bright, how could this be all?"

Ari laughed a little and shrugged it off. River could see they hadn't understood, and a flicker of that familiar frustration lit in her chest.

"You'll do it," River said insistently. "You want to use your brain. You love to dance but you want to do it wrapped in numbers, a *pas de deux* with the threads that tie the universe together. You want to discover and solve and teach and rise up. And you will. You'll do it."

Ari sat stock still, barely breathing, captivated by the power and certainty in River's voice.

"I don't know how you know all that," they finally whispered. "But you're right. I want that. Don't get me wrong, I love to dance, and I'm so lucky to be able to do it for a living."

"But is it living?" River asked, interrupting. So many people, all of them wrapping their dreams in layers of excuses, blocking themselves from destiny with a wall built brick by brick with their own doubts and fears. "They're not mutually exclusive. You can love this and still want that. I do."

"You do?" Ari asked, almost pleading.

The poor thing. River hated that it took meeting a mind reader of sorts for them to feel seen and understood. But then, there were others, too. There would be more. Things would change. It would be better, soon. Or… not soon? But eventually? River clutched her head, wincing as all the things she knew or maybe knew or heard or saw or *something* went crashing around, destroying the calm and clarity she'd hard earned from her dance.

"Ocean, you want to dance again?" Ari asked, relieved to change the subject and having enough experience by now to know when River's mind was taking a bad turn.

River hopped to her feet, keeping her eyes closed as her thoughts clamored. It was nice, having someone who didn't just flee or panic when the effects of what had been done to her flared to the surface. Someone who enjoyed her company anyway, and who cared enough to help her through it.

"Want to learn a new step?" Ari asked, taking River's hand. "I've been working on some new choreography for a piece the band is working on, and—"

"Can't," River said wistfully, finally opening her eyes. "It's time to go. I'm sorry."

"What?" Ari blinked. "I thought you were here for two more days. What do you—"

"Hey, Ocean!"

River turned to see Kaylee approaching with a wave. She lifted a hand and gave a funny little wave back.

"My ride's here," River said. She met Ari's eyes again, knowing her direct gaze was too intense for most people, and put her hands on their shoulders. "Thank you for dancing with me. You're a great friend. I'll see you soon, and then you'll have your dream."

Ari opened their mouth as if to protest, or to ask for details… then closed their eyes with a pained expression.

"Promise?" they whispered, squeezing one of River's hands where it rested on their shoulder.

"Promise."

Then, without another word, River spun on her toe and skipped over to Kaylee.

"I'm ready. Let's go."

Kaylee threw an arm around River as they left the hall. "You already know what's going on?"

"More than most," River sang in response. "Do you?"

Kaylee laughed. "Probably not, if I'm honest. Not like you do. But the cap'n will tell us what's what, and we'll all come out the other side all right. Ain't it so?"

"It's so," River replied with the utmost confidence. "From a certain point of view."

Kaylee looked down at her, puzzled. "What d'you mean, 'certain point of view'?"

River sighed internally but didn't let her exasperation show. Kaylee was a sweet soul, and she cared for River, even though River still scared her a bit. Wouldn't do to make her feel talked down to. She tried to explain.

"Who defines the parameters of 'all right?' You, me, Mal, the duke, the duchess, your friend Oganya, my friend Ari, and every other person who ever has or ever will exist. Everyone has a different definition of 'all right.' So, we have to define the variable before we can determine with any degree of certainty the correct solution to the equation."

"Okay then," Kaylee said, clearly getting a bit lost in the math analogy but accepting it regardless. "Well, my definition would be all of us crew and our friends getting out of this safe and unhurt. And *Serenity*, too, of course."

"Oh. Well." River thought for a moment. "I can't promise anything."

Kaylee visibly paled.

"Uh. Okay then. We should… probably get to the ship, then, shouldn't we?"

"Yes, that's for the best," River said with absolute certainty. "That's our role. Time to dance the steps. Thankfully, I've had a good warmup."

"I guess I have too, in a way," Kaylee said. "Sad to be leaving, though."

River smiled up at her. It was almost like Kaylee understood.

"Don't worry. We'll be back."

14

Simon wasn't sure if he felt better or worse with both River and Kaylee gone. On the one hand, they were safely in orbit and out of danger, on their way to Kerry's moon, and that was a comfort. On the other… well. He always felt better when they were near.

Regardless, he was happy to be occupied and useful, tending to some of the guards injured in the brief fighting that had happened just outside the duke's compound. From the tales he'd heard, it seemed the other side had come out considerably worse for wear. However, thanks to an opening salvo involving a rocket and falling chunks of concrete, it was no surprise that only two soldiers had emerged without injury.

The duke's medical staff did not need the help, per se. They were professional, well trained, and adequately staffed. Simon didn't handle being alone and idle well, though, so he'd offered his services and they'd gratefully accepted. And when one soldier had been carried in with a severe trauma to the head and ribs from falling debris, well, a top-notch trauma surgeon had suddenly come in very handy. After eight hours in surgery, Simon emerged exhausted yet elated, with the satisfaction of a job well done. He lived to heal people, and it felt good to be fulfilling his calling once again. *Serenity* had gotten into a fair number of scrapes, and he'd been called into action often enough. It was a very, very different situation though, working on people you considered friends, even family, as the only medical professional in an understocked ship's infirmary, versus being part of a care team in a professional medical setting with all the supplies and support one could need.

He felt a twinge of regret—one that came less and less often these days—as he thought back on his old life. The comforts of the Core. His family, back when they'd acted like real family. A job he loved, was good at, felt fulfilled by. A lackluster social life, sure, but he'd been plenty happy anyway.

But then there was River. If he had to give it all up again to keep her safe, he would. He still remembered, viscerally, the panic and helplessness he'd felt once he'd gotten her message— that she was being tortured at the so-called "academy" she'd been attending. Because of the ten-year age gap between them, he'd always felt extra protective, almost parental toward her. So when his parents had completely failed to come through for River, he'd done the only thing he could do. He couldn't fathom how someone in his situation could do anything else.

After thoroughly scrubbing up and sending his PPE down the chute to be disinfected, Simon bid the head doctor a brief farewell and headed out into the fading light of evening. It was nice, at least, to know he had an incredibly comfortable bed and a private room bigger than a closet to go back to. Another vestige of life in the Core, and one he sorely missed. *Serenity*'s crew quarters weren't too bad, but Simon didn't get one of the crew rooms. No, he, River, and Shepherd Book were still relegated to the passenger dorms, which were barely big enough to fit a bed. There was one crew room available, thanks to Zoë and Wash sharing, but Mal "didn't think it'd be fair" to play favorites between Simon, River, and Book. And so, the room sat unused, and Simon tried to forget it was there and not get claustrophobic. Not for the first time since arriving on Kerry, Simon had the fleeting thought that he could get used to life here. If he could bribe enough people, disguise him and River well enough… but no. They'd never be safe staying in one place, and certainly not in a place with Alliance loyalists. Would they?

A tempting thought, realistic or not.

As he walked the white stone path from the hospital to the guest cottage, he passed the local tavern, which was busy with folk ordering dinner and enjoying end-of-the-day drinks. At one particularly boisterous table, Simon caught sight of a familiar face. One that did not inspire endearment or warm fuzzy feelings, unfortunately.

Jayne Cobb sat at a long rectangular table with what looked like a group of off-duty soldiers, his chair precariously tipped back on two legs and a mug of ale in one hand. His cheeks were flushed and his hair was mussed up, much as he'd looked on New Canton when they'd all gotten quite into their cups drinking with the mudders. His laugh was loud enough to tell Simon exactly how drunk Jayne was. Considering the message he'd gotten from Mal right before he'd gone into surgery, that he was sending River and Kaylee into orbit and that the rest of the crew was staying combat-ready… well. Jayne definitely wasn't looking combat-ready at the moment.

"Doc! Hey, Doc!" Jayne called, and Simon winced. He'd been spotted. The soldiers turned and raised their mugs to him with a cheer, likely assuming he was a friend of Jayne's. He forced a smile and strode over to the table, leaning on the low fence surrounding the outdoor seating area.

"Hi," he said cautiously. "How's it going?"

"It's going ruttin' great, Doc. Have you tried the ale here? It's great stuff!" Jayne said, which was apparently worthy of another round of cheers and hoisted drinks.

"Are you sure you should be drinking right now?" Simon kept his voice low so as not to make things worse between them by humiliating Jayne in front of his new drinking buddies. "Won't the captain want you combat-ready?"

"Bah, screw the captain," Jayne said far too loudly, shattering any discretion Simon had managed. "He's overreacting. As always."

Jayne lifted his mug of ale in a wobbly toast to the soldiers ringing the table.

"These fine folks here told me we ain't got nothin' to worry about. They're well prepared to deal with anything those *gǒu cào de* insurgents throw at them."

Simon sighed and rubbed at a spot of tension developing between his brows.

"If that's the case, then why did I just perform eight hours of surgery to save a man's life who was injured in the attack today?"

The table suddenly fell quiet, and one man stood, staring Simon down.

"He lived?" the man said, eyes intense. "Murphy? You were able to save him? We hadn't gotten word yet."

Simon blinked and nodded slowly. "Yes. I'm not supposed to talk about patient condition, only the listed next of kin can receive that kind of information, but I suppose there's no harm in telling you the basic facts. He's alive, and I expect him to make a near-full recovery."

The whole table collectively let out a flurry of released tension, with sighs of relief, cheers, and much shoulder-slapping. The one who had stood rushed around the table to take Simon's hand and shake it vigorously.

"Thank you for saving him, Doc," he said. "I—we all were really worried he wouldn't pull through. It's half the reason we're all drinking right now."

"And now we have a better reason to drink," a woman at the table said, lifting her mug to the sky. "To Murphy, and to… this fancy doctor bloke right here!"

"Huzzah!" the others at the table cried, and they all knocked back their ales, Jayne included. The man standing before Simon looked more serious and solemn, though.

"They caught us by surprise, Doc," he said, quiet and intense. "To answer your earlier question. That's the only reason they got us bleeding. Next time, we'll be ready, and they'll be sorry."

Jayne, missing the man's tone entirely, let out a guffawing laugh.

"See, Doctor Prissypants, no need to get all uptight and fussy. These fine folks have got everything under control." He stumbled to his feet and attempted a wink, which instead looked like an uncontrollable facial spasm. "So I'm gonna have another drink, an' I don't wanna hear a word from that pretty little mouth of yours."

He turned and stumbled away as Simon mouthed, "Pretty mouth?" to himself… then shook his head to clear it away. Best to let the ramblings of a drunk Jayne be as clouds in the sky and let them float on by.

"Well then," Simon said, looking around awkwardly. "I suppose I'll take my leave then. Enjoy your celebration. I'm glad your friend is okay."

"Aw, come on, you won't have one drink with us, Doc?" the woman who had spoken earlier shouted far louder than necessary.

"No," Simon said. "But, uh, thank you. It's just, eight hours of surgery is pretty draining. I need to rest in case I'm needed again."

"Oh, don't you worry about that, Doc," another of the soldiers called. "Only casualties next time will be on the other side, and there won't be no saving them. It's gonna be a bloodbath, you wait!"

The whole table cheered again and went back to their drinks, seemingly forgetting about Simon altogether. A chill went down his spine at the words, but he shrugged it off as soldier bravado. He couldn't imagine having to face down violence as a job, and they must have had to do all kinds of mental gymnastics to make the morality equation balance and face the constant fear of injury and death. That's all it was.

Simon had gotten better at that kind of mental calculus since taking on the mission to save his sister and joining the crew of *Serenity*. But he was never going to be one of the hardest members of the crew. Even now, knowing the threat of violence was high, he couldn't silence the constant low-level hum of alertness and fear.

Nothing to be done about it now. All he could do was rest, recharge, and make sure he was ready for the next person to be rolled in on a gurney.

Hopefully it wouldn't be a familiar face staring up at him from the operating table.

15

Zoë woke with a start, scanning for enemy ships on the horizon, muscles tensed in readiness. She searched for the source of the explosion, of the flash still lingering on the insides of her eyelids with every blink, and the tinge of acrid smoke in her nose, the too-familiar scent of Alliance artillery. Serenity Valley hadn't been lost yet, and it wouldn't be so long as she drew breath. Sleep be damned. She patted around for her weapon, which should have been right beside her. She never slept without it in arm's reach.

But her hand found only soft blankets, fluffy pillows, and the empty space where there should have been a man sleeping next to her. Wash. Her husband. Who she had married after the war. The war that was over.

Just like that, the flash and smoke disappeared from her senses like the ghosts they were. Zoë flopped back onto the pillow and groaned, covering her face with both hands. It happened less often these days, but still far more often than she'd like. Still, something had woken her, and her every muscle was tense, on edge. Her body knew something was wrong, even if her mind hadn't caught up. She threw back the covers and grabbed her pants with one hand and her comm with the other, dressing quickly as she called up to *Serenity*.

"Wash, baby? You up?"

A beat of silence, then Wash's sleep-drunk voice came over the connection, sounding like his face was still smashed against the pillow.

"Whaz goin' on?" he murmured.

"Dunno yet," Zoë said, tying off her boots. "Wake up and get to the bridge. We need *Serenity*'s sensors looking down on the duke's compound."

"What 'bout you? Safe?" he replied, sounding slightly more conscious and concerned.

Then a not-very-distant explosion rattled the windows, and Zoë knew instantly what had brought her out of her dreams and into another Serenity Valley nightmare. Her brain finally processed the fading echo of the explosion she'd heard immediately after waking.

"That's not the first blast," she said to herself, and burst out into the hallway at the same time as Mal.

"Rooftop," Mal said, already turning down the corridor toward the stairs. "There's a reinforced lookout point, should be able to see what's going on."

"Yes, sir. Blast sounded like it came from the east," Zoë said.

"Direction of town."

"My thoughts exactly, sir."

"Can someone explain what's going on?" Wash's voice chimed in over the comm.

"Not now, baby. We'll be in touch," Zoë said, then cut off the connection with a tinge of regret. Wash would be worried and panicking but, as much as she loved him, in a combat situation she needed his voice completely out of her mind.

Zoë and Mal sprinted up the stairs two at a time, but slowed when they approached the rooftop door, both drawing their weapons. Once ready, Mal nodded and eased the door slowly open, following it with the business end of his Liberty Hammer. Zoë kept her finger safely off the trigger of her Mare's Leg until Mal was clear, following him out to sweep the rooftop. Once they verified they were alone, Mal pulled out his comm.

"Jayne, Doctor, get your asses to the rooftop," he snapped.

Jayne's groggy voice replied faster than Zoë might have expected, considering the state he'd been in that evening. "Aw, Mal, c'mon—"

"Now, Jayne, don't care if you're still in your skivvies. You get your lazy ass up here," Mal snapped back.

"You bring binocs, sir?" Zoë asked, peering over the edge toward the east, the town on the horizon. "I see muzzle flashes, but not much else."

"Surely did," he said, switching them to night mode and taking a quick look through before handing them over. "Looks like combatants right outside the wall trying to break through."

"Well, good luck to them. Ain't gonna work," Jayne said as he stumbled through the door wearing nothing but trousers and his favorite gun, a Callahan Full-bore Auto-lock he called Vera. "The folks I was talking to said there's steel running through the whole heart of it, no weak points to speak of. They can fire rockets at it all day if they want. Don't see how attacking it from the outside's gonna do much good."

Simon finally joined them, rounding out all the crew still staying at the guest cottage. Shepherd Book was still at the abbey, theoretically safe.

"What's going on?" Simon asked.

"Dunno yet," Zoë said. "This is the second time the insurgents have made an attack on the wall itself. They should know by now what they're dealing with."

"Unless it's a distraction," Mal said, racing to the other side of the roof. Zoë followed, taking up position behind a low wall protecting the building's air conditioning units. She aimed the binoculars out toward the opposite side of the compound, but empty fields were all that lay beyond the walls. She returned to her original point and searched along the wall up to the eastern gate that led into town… and finally spotted the answer.

"Enemy at the gate," Zoë reported. "It *was* a distraction. Pulled the guards away from the main entrance."

"Everyone ready yourselves," Mal said. "This ain't our fight, and I don't want no one involved, you hear? But I mean for us to defend ourselves if it comes down to it. Got it, Jayne?"

"Why you askin' me?" Jayne said, finally sounding fully awake.

"Because your new best buddies are the duke's soldiers, and you might be feeling some kinda kinship there," Zoë said.

"They're good folk," Jayne said, defensive. "But I ain't about to go charging into battle to save them."

Zoë gave him the side eye but didn't say anything further. For all his protestations, Jayne Cobb did have a strange streak of heart that very occasionally cropped up at unexpected times. He'd never be a saint, or even a good man, really. But he wasn't a pure selfish crook either. At least, not all the time.

"Should we be… I don't know, leaving or something?" Simon asked, shifting his weight from foot to foot nervously.

"Can't bring *Serenity* down with this going on," Zoë said.

"And I don't mean to," Mal said. "Unless this fight gets worse, I mean to give the duke the time he needs to find us extra cargo to haul out to Silverhold. We could wait it out in orbit, but there's Inara and Book to consider, and I don't fancy offending the duke when he's bankrolling our next six months of rations, by the sound of it. I'm not seeing anything yet that'd provide any real danger. Just more of the same."

"You can go back inside if you're scared of a little gunfire," Jayne taunted. Zoë tuned out the bickering. She and Mal had both slept with the sounds of war in the background more times than she could count, but not everyone had. No shame in a noncombatant taking shelter, far as she was concerned.

The clatter of gunfire and the occasional explosion of larger artillery continued at the original attack site, but Zoë focused the binocs in on the party attacking the gate.

"This attack *is* much larger, sir," Zoë reported back. "Maybe thirty at the original attack site, but I'm seeing as many as forty outside the gate."

"Seventy?" Mal said. "If these folks are drawing forces from the town, must be a damn large share of the folks living there, small as it were. Just about every combat-ready adult."

"Yes, sir. Could be they've drawn troops from the surrounding towns as well. If this attack is about unseating the duke, they could be from anywhere on the continent," Zoë said. "They're nearly through. We might want to consider sheltering."

"Movement on the rooftops," Mal snapped, interrupting. "Two o'clock."

Zoë swung the binocs around and focused in on the only buildings in the compound taller than the guest cottage: the palace and the barracks. Sure enough, she spotted a group of soldiers atop each, preparing to return fire.

"Shoulder-mounted launchers of some kind," Zoë said, handing the binocs to Mal. "Two on each rooftop."

"Risky, having two in such close quarters," Mal said. "The backblast, depending on what they're firing—"

All four launchers fired simultaneously, with three streaking out toward the gate party and one toward the distraction party. Zoë narrowed her eyes.

"What was that?" she asked. "Didn't look right for a rocket."

There was a pop and a flash as the ordnance exploded in midair, then disappeared into the dark.

"*Wǒ de tiān a*," Mal said, his voice rough. He dropped the binoculars and looked to Zoë, shaking his head. "Tell me I'm not seeing what I'm seeing."

Zoë, shaken by the tremor in Mal's tone, took the binocs back and focused in on the closest group of insurgents, bathed in the floodlights mounted on the outside of the walls. What she saw froze her right down to the core.

The ordnance had burst, raining thousands of tiny pieces down on the combatants with enough force to pierce their skin anywhere that wasn't covered by body armor. And, considering these plainclothes insurgents had almost no armor to speak of, that meant everywhere. Tiny metallic shards drilled through skin and bone, leaving small spots of blood at each of the many entry points.

Those insignificant wounds were not what had inspired the horror in Mal's voice.

"Devil's Thorns," Zoë breathed, lowering the binoculars before she could see what was to come.

"That's impossible," Simon said, puzzled. "That was outlawed by the Alliance during the Unification War in the absolute strictest terms."

"Not soon enough," Mal said, his voice ragged.

Zoë squeezed her eyes shut, but it did no good. The images before her weren't real-time input from her eyes, but horrific images from the past burned deep and hot into her brain. She didn't have to see with her eyes to know in excruciating detail precisely what was unfolding second by second. She had seen it once before, and once was enough to make sure she'd see it again and again in her nightmares for the rest of her life.

"Can someone please tell me what the hell is going on?" Jayne asked. "I'm tired of your cryptic war buddy game."

Zoë opened her eyes and looked to Simon. "Do you know?"

Simon seemed to understand her request, and he nodded, his face sympathetic.

"Devil's Thorns are a sort of shrapnel grenade that rains down almost microscopic pieces of nanorobotic metal coated in a fast-acting toxin."

"So what?" Jayne asked. "Shrapnel grenades have been around since Earth-That-Was. Wouldn't wanna be hit by one, but what's with you two looking like you're gonna chuck your dinner?"

Seeing Mal and Zoë were still not fit to speak, Simon continued the explanation, as if repeating a lecture or a passage from a book. Zoë let his voice be dry and robotic and factual in her mind, to disconnect from her very real and direct experience etched into her memories.

"The shrapnel is self-replicating. First, the toxin paralyzes you within seconds. Then, as you lay there unable to move, the tiny pieces of metal under your skin begin to grow. They branch out like the roots of a new plant under your skin, but really slow, piercing anything they come into contact with. Muscle, organs, you name it. While that happens, the toxin goes to work on your amygdala, ensuring that you feel every second of the process. It's quite similar to what was done to River, in a way. It disables your brain's ability to regulate pain, so there's no checking out, no going numb, no pain receptors overloading and shutting down. Eventually the thorns will pierce your lungs and you'll suffocate or drown, or they'll cause enough internal bleeding that you die from that, or—"

"Okay, okay, I get it. Gorram, Doc. Coulda just said it's the worst possible way to die and left it at that," Jayne said, looking a little green around the gills.

"It is hours of absolute agony," he agreed. "The Alliance Ethics Review Board banned their use after only a few field deployments. It was declared too inhumane even for war, and with too much risk of friendly fire and unintended civilian casualties, same as weaponized pathogens."

"Yeah, that message took a while to filter out through the ranks," Zoë spat bitterly, finally finding her voice once more. "Else some fine Alliance brass thought they could use the excuse they hadn't heard the news yet."

"We lost a lot of people to that weapon," Mal said. "Fine soldiers, young kids barely of legal age to fight, all of them tortured to death. And we didn't know what it was at the time, so we couldn't even do them the courtesy of shooting them.

Still called for med evac like we was doing them a kindness instead of making 'em suffer."

Zoë choked on the rage Mal's words brought roaring back, clenching her fists to keep herself from hitting something. They'd seen the Thorns deployed for the first and only time during a battle on Three Hills. It had been a disaster from the start; poorly planned, poorly led, and based on bad intel likely fed by a mole hoping to annihilate two whole platoons of Independents. And they'd just about managed it—three-quarters of their force had been hit by Devil's Thorns. Zoë and Mal had taken cover in time. But they'd had to watch. They'd had to hold position and tend to those suffering until air support could cover their withdrawal. When the evac arrived, they'd been ordered to abandon the position and leave their suffering comrades behind.

That decision still haunted Zoë. She and Mal had only been following orders, and they didn't know any better yet. The weapon didn't yet have a name, and its reputation hadn't yet filtered down through the ranks. It was only after the fact that they knew the truth: that there was no separate med evac coming for their comrades. That there was no saving any of them. That the merciful thing to do would have been to go from trench to trench and shoot them all before they left.

"What I can't understand is where the duke got his hands on the gorram things, much less how he could stomach using 'em," Mal said, rubbing a hand over his face. "Far as I know, they stopped production after they were outlawed. Don't imagine there could be more'n a few dozen crates floating around the entire 'verse, and they'd be the blackest of black-market goods."

Jayne took a step back, glancing between Zoë, Mal, and Simon with a puzzled look on his face.

"What do you mean?" he asked with genuine confusion. "We know exactly how the duke got 'em."

"We do?" Simon asked.

But the horror was already dawning cold and red in Zoë's heart.

"Well, *yeah*. That's the cargo we just brought in," Jayne said.

The answering silence between them wasn't punctured by any gunfire, explosions, or grenade launches.

There was no need. The fighting had ceased.

16

All at once, the picture snapped into clear focus, and Mal was *pissed.*

"*Nǐ tā mā de. Tiān xià suǒ yǒu de rén dōu gāi sǐ,*" he swore, long and profane. "When were you thinking of telling us this, Jayne?"

"I just said, I thought you knew!" Jayne shouted back. "Also don't know why you care. We did a job, we got paid for it, and we ain't the ones killing folk, so I don't much see an issue here."

"Don't see an issue?" Mal said, his voice going high and hoarse in a way that he'd be embarrassed about any other time, sounding like a prepubescent boy. Right now, with the vision of his comrades being slowly tortured from the inside still superimposed over the present, he couldn't care less what he sounded like. "Jayne, those people out there are being killed in the worst way imaginable and we're the ones what put the weapon into the duke's hand. Not to mention we were apparently party to a trade in the most deeply illegal sort of weapon there is. Not even the Alliance special forces are allowed to use it. Think on that for a second, Jayne. Put every brain cell in your thick skull to work on solving that little equation."

"We haul illegal things all the time," Jayne countered. "It's kind of our whole business model, ain't it? Our last, what, three cargos have all been contraband, in case you hadn't noticed."

"This is different," Zoë said.

"It's no different! You're both of you just getting all in your heads about the gorram war that's been over for years, and no one give a *niú fèn* about it anymore except you."

Mal surged forward and grabbed a handful of the strap holding Vera to Jayne's chest and used it to slam him against the wall at his back.

"*Hún dàn!* Now is not the time to be running that mouth of yours, Jayne. You don't know what you're talking about, and you're mucking about in things you can't even imagine. Life as a petty crook ain't nothing on fighting a war and you best remember that. Zoë."

"Sir."

"Things calmed down enough that we can do what needs to be done?"

"Will be by the time we get there, sir."

"Good." Mal pulled out his Liberty Hammer, checked it, then turned to Jayne and Simon.

"Me and Zoë are going to go put those poor bastards out of their misery. You're welcome to stay here or come and help as you choose, but there'll be no bellyaching about it neither way. Clear?"

"Yes," Simon said. "Though I'd rather not use a gun, if you don't mind. I have a few injections I can administer in my kit."

"Mercy will be welcome no matter how you choose to bring it, Doc. And you, Jayne?"

"Yeah, yeah, I'm coming. Gonna need a smaller gun, though."

At Simon's surprised look, Jayne's eyes narrowed.

"What're you looking at? Just because I don't much care about hauling the cargo, don't mean I like the idea of them people out there dying all slow and torturous. Never let it be said that Jayne Cobb ain't a merciful man. Mama Cobb raised her boys right."

Mal restrained himself from amending that remark with the obvious fact that Mama Cobb had, in fact, raised a criminal who had quite a body count to his name and didn't see the moral dilemma of hauling instruments of torture. Jayne wouldn't see the contradiction and it would only lead to a fight that Mal was very much not in the mood for. Instead, he pulled out his comm and called Shepherd Book. Despite the late (or very early) hour, Book answered almost immediately.

"Captain Reynolds. Is everyone unhurt?"

"We are. Guessing the same holds for you, seeing as you've answered without any screaming."

"I'm intact. I'm afraid the same can't be said of Brother Hewson, one of the residents of the abbey. He's a habitual early riser and happened to be out for a morning walk at the time of the attack."

"*Zhēn dǎo méi,*" Mal said, closing his eyes. "I'm sorry to hear that, preacher. Were any other civilians from town hit?"

"Just one farmer who was up early to tend her animals that we know of. We're out among the victims trying to assess the situation, but…" Book trailed off. "Mal, are you familiar with Devil's Thorns?"

"All too familiar, Shepherd. We're on our way out to bring mercy to those fallen. I trust you and your holy folk can see to them from there?"

"We'll be going around to perform last rites, then assisting the families in recovering the remains. But there are near on sixty dead. It will be some long hours. And Captain?"

He paused for a moment, and when his voice returned, it was heavy with the terrible knowledge of exactly what was happening to those fallen.

"Thank you. For doing what needs to be done for these poor suffering souls."

Mal wondered for the thousandth time what kind of holy man had knowledge of a weapon as soul-scorchingly horrific as Devil's Thorns, but he just as quickly dropped the train of thought. There was no time to wonder about mysteries the man clearly didn't want solved.

There were people in pain. People in need. It felt an impossible task, and certainly another deeply etched memory in the making.

But we do the impossible when it's right.

"Come on," he said to the others, holstering his gun again. "Zoë, call Wash back and update him on the situation, then let's stock up on necessities."

He sighed, rubbing a hand over his eyes.

"We're going to need extra ammo."

Once loaded down with enough ammo to take care of the entire fallen insurgent force, Mal led his contingent to the smaller side gate they'd used the previous morning. There were two guards stationed there despite the early hour, which Mal had expected given the circumstances. He hoped he wouldn't have to use violence to pass, but he would, if necessary.

"No one in or out by order of the duke," the guard on the left said as they approached. "Turn on around. Should be good to travel in a few hours' time."

"I'm Captain Reynolds, on my way to retrieve my crewmate who's been staying at the abbey. I need to check on him after the deployment of those Devil's Thorns."

The guards looked at each other, blinking and unsure.

"Yes, we already know what happened out there and exactly what we'll see when we walk through that gate," Mal said. "Seen it before, back during the war. So there's no reason to be keeping us in when we've got a man on the outside. Let us pass and I'd consider it a kindness."

The guard on the right shrugged, her hand still hovering near her sidearm as she scanned the array of weaponry they carried.

"We're gonna have to report this to the duke," she said.

"You do that," Mal said. "You let him know Malcolm Reynolds is coming to see him soon as we get back."

The other guard spotted Simon's medical bag and spoke up.

"No one is to give aid to the insurgents wounded in the attacks," he said, pointing to Simon.

Simon glanced to Mal, who smiled in a way that a goodly number of people around the 'verse had come to dread. Unless you were a friend, it was wise to be wary of a Malcolm Reynolds smile; he was likely lying, about to strip your pride from you with a fearsome bit of tongue-lashing wit, or a hairsbreadth from drawing his gun.

This time? Bit of all three.

"Well, well! What have we got here, Zoë?" he said, gesturing to the two puzzled guards.

"Seems to me we have a pair of soldiers party to a war crime, sir."

"There ain't no war on," the left guard protested, but Mal carried right on.

"Devil's Thorns is just about as illegal as a thing can get. When the Alliance Ethics Board deems a thing inhuman, well then, you really know, don't you?"

"Sure do, sir. Downright sickening, it is."

"Ain't it just. Wouldn't want to be part of such a thing myself."

"Me neither, sir. Couldn't live with myself."

"Nor I, Zoë. Takes a special kind of person to be able to stand by while people are suffering the worst kind of death."

Both guards bristled. The one on the right started to draw a gun.

"Our orders are to prevent anyone from interfering with the insurgents. This is meant to prevent any further violence in the future. I can't let you—"

She was far too slow a draw. Mal had his Liberty Hammer pointed straight between her eyes before her gun ever left its holster.

"We'll do as we damn well please and nothing but," he said. And he smiled again.

"Now then. We—" he gestured to the assembled crewmembers "—are going to go out there, put those poor people out of their horrific torturous misery, and retrieve our crew member. And you, good little wind-up soldier you are, can run off and tell the duke right away, if you like. Wake him from his bed, in fact! I'm sure he's sleeping soundly while these people are suffering. Probably got up just long enough to order the weapon used, then went back to bed with no trouble at all."

The guard on the left sputtered. "The duke is—"

"I don't give a damn what you think the duke is," Mal said, his smile dropping off his face so fast the guard took a step back. "He's a sick man for even owning Devil's Thorns, much less using it. And I intend to tell him so to his face, soon as what needs doing is done. Now. Get out of our way."

They got out of the way.

Mal stomped through the gate at the pace of his righteous fury, so single-minded that he forgot to prepare himself for the fact that the insurgents had been trying to break through that very gate. And so the bodies of the fallen were barely ten paces outside the wall.

Mal stopped short, fighting the surging nausea threatening to shove his dinner right back out his throat. His vision blurred, half in the present and half in the past, seeing comrades and strangers alike lying at his feet. For most of them, the paralytic had kicked in while their eyes were wide open, terrified, their brows knitted in pain and their jaws hung low in a silent scream. Some lucky, blessed few had been squeezing their eyes shut against the agony when the toxin had taken hold, and so at least didn't have the drying eyes unable to blink as an added part of their torture.

From his right, a warm brown hand gripped his arm tightly, bringing him fully back to the present. Zoë. He looked up at her, seeing her pain in the tension at the corners of her eyes, and knew she must be seeing the same ghosts. She'd always been better at compartmentalizing, though. His rock, always anchoring him so he could focus on what needed doing. He gave her a nod, then spoke loud enough for all those nearby to hear.

"We'll be back to help you shortly. This will end soon. You have my word."

"We're not going to just start here?" Jayne asked. "Why we wasting time?"

"We're meeting up with Shepherd Book and the folks from the abbey first. They're performing last rites for everyone. We'll start where they did and work our way through."

Jayne grumbled something unintelligible but wisely (for once) didn't say anything else.

They walked through the field of bodies around to the area of the initial attack against the wall, where they quickly spotted three figures in the black vestments of the church moving from person to person. They performed the sign of the cross, prayed, anointed with oil, and closed eyes in whichever cases it was possible to do so, moving as efficiently as could be done respectfully. Mal approached Shepherd Book and waited until he was done with his current victim before speaking.

"Where should we start?" he asked.

Shepherd Book's expression was pained and deeply, terribly sad, but he pointed back toward the abbey.

"We started with those closest to the abbey and have been working in this direction. We've let them know you'll be coming, but… you'll say something to them first, won't you?"

Mal nodded, looking around to the others to ensure they all got the message.

"Will do, preacher. We'll bring these people peace."

Book's mouth quivered, and he placed a hand on Mal's shoulder, squeezing.

"Thank you for this great and terrible duty. May God look down on you and guide your hand as you bring mercy to these poor souls. Amen."

An echoing "amen" nearly escaped Mal's own lips, but he tightened them at the last moment. That wasn't his way anymore, but he clapped the Shepherd on the shoulder all the same, then led his crew away to the far end of the killing fields.

"You heard the shepherd. Introduce yourself. Make it quick and clean. Say something before you do the deed."

"Like what?" Jayne asked.

Mal thought for a moment, then decided to lead by example. He drew his pistol, checked the chamber to ensure it was loaded, then approached the closest casualty. He was a young man, no older than twenty, with pale skin and dusky brown hair cropped close. He could have been any number of kids who served at Mal's side during the war. His clothes were ragged and patched, his boots peeling at the sides and barely held together with fraying laces. He was lying on his back, frozen with his knees pulled together and his hands clawing at his chest. His eyes, thankfully, were closed, by either luck or intervention. That made it easier.

Mal cleared his throat.

"My name is Malcolm Reynolds," he said, voice roughened with emotion. "I'm going to end your pain and stop the man who did this to you. Be at peace, brother."

Then he aimed his Liberty Hammer true, right between the boy's eyes, and pulled the trigger without looking away.

17

By the time the sun had fully risen, the grisly deed had been done.

Mal led Zoë, Simon, and Jayne back through the gate, spattered with blood and other unspeakable things, the silence vast and weighty between them. Their souls had never been heavier, Mal thought, except perhaps that day in Serenity Valley. Knowing that their killings had meant an end to pain and suffering did not diminish the scarring it left on Mal's psyche, the nightmares that would likely follow, or the hot, heavy feeling behind his eyes.

And it did nothing for the heavy burden of guilt Mal carried at having brought the godforsaken weapons to the planet in the first place.

"We going to head back and clean up first, sir?" Zoë asked, her voice quiet as if they still walked among the dead.

"No," Mal said flatly. "I want him to see exactly what he's wrought. People like him, they sit on their pretty thrones and pull the trigger from a distance, acting out their violence through other people. He never has to see the spray of blood and brains or smell the piss of the terrified soldiers beside him. I'd be willing to bet he's never seen a battlefield in his life."

Mal took a deep breath in through his nose to calm himself before he got too fired up, then continued.

"So, we're bringing the battlefield to him. Let him see. Let him dare send us away for the state of us. I'd love to see him try."

"Could it be the duke didn't really know how horrific they were?" Simon asked, naively hopeful. "As you said, he doesn't strike me as someone experienced in the craft of war. Maybe he just deployed them without really knowing what exactly they did."

Zoë shook her head. "No."

"No," Mal agreed. "That's irresponsible at best, and damn unlikely to boot. The duke is not a stupid man, and you don't jump through the hoops to buy something that heavily restricted unless you know exactly what you're getting. He knew what he was doing, and he did it to his own citizens."

"And to deploy it that close to town, too…" Zoë trailed off, shaking her head again. "Those weapons have a huge splash radius. Excess casualties were almost guaranteed."

"Right," Mal said. "There won't be no worming his way out of this one with fancy words and jingling coin, no matter how much work he promises us. I won't be party to another massacre like this."

"What? Mal, come on, be reasonable—" Jayne started, but Mal whirled on him and shut him up with a finger pointed in his face.

"One more word, Jayne, and so help me I will shoot you right here, right now. You love the duke and his soldier folk so much, you ask him for a job and get your carcass off my boat."

"You know, that's a damn good idea, Mal," Jayne said. "Might just do that. Who would want to stay on a falling apart junk heap of a ship with a crazy girl waiting to stab me again and a captain who can't keep the work flowing so we can actually, you know, eat something other than protein goo? Maybe enjoy a drink and some paid company on whatever planet we put down on? You ask me—"

Simon bristled at the comment about River, but Mal charged ahead before he could react.

"But that's the thing," Mal snapped, getting right in Jayne's face. "No one asked you. And I ain't interested in hearing another word. You hate life aboard *Serenity* so much? Fine. Shiny. We'll drop your belongings on the landing pad before we leave. Have a nice life, Jayne Cobb."

Mal turned away and continued his stalking toward the palace, Zoë at his side. He hadn't thought his heart had any more room for anger or disgust and yet, as always, Jayne Cobb rose to the occasion.

"Now, wait—" Jayne started, but Zoë shot him a glare over her shoulder.

"Go back to your room, Jayne. You ain't needed for this."

Mal refused to look back as the sound of Jayne's footsteps paused, then trailed off in another direction with accompanying grumbled commentary. It was probably for the best if Jayne weren't around for this little confrontation anyway. One less volatile element to consider.

"Do you really think he'll leave?" Simon asked, turning to watch Jayne walk away.

Mal shrugged.

"Who knows, and who cares? Bigger worries right now than Jayne Cobb's life goals."

As they approached the large double doors of the palace, the guards straightened, and the footman shifted nervously.

"Captain Reynolds," the man said, his voice a mite unsteady. "The duke is taking his breakfast in the dining hall right now. Perhaps you would like to—"

"Join him? Yes, think I will, thanks," Mal said, shouldering his way past with Zoë and Simon in tow.

"No, actually, Captain, I meant—that is, perhaps—"

The man's gibbering faded into the background as Mal retraced his steps from the night of the dinner party, locating the dining hall partly by memory and partly by smell. His stomach rumbled at the sweet, heady scent of pastry on the air, but Mal ignored it. Just another part of the duke's tainted hospitality. Besides, Mal wasn't sure he could truly stomach food until he got the evidence of their early morning work showered off him.

The doors banged open as they entered the dining hall, and every head turned toward them—quickly followed by horrified gasps as the nobles took in their appearance. The duchess, seated at the duke's side, covered her mouth with one hand, her face going pale. Mal stared straight into the eyes of every person who looked his way, letting them witness the flecks of blood on his face and the cold horror in his eyes. They needed to see. They all needed to wake up.

"Ah, Captain Reynolds! Good morning," the duke said in a jovial voice, attempting to break the spell. "I have fine news for you. I've managed to secure cargo for your trip to Silverhold after all. We can have it loaded in your hold this afternoon, if you'd like to recall your ship now that the minor threat has passed. It's quite a lucrative job, too, I think your crew will be well pleased."

Mal almost laughed at the duke's ploy. He'd no doubt already received a report about their activities out in the killing fields. Still, Mal played his role all the same for the benefit of those watching.

"Deal's off. Won't be carrying no cargo for you anymore, Tarmon. Never again."

"Why, Captain," the duke said, putting on an air of concern and hurt. "I'm surprised. I thought you were first and foremost a businessman who prided himself on taking care of his crew. Are they all in agreement about leaving behind our hospitality and paying work?"

"Ain't their call. It's mine, and I say we go," Mal said, refusing to let himself be manipulated. "'Sides, near all of 'em agree that we want nothing to do with you anymore after what you've done. 'Cept Jayne, maybe, but you're welcome to him."

"What I've done?" The duke blinked, the picture of innocence. "Captain, all I've done is avert a lengthy bloody conflict with one quick, decisive strike. If the first attack is so costly, then they'll decide it's not worth it and stop fighting. They'll finally come to the negotiating table. You're a former soldier, are you not? Is it not better to end the conflict altogether with such a strategy than to drag it out and ultimately take more lives in the process?"

"Not like this. Not using Devil's Thorns. It was banned for a reason. Because it's torture. The most inhumane way there is to kill a large number of people all at once. Does that not make you sick? Are you so dead inside that it doesn't even register, that those people suffered in the worst way imaginable?"

The duke frowned. "Those are strong words, Captain. Dead inside? Do you truly think me so horrid? Everything I've done, I have done for the good of my people, both within these walls and without."

"And how exactly was it for the good of the people in the town? How was it good for the brother from the abbey and the farmer out tending her flock who both got caught in that fire?"

The duke shook his head. "Malcolm, you know not of which you speak. It is regrettable that any civilian should be caught in the crossfire, and I will ensure their families are compensated, though I know there is no making up for the loss. But this is the result of many years of back-and-forth struggle of local powers that you have not been privy to. I have spent enormous amounts of time, money, and resources attempting to reach an agreement with the town and other surrounding territories. This is the result, sadly."

The duke looked away, his voice low and heavy. "Would that things had been different."

For one moment—one very brief moment—Mal faltered. Was he overreacting? The duke seemed completely sincere, not a drop of dishonesty in his voice or expression. He truly believed every word he was saying. The people around him were all nodding their agreement, sad but resigned.

But Mal knew there had to be pieces missing. The duke being convinced of one truth didn't make it the only truth. It was Simon who spoke up with the critical question.

"And the people in your territories—what exactly is it that they wanted that you couldn't reach an agreement for?"

The duke laughed bitterly. "What *didn't* they want?

Each and every little town in all of Killarney, spread over hundreds of kilometers, they all wanted the best of everything, and they demanded it done their own way. They wanted me to build hospitals, transportation systems, schools, and a dozen other things, and they wanted their own people deciding all the where and when and how. They've even fought me over farming and mining techniques, as if they know better than the Alliance engineers who designed the best practices. I've had to enact and enforce laws just to get them to farm correctly. It makes no sense. Why not use the proven techniques and fertilizers I've supplied? Why build a hundred of everything? Why not have one hospital with the absolute best resources available in one central location?"

"Meaning your location, I assume," Mal said.

"Well, of course," the duke replied. "Why would it be anywhere else?"

Simon blinked, glancing at Mal as if to say, "Can you believe this guy?"

"Because time means lives," he said. "For a gunshot, for a heart attack or stroke, for so many of the common injuries befalling farmers and miners, the time it takes to get to a doctor is critical."

"A doctor in every town," Mal said, disbelieving. "You're fighting this battle, killing people, because they wanted a local doctor in every town?"

"Bet they wanted a sheriff and clean drinking water and food, too," Zoë said. "How unreasonable."

"Can hardly believe it, myself," Mal added, voice heavy with sarcasm.

"You misunderstand," the duke said with another sigh. "With limited resources, it only makes sense to consolidate. We simply can't afford to do otherwise."

"You can't afford it?" Mal barked a harsh laugh. "Look around you, *Tarmon*. You've an embarrassment of riches in your court here. You could cut back on serving wine from the hours of eight to ten in the morning and pay a doctor's salary for a year for every town in your flock."

The nobles dining with the duke all cast guilty looks at their early morning wine glasses, save for two, who drank defiantly. Mal continued.

"You could hold one less dinner party and fix a well in one of your territories, or provide reliable Cortex access so your local children could get their learning. You could provide enough food or lower your quotas for your farmers and miners so they could actually raise their children instead of leaving them as shopkeeps. You could even—and I know this is crazy, but hear me out—you could actually *listen* to the people who've worked this land with their own hands and trust that they know best, not some Alliance scientist in another gorram system."

Mal shook his head, disbelieving. "It would take so little effort on your part. But you choose not to. You play at being master of your own little kingdom out here, getting your kicks by sneaking black-market goods under the Alliance's nose. But when it comes right down to it? You're just like them. Hoarding all the resources at the center of your own universe and letting everyone else rot."

"Honestly can't imagine why people still live here at all, sir," Zoë said.

"Me neither, Zoë. A mystery for the ages, ain't it."

"Oh, it's no mystery," the duke said sharply. "If I were to open up emigration, these people would abandon their neighbors in a heartbeat. If Killarney's farmers left, how would the people of Kerry eat? No sense of loyalty to their countrymen."

Zoë let out a snort and shot Mal a glance. "Does he think that makes him sound better?"

The duke's expression darkened. "You would do well to remind certain crew members to hold their tongues in polite company, Captain."

Mal and Zoë locked eyes and burst into amused laughter, shaking their heads. Simon forced a nervous chuckle in solidarity.

"Oh, Tarmon," Mal said, wiping his eyes. "You really do not know my crew."

"Clearly not," the duke said. He pushed his plate away and seemed to not even notice as a servant scurried forward and made it disappear. The duchess's eyes locked onto Mal's fingers as they swiped a drip of blood from his cheek, then she wrenched her gaze away, quietly excusing herself. She fled the room nearly as fast as the servant had. Unable to stomach the gore resulting from her husband's actions, apparently. The duke hardly seemed to notice.

For the first time, Mal saw with absolute clarity the kind of person they'd been dealing with all along. The most dangerous sort of enemy—one driven by an unshakeable belief in his own righteousness. He had never given off anything but complete sincerity in every conversation because he was absolutely convinced of his own cause. And that sealed the deal for Mal. There was nothing more to be gained here.

"One last thing," the duke said before Mal could come up with a quippy rejoinder to part ways on. "I got word you've been out in the fields around town this morning, giving aid to the insurgents."

"Mercy. Not aid," Simon clarified.

Mal nodded. "You and me both know those folks were far beyond any aid we could possible give."

The duke waved a hand to concede the point.

"I cannot say I was pleased to hear it," he said. "But I do understand it, given your particular history. I'm willing to overlook it and give you one last chance to accept my offer of work. I truly do like you, Mal, and there are so few people in the world willing to haul cargo of the sort I need."

Mal blinked and shook his head, sure he'd heard wrong.

"Wait, you—" He paused and shook his head again, laughing. "Since it wasn't obvious enough the first time, let me say it plain, if I had known those crates were full of Devil's Thorns, I never would have taken the job. Hell, I probably would have stolen them from the supplier and dropped them into a sun. Sounds like something I'd do, don't it, Zoë?"

"Sure does, sir," she said.

"And I'd have had fun doing it. So, in conclusion, I think you're a scumbag, I'm never working for you again, and I hope your people storm this little castle of yours, eat all your fancy food, and put you out to pasture. But," he said, holding up one finger, "I don't wish for them to use the Devil's Thorns on you in retaliation, just so you know how it feels. Because unlike you, I'm not a *zhēng qì de gǒu shǐ duī*. Farewell, Tarmon. We'll be in orbit for exactly as long as we have to be for Inara, and then we're never coming back."

"Yes," the duke said, drawing the word out as he picked up his wine. "Well, I'm afraid I've had to recall my general from her time off with your Companion friend. After the attack last night, you see, it only seems prudent. Especially in light of the new enemies we seem to have made."

Mal brightened. "Fan-*tastic*. Then there's absolutely nothing keeping us here. We can leave early, and thank the stars above for it. I'd say it's been a pleasure, Duke Farranfore, but—well, you know."

With that, Mal turned on his heel and marched out of the dining hall, Simon and Zoë right on his heels.

18

Mal stormed out of the duke's palace with Zoë and Simon close behind, practically floating on the sheer force of his incandescent rage. The nerve of that guy, trying to offer work again after all that. What a sick, twisted excuse for a human being. And Mal had bought into his whole act.

The second they were outside the double doors of the palace entrance, Mal pulled out his comm and called *Serenity*.

"Wash? You there?"

"Absolutely, Cap'n!" Wash said, with a faint clattering sound in the background that Mal recognized as Wash's toy dinosaurs tumbling down behind the flight console. "We're up here working hard, making sure *Serenity* is in tip-top shape for our next gig, wherever it may take us."

"Right," Mal said, moving right on past the obvious lie. Mal tried not to micromanage the crew too much, especially when he had to send some people away for safety. They could have a party up there for all he cared, so long as the work was done and they were ready to go at a moment's notice. Like now. "We're leaving. Inara's gig is over early, so get

Serenity ready to pick us up. Were y'all able to get everything we needed up on Madcap?"

"Most all. Few bits and bobs we couldn't find or didn't want to pay extortionate prices for, but we've got what we need to be underway, at least."

Mal threw open the door to the guest cottage and stalked up the stairs as they talked, heading straight for their suite of rooms so they could pack.

"Great. Find yourself a nice landing zone outside of town. I don't want *Serenity* back inside these walls. We'll meet you out there, wherever you choose. Let me know—"

Mal cut off as soon as he opened the door to his room to find a young servant from the duke's palace standing there. One finger was pressed to her lips to ask for silence. Mal's hand was on his gun in an instant, but the woman held up something in her right hand that caught his eye. It was a silky blue scarf, edged in gold and stitched with fine, delicate patterns that he recognized.

It was Inara's.

Mal tensed. Had something happened to her? Where was she? He opened his mouth to start interrogating the woman, but she gestured again with the finger over her lips, then dropped the scarf to reveal a handwritten note beneath it.

> Your room is bugged with listening devices.
> Follow Fia. She will lead you to me.
> Please come.
> —Inara

Mal passed the note to Zoë, his lips pressed together in

a firm line. Nothing ever went smooth. They couldn't just hop in their ship and go. Nooo, there had to be some kind of mysterious detour right as they were about to be rid of the duke and his gorram cursed planet.

"Mal? You still there?" Wash asked over the comm, worry in his voice. "Everything okay? Zoë?"

"Not now, baby," Zoë murmured into her comm. "Everything's fine. We'll call you back."

"Stay where you are for now," Mal added.

He could practically feel Wash vibrating with curiosity over the line, but he wasn't about to say more when his room was apparently bugged. Wash didn't handle not being in the loop very well, though, and they didn't need him acting rashly or making his own decisions out of fear for Zoë. They'd have to update him as soon as they could.

"Should we go find Jayne?" Zoë asked, though her expression said she didn't think it was a good idea. Mal shook his head and chose his words carefully, so as to be innocuous to anyone listening.

"No, let him sulk. We'll find him before we leave."

Mal gestured for the servant woman, Fia, to lead on. She nodded and poked her head out into the hallway before leading them quickly to a hidden staircase near the rooftop entrance. It was narrow and dimly lit, clearly designed for servants rather than guests. They climbed down and down, farther than Mal expected and definitely below the ground floor, until they finally emerged into a basement packed to the brim with supply crates. Fia led them through a maze of stacks Mal didn't think he could retrace without guidance, until they finally reached the mouth of a poorly lit tunnel.

Fia took two heavy-duty flashlights from behind a crate and handed one to Mal, keeping the other for herself.

"There's enough light to see by, but only just," she said. "I thought this might make you more comfortable."

"You'd be right," Mal said, clicking the flashlight on. "I do prefer to see where I'm going, if anything's going to try to kill me, and so on. This mean we can talk now?"

Fia hesitated. "Not quite. These are the servants' tunnels. They aren't typically busy this time of day, as everyone is serving breakfasts or turning down beds, but…"

"Got it. I can be patient," Mal said. Zoë and Simon both hummed their uncertainty at that statement but said nothing further when Mal shot them both a look.

Mal took Fia at her word and followed in silence, analyzing the tunnels around them as they went. He shouldn't be surprised that a man like the duke would want his servants running unseen between all the various noble houses, considering the way he thought about his people outside the walls. Now that he thought back on it, the servants he'd seen during their audiences and the dinner party had been nearly invisible. Silent, efficient, and frictionless in their service. Mal studied the back of Fia's head, watching her braid swing as she walked, and wondered what her life was like under the duke's rule.

And more than anything, he wondered where the hell they were going, what he would find when they got there, and what Inara was playing at with that note.

They came to a large central junction, and continued down another tunnel, passing doors and smaller branches as they went, until finally they came to a plain wooden door that seemed absolutely no different than all the rest. It wasn't until

Fia's flashlight beam passed over a tiny collection of scratches that Mal saw anything to distinguish it at all. Upon closer inspection, the scratches formed the rough head of an animal of some sort. A wolf? A cat?

Fia withdrew a set of keys from a hidden pocket inside the waistband of her skirt and inserted one into the lock. With a click, the doorknob turned, and the door swung open. Two figures stood immediately inside facing the door, guns with silencers drawn but aimed at the ceiling, fingers near but not on their triggers. When they saw Fia, they relaxed and stepped aside, allowing them up yet another staircase.

"This is the last one, I promise," Fia said, shooting them a wry look over her shoulder.

She led them up past the first floor, and past a second floor, too. That narrowed down the number of buildings they could be in. There were only a handful of buildings in the compound that were three or more stories tall. When they finally arrived at a door leading out of the staircase, Fia paused and peeked her head out, then beckoned for them to follow her into a hallway full of heavy curtains drawn over windows. At the end of the hallway were two double doors that stood open, leading to what looked like... an enormous professionally appointed kitchen?

Through the doors, Mal could see people of all sorts milling about, chatting, sitting atop workbenches and commercial-grade appliances. Servants, guards, soldiers, ground crew, farmers, people of all genders, though the group was skewed heavily toward women. He spotted River's dancer friend talking with several of the ladies he'd seen in Kaylee's company. As they approached, more and more people came into view, more than Mal had originally thought. Nearly thirty, it seemed, all of whom turned to look as they walked into the room. As soon as they crossed the threshold, Fia's shoulders relaxed, her body language changing completely, as if she were no longer on guard.

Then Inara's voice cut through the din.

"Mal, you came," she said.

All at once, the chatter fell to a low murmur as Inara strode to meet them, her graceful confidence drawing every eye. She smiled as she stopped before Mal, lifting a hand in greeting to Zoë and Simon.

"Thank you all for being here. Please, may I introduce you to those who have asked you to come?"

"Please do," Mal said past the tightness in his throat that always seemed to crop up when he saw her for the first time after days apart. "I admit to being a mite curious to know what this kitchen party's all about."

"It's quite a situation, to be sure," Inara said, taking him by the elbow and guiding him up to the front of the kitchen. A group of people stood before a row of shiny stainless-steel refrigerators, heads bent in discussion.

With a start, Mal realized he recognized every single one of them, either by face or dress.

Shepherd Book.

The abbess.

The general.

And the duchess.

"Captain Malcolm Reynolds," Inara began. "May I present General Li Xiùyīng and Her Grace the Duchess Jīn Mèngyáo, leaders of the Killarney Liberation Forces."

"Oh, *gǒu shǐ*," Mal said.

19

River Tam loved moments like these. The rush toward inevitable conclusion, everything tick-tick-ticking down toward the thing she had always known. Or if not known in hard detail, in the exactness of fact and photographic detail, then known in a bones sort of way. In a way that she could feel the threads of events around her, pulling tight and falling slack like a game of cat's cradle, twisting and dancing until they finally came together into the shape they were always intended for. And always, eventually, they would come to a point: the moment of clarity that would catch everyone up to where she'd been standing all along.

Most of the time, the people around her struggled to understand her words, no matter how clearly she communicated. It brought her near tears, sometimes, as she fought to make herself heard. It all made perfect sense to her, and she couldn't get how they didn't see. It was all right around them, and she tried to show them, to point and say, "Look! Here! This is what you're missing!" She even tried metaphor when exact words didn't seem to help.

And yet, it rarely worked. They labeled her crazy, labeled her words as disturbed ramblings, rather than considering that there might be something of value, something real she needed to communicate. Even Simon, whom she loved to the ends of the universe, could be dismissive of her because of her condition. She understood why, but it still frustrated her. It wasn't that River was unaware of her challenges—she fought the brain fog, the paranoia, the full-blast panic on an almost daily basis. But she knew, inside her own head, that she was still more than those moments. That she still had value to bring to the crew.

And so, she kept trying. Even when she knew it was likely to result in naught but frustration for her and confusion or fear for the others, she always kept trying. Like now.

River had been sitting quietly in a corner of the engine room, watching Kaylee work as she performed routine maintenance and cleaned everything top to bottom, for lack of anything else to do. With just the three of them on the ship—her, Wash, and Kaylee—the Firefly felt much larger. Emptier. It made her want to stick close to one of the others. Besides, it was fun to watch Kaylee at her work. She felt a sort of kinship with her. Felt, in a way, that Kaylee was the most likely to understand how she saw the world. Kaylee knew things about machines on an instinctual kind of level. She could look at *Serenity* and, by some combination of intuition and noticing small details on a subconscious level, follow her fingers right to the source of a problem. Simon may have been the one who was closest to her in sheer intellect, but it was Kaylee whose brain was the closest to working like hers.

"Kaylee," River said as she pushed herself to standing.

Kaylee jumped, banging her head on the underside of *Serenity*'s drive core.

"Ow!" she yelped, backing out from underneath the core's housing with a grimy hand pressed to her forehead. River winced in sympathy.

"Sorry," she said. "I should have waited another fifteen seconds for you to finish tightening that bolt and come out from under there. It won't happen again."

Kaylee, always the most forgiving sort, sailed right past the exact detail in her statement that would have tripped up most other crew members.

"You were being so quiet over there I forgot you were in here with me. Good thing I didn't start singing."

"I like your voice," River said. "Don't insult it. It doesn't like that."

Kaylee smiled, sweet and genuine, with the dimple and all. When her hand fell away from her forehead, it left a black smudge behind, streaking from hairline to eyebrow.

"You're right, that was rude. I apologize, voice!"

River returned her smile and grabbed Kaylee by the hand, despite the grease.

"Come on. We need to go talk to Wash."

Kaylee blinked. "We do?"

"Yes. We're needed."

Kaylee shrugged and let herself be led through the ship, all the way from the engine room at the stern to the bridge at the very front. As they entered, Wash had his feet up on the console, a warm cup of half coffee/half hot cocoa in one hand and a tablet with a romance novel in the other. Not that there was any way to tell the latter, just looking at him, but River knew, in that way that she knew things. He only ever read them when most of the crew were off the ship.

She also knew because Kaylee's cheerful greeting made Wash jerk in surprise and throw his tablet across the room.

"*Wǒ de mā!*" Wash said, clutching at his chest with his now-free hand. "Give a man a heart attack, why don't you!"

"Sorry, geez," Kaylee said, trying to hold in her laughter. "What's got you so on edge?"

"Nothing!" he protested, folding his arms and sipping at his drink with feigned casualness. "Just, you know... researching. Ship things. And contemplating this here view in a... philosophical sort of way."

"Uh huh," Kaylee said. "Then why are you blushing?"

"Why are you?" he shot back. Kaylee wasn't flushed at all, but neither of them deigned to point it out.

"Anyway," Wash continued, pointedly changing the subject. "What are you two doing up here? Things get lonely without the others around? You come in search of my charming company?"

"It's time to go," River said simply. Wash, of course, didn't understand the first time around. He never did.

"Nah, not quite yet. Mal called a few minutes ago saying they were ready for early pickup, but then he suddenly changed his mind with no explanation and hung up on me."

"How rude," Kaylee said, feigning affront. River tried not to roll her eyes. Wash was uneasy in this place, thinking of past dangers, comfy in *Serenity*'s hidey-hole and reluctant to poke his head out.

"No, we're not leaving yet," River said. "There's still a whole other act to the play and it's rude to leave before it's done. We need to respect the performers. But we can get in position. Take our marks. Be ready when our cue is called."

Wash opened his mouth to say something, then looked over her shoulder at Kaylee instead with a shrug. River hated that. She was right here, she could see them exchanging looks about her. She could feel the frustration and tears building in her, and the dread that accompanied them—dread because she knew she no longer had the ability to regulate those emotions anymore. Or at least, not fully.

Things had gotten somewhat better since Simon had scanned her brain on Ariel and started her on a new course of medications. But despite everything that had been done to her, River retained her ability to be logical and realistic. She knew that her amygdala had been physically altered, and that without some kind of breakthrough surgical fix to restore it, she would never be completely the same. If anyone could figure out such a fix, it would be her prodigy trauma surgeon brother. He always came through for her.

In the meantime, she had to work with what she had. She reached deep into herself to summon whatever level of self-control was still possible for her and used it to force back the frustrated tears that threatened. She focused on that thing she loved about her new self—that feeling of the threads coming together, a sense so strong it was like taste.

With that feeling firmly in her mind, she turned and looked Kaylee right in the eyes.

"I know what I say doesn't make sense to you. That doesn't mean it isn't right."

She turned back to Wash, listing the facts as clearly and succinctly as she could.

"The most fuel-efficient route back to Kerry is to slingshot around Madcap. To do that, we'll need to exit the atmosphere on the opposite side of the moon. The place we need to go is in that direction. What does it hurt to leave a little early? To trust that I'm telling you this for a reason?"

A crack formed in her hard-won calm, and she covered her face with her hands, holding the tears physically when she couldn't do so mentally.

"There's a reason, we need to go, please go, we have to go, just take the ship and let her fly where she wants to go and then we'll be ready. There are promises to fulfill, and we have to reunite the pack. It'll be our job. Can we please just please, please, please—"

"Okay, fine! Fine." Wash waved his free hand to make her stop, then looked to Kaylee. "She's right, we'd need to head that way eventually anyway. Dunno how she knows that, but she always does, doesn't she?"

I'm right here, River wanted to scream. They always talked about her like she wasn't standing right next to them. But Wash was finally accepting her word, so she held her tongue and screamed the words inside her mind instead.

"Head for Thompson's Wake," she said, speaking of a settlement nestled at the foot of a mountain range known for extreme climbing. Wash punched the destination in and received some coordinates and a heading back from the ship's computer.

"As you wish, milady. Heading for some random place I've never heard of for completely unknown reasons. Here's hoping Madcap's mad weather will spare us its wrath," he said, then swapped over to the comm. "Firefly *Serenity* requesting clearance for takeoff."

As Wash chatted with the air traffic controller at the tiny local dock they'd put down at, River felt a tingle of unease at the back of her neck. Or the back of her mind? She searched within herself for the source, looking, looking... then finally found it outside herself.

Kaylee. For all that sweet, sunny Kaylee was the one who played games with River and treated her the same even she occasionally got spooked. Now was one of those times. River turned and reached out to Kaylee, squeezing her hand.

"I'm sorry to creep you out. I don't mean to."

Kaylee looked stricken and immediately started to protest. "No, River, you don't—"

"I do. It's understandable. People fear what they can't see or touch or experience for themselves. It's me, though." She squeezed Kaylee's hand once before letting it fall. "It's just me."

Kaylee's expression softened, and she threw an arm around River's shoulder to give her a sideways hug.

"You always have our backs, don't you?" she said softly. "Even when we don't have yours."

"Of course," River said simply, then grinned. "Simon's too much of a boob to function otherwise."

A surprised laugh burst out of Kaylee, and she clapped a hand over her mouth to stifle it.

"Well, that's for dang sure," she said.

"Hey, hey, trying to do important pilot-y things over here," Wash shouted over his shoulder. "Keep it down in the peanut gallery."

"Firefly *Serenity*, you are cleared for takeoff," the controller said, a note of amusement in his voice. "Safe flight, and good luck with your important pilot-y things."

Wash turned red but kept his voice neutral and smooth, as if impersonating a commercial pilot on a big shipping liner as he replied: "Thank you, control. Have a wonderful day."

As Wash eased the ship off the ground, one of the many threads pulling at River fell slack, and she nearly collapsed into Kaylee with relief. One more piece slotting into place. One step farther along their path.

Before long, the pack would hunt.

20

Had the circumstances been less dire, Inara would have laughed at the utterly gobsmacked expression on Mal's face. Simon too, for that matter—he was terrible at hiding anything, and his face showed every inch of his surprise.

Zoë, on the other hand, simply hummed in acknowledgement and nodded.

"That tracks," she said.

Inara smiled. If she were to have bet money on which crew member would pick up on the grim undertones of Duke Farranfore's court, she would have bet on Zoë a hundred times over. Her gut was infallible. She would have also bet on Mal choosing not to listen to it in the face of a lucrative offer of work from the duke. Someone should really start paying her for her predictions. She was nearly at River's level on this one, really.

As it was, Mal turned to Zoë, his brows knit tight. "You knew about this?"

Zoë shook her head and shrugged at the same time. "In a manner of speaking, sir. I told you something ain't felt right from the start. Knew there was something about the duchess here that didn't click for me. Begging your pardon, Your Grace."

The duchess paused in her quiet murmured conversation with the general, switching from Mandarin to English.

"No pardon needed," she said. "Your instincts are admirable."

Mal then turned to Inara instead. "*You* knew about this?"

"I did," she acknowledged with a nod. "From the first evening we arrived."

"Why didn't you tell me then?" he nearly shouted, then mastered himself when he noticed the duchess watching him carefully. "Could have potentially saved a lot of lives, is all. No offense, Your Grace, but your forces haven't exactly made the best showing for themselves. Why didn't you come to us right away? Coulda saved us a whole lot of waiting around, playing nice with a murderer. Coulda even struck before he managed to use those God-awful weapons."

"That is my fault, and I beg your forgiveness," the general said, stepping forward. "I was moving our pieces into place and trying to convince our renegade forces to come back into the fold for our final offensive. I thought if everything were tidy and ready to go by the time we requested your aid, you'd be more likely to help us. Inara told me to just ask, but… well. This has been the biggest mistake of my military career and it has cost many lives. I'm ashamed."

The duchess placed a consoling hand on the general's arm and spoke. "You made the best decision you could with the information you were given, as all leaders do. You should be more gentle with yourself, Xiùyīng."

The duchess squeezed once before letting the general's arm go, then turned back to Mal and the others. "But we're getting far ahead of ourselves here. Let us start at the beginning, shall we?"

"Yes, please, because I'm still struggling to find a grip on this here business," Mal said, then looked around at the various appliances as if he'd forgotten they were, in fact, standing in a fully functional kitchen. "To start with, where are we, exactly?"

"My private residence," the general answered. "In my enormous and rather unused kitchen, specifically. My predecessor had a penchant for dinner parties and employed a full kitchen staff. I... do not. Much to the duke's displeasure."

The duchess snorted in amusement, then mastered herself quickly, the brief glimpse of genuine emotion disappearing so fast Inara would swear it was never there. She had impressive control over her external expression. Then again, Inara supposed she'd had to.

"He really doesn't know you at all," the duchess said.

The general gave a wry grin. "Indeed."

"Fascinating," Mal said, clearly not fascinated at all. "Not a very discreet location you have here. Not even very far away. Isn't this an awful big risk?"

The duchess pursed her lips and nodded. "My movements are... quite controlled. I can't get far, not for very long. The location *is* a risk, but a necessary one. It has served us thus far."

"I think you'll find, Mal, that every member of the duke's court who is not a man has a similar story to tell," Inara said, looking over the assembled group to meet the eyes of servants, gardeners, nurses, and even a few nobles, all nodding. "Think back over the last few days. Have you seen the duke speak directly to or acknowledge the words of anyone other than a man? Even once?"

Mal blinked, his mind reaching for examples and coming up empty. "I... didn't really notice, no."

"Unsurprising," Inara said wryly, meeting Zoë's eyes for a shared moment of solidarity. "Because it didn't affect you."

"Now, I don't agree with him or nothing, I just didn't—" Mal sputtered, backpedaling, but Inara cut him off.

"No one said you did, Mal. But we're telling you how it is. How it's always been, apparently."

Mal rubbed a hand over his face. "Wow, just when I thought I finally had a handle on just how bad this guy is, I find out he's even worse. Great. Just dandy."

The duchess nodded. "It didn't used to be quite so bad, when I was first married off to the duke. It's gotten worse with every passing year, the more he settles into his power. What started as casual disrespect and infantilizing eventually progressed to watching my every move, reading my communications, having me followed, and encouraging the same among the men of his court. And I, as the duchess, am in a place of privilege and under the public gaze, which affords me some protection. You can only imagine how his influence has affected others."

She pursed her lips and took in a slow breath, mastering some emotion before she continued.

"His attitudes toward the towns under his stewardship deteriorated as well. You heard him this morning. It took years for him to get to that point, but we've all been watching it happen and knew we could not let it go further. We started to organize, quietly, about eighteen months ago."

The general sighed. "It's been slow, careful going, and we have to be incredibly careful about who we talk to. The duke inspires a near-fanatical loyalty in many people. You've seen what his court is like, the comforts he offers. For many people, as long as there's good food and drink flowing and a comfortable bed at the end of the night, they're willing to suspend their own doubts or overlook flaws, convince themselves they aren't seeing what they think they're seeing. They're spoiled by the lifestyle the duke offers. But many, like you, Captain, genuinely don't notice. Unfortunately, many of my own soldiers are in that camp."

Inara saw the pain in Xiùyīng's eyes as she spoke. She loved her people and her job. She was a guardian right down to her heart, and seeing her people fall under the sway of the duke had been a constant source of stress. Inara was glad their time together had been able to relieve some small amount of that stress, but it hadn't erased the worry lines at the corners of the general's eyes.

"I was appointed by the duke's father only a year before his death, and I've built up considerable goodwill among my troops. Getting rid of me wasn't an option, so the duke simply installed a second-in-command beneath me who he could manipulate, and who he speaks to instead of acknowledging my authority."

The general's expression darkened.

"My second-in-command obeys the duke without question. In fact, the duke recommended I take a vacation at the same time he was expecting your shipment to arrive, and I suspect that's no coincidence. He didn't tell me he had ordered the Devil's Thorns, and he knows me well enough to know I never would have authorized its use. So he made sure I'd be out of the way so my second could sign off on it."

"You don't think your troops would follow you if you were to attempt a full coup? Or enough that the rest would go along with it, at least?" Simon asked.

Inara met Xiùyīng's eyes with a wistful smile. Sweet, naive Simon, always hopeful that people will ultimately do the right thing, even after his and his sister's horrific experiences. If only that were the 'verse they lived in.

Xiùyīng shook her head. "Not enough of them, no. I've spent the last year and a half testing the waters with as many as I could, but we've had to take caution to an extreme to avoid the whole thing collapsing around us. One wrong word to the wrong person and the duke would use my second-in-command to take over his standing forces and oust me. Thankfully, we also have some brave townsfolk from around the continent who have joined our cause."

At that, she turned to the abbess, who came forward and held out a hand for Mal to shake. "Captain Reynolds, my name is Mother Serrano. I'm abbess at the Dunloe Abbey. I've been recruiting and coordinating the civilians outside the duke's compound, as well as monitoring the labor conditions and environmental consequences of the duke's operations. What direction did you approach the duke's estate from on your flight in, may I ask?"

"The south, I think," Mal answered, taking her hand in a firm shake. Mother Serrano continued with a nod.

"Then you would not have seen the damage to the northern reaches of the continent. Many of our civilian recruits came to us because of the working conditions and methods the duke insists on in his mining, logging, and farming operations, all in the name of increasing output and filling the duke's accounts. Workers are injured or grow sick and die without adequate care, and many accuse the duke of stripping Killarney to the point of uninhabitability. More than one comparison to Earth-That-Was has been made, and the people are scared."

"That does track with some things we've seen and heard," Zoë said. "The issues the farmers are having in Dunloe, and that abandoned quarry we flew over, among others."

Mother Serrano's expression was grim. "Ah, see, even in your short time, the cracks begin to show. There are many layers to this conflict that go back years. Though I wish the Devil's Thorns had never touched Killarney, the fact that it's *your* crew here with us now, at this inflection point, is a bit of unexpected grace."

She turned to acknowledge Shepherd Book with a wave of her hand.

"We're grateful to have had your Shepherd Book at our side these last two days as we've suffered the incredible losses you've witnessed."

"It's been my pleasure to assist," Book said with a nod.

"Well, Mother Serrano, I appreciate your insight into the situation," Mal said. "It's good to finally meet you."

"Good to find out I'm not actually a tyrant, more like. I'm sure you've heard plenty about me from the duke and the good shepherd here," Mother Serrano said with a raised eyebrow.

"I may have mentioned your… stony demeanor," Shepherd Book said diplomatically. "To be fair, you had no idea who I was or if I could be trusted."

"To be even more fair, I absolutely was stonewalling you on purpose," Mother Serrano admitted. "But you just wouldn't leave. I suppose I'm glad of it now."

Inara could see Mal's impatience in the twitch of his hand and the tiny downturn at the corner of his mouth, until sure enough—

"Cute, very cute," Mal said. "Can we get back to this whole revolution thing y'all have apparently been cooking up? And, no offense intended here—"

Oh, how Inara wished every sentence that started with those words would simply end with them. Especially coming from Malcolm Reynolds. Offense was almost always both intended and received.

"—but," Mal continued, "I'd love to know what in the hell happened with your past attacks, and what exactly the plan for the future is. I'm assuming you're wanting us involved somehow, but I can't say I'm much inclined, given what I've seen of your operation so far."

The duchess and the general looked at each other with shared anguish. Inara marveled at their connection, their silent communication and the bond born of years spent suffering the same indignities. She completely understood what Xiùyīng saw in the duchess: her quiet strength, her conviction, her leadership, and the spark of wit and humor underneath it all that had yet to be snuffed out.

"It's been the slow work of nearly two years, bringing this all together," the duchess said, turning back to Mal. "And now I'm afraid it's impatience that's threatening to bring it all crumbling down. A few months ago, a small subset of our forces began to unite under one of the townsfolk who thought we were taking too long. I have to admit, it's understandable. We're in here living our comparably comfortable life, and they've rightly pointed out that every day we take arranging our chessboard is another day they are living in poverty without basic resources and support, risking their lives in the duke's quarries and fields. We've done our best to funnel them food, medicines, educational materials for their children... but obviously it was never going to be enough. Not when we were promising an end to all this, but offering them a pittance instead."

"Be that as it may," Mother Serrano said, rather more stern, "that was no excuse for leading those half-cocked attacks that got so many killed. There are children without one or both parents now because of that man and I will see him punished for it."

The general raised both hands in a "don't shoot" gesture and spoke in a soothing voice. "You are absolutely correct. But what's done is done, and what's important is that we seize the opportunity before us. Captain Reynolds, here is our situation at present."

She removed a small handheld projector from one pocket and hit a button to project a map onto the ceiling for all to see. It showed the duke's estate in the center with all the important buildings labeled, plus a large amount of the open countryside around it. Small settlements dotted the landscape, nearly two dozen of them scattered across a few hundred kilometers. The general continued.

"The fact of the matter is, the presence of the Devil's Thorns has escalated the situation considerably," she said, illuminating a building in the duke's compound labeled ARMORY with a red outline. "A source at the armory has confirmed that several crates of Devil's Thorns remain after the initial attack, enough to respond to any attack we might launch many times over. A not-insignificant portion of our force has threatened to desert. Another portion is threatening to strike again, no matter how ill-advised."

The duchess huffed an impatient sigh at that, and Xiùyīng shrugged helplessly.

"It is what it is, unfortunately. We created this situation, and now we have to work with it." She added several blue circles to the towns closest to the duke's compound. "We've begun mustering our troops for a final offensive. We have standing forces in all of these towns awaiting the order to march.".

She zoomed the map way out to show the planet and its orbiting moon, then illuminated a section of Madcap in blue as well.

"We've also managed to smuggle a fair amount of people off-world to Madcap to start new lives, despite the duke's emigration ban. Just one or two people at a time, unfortunately, but they've remained part of our efforts. And this is where the final obstacle to our plans lies. Ship traffic is tightly regulated in this compound, and the air traffic controller is not one of ours, nor is the one who approves ship manifests. The duke has begun personally vetting any coming or going that isn't a regularly scheduled supply delivery. And yet, if we have any hope of succeeding, we will need a large number of forces inside the walls right from the start of the battle to tackle three objectives: destroying the Devil's Thorns so it can't be used during the battle, occupying the significant portion of the duke's forces that are not loyal to us to keep them away from the palace, and storming the palace to take down the duke himself."

General Xiùyīng stepped back from the projector and looked to Inara for a moment, seeming to gather her strength for the most important ask of her life. Inara gave a slight nod of encouragement. Xiùyīng blew out a breath and met Mal's eyes directly.

"This is where we hope you will come in, Captain

Reynolds. Your ship, *Serenity*, is a known entity. The duke is expecting it to land within the next twelve hours to pick up the remainder of your crew, and we've confirmed with traffic control that your ship has standing permission to land. We are hoping *Serenity* will bring our people on Madcap with her when she comes. Your involvement could end there, if you choose, but as your people are skilled combatants, we do hope you will stay to fight alongside us as well."

Inara studied Mal's expression carefully, looking for any hint of what his answer might be. She'd spent the last two days assuring Xiùyīng and the duchess that Mal was a good man, that he always stepped up to help those in need. And more than anything, that he had a chip on his shoulder as big as an Alliance cruiser and would always help those little folks getting stepped on by a giant, no matter how much he protested. He may or may not be moved by the plight of those at court suffering under the duke, though she suspected he would. There was always a chance that his outrage over their luxurious lifestyle would override it. He would most certainly boil over with fury at the mistreatment of the small towns under the duke's purview. Would it be enough for him to risk his crew, though?

She prayed as hard as she could that he would accept.

When he still had not spoken after a full minute of silence, Inara stepped forward and laid a hand on Mal's arm.

"You have the power to turn the tides here, Mal," she said. "A whole continent of this world will have a better life if this succeeds." The expression on Mal's face flitted through a dozen different emotions. Among them, most certainly, was irritation at being manipulated. But she thought—or at least, imagined— that there was something approaching tenderness there, too.

"Here's what I don't get," Mal said, shrugging her off and approaching the duchess directly. Xiùyīng shifted almost imperceptibly closer to the duchess, ever protective. Quite sweet, really. Mal posed no threat, though. He stopped several paces away and looked the duchess directly in the eye.

"You're a part of this fake nobility system, same as the duke is. If you're asking me for help, I imagine you know a bit about my personal history and how that might not sit so well with me. What assurance do I have that you won't just be a different kind of problem?"

That was a fair question, and one Inara had warned them they'd have to answer. It took a lot to convince Mal Reynolds that any sort of authority other than his own deserved following.

The duchess acknowledged the point with a smile.

"Ultimately, Captain Reynolds, the same system that allows him to get away with abuse will allow me to get away with dismantling it," she said. "The Alliance stamps a certificate of authority and sends it along with our portion of Kerry's operating budget once per year, and other than that they couldn't care less about the day-to-day running of anything outside the White Sun system. Their ignorance provides us all the room we need to create a society where everyone has access to the things they need for a good life. I will be a figurehead and smile at the Alliance whenever they look our way, but the people themselves will establish whatever form of rule they choose and elect their own leaders. I have no need or want of governing power. But ultimately, it's not my word you should care about. Ask them."

She gestured over Mal's shoulder to the people assembled in the room. He turned, scanning the room over as miners, farmers, representatives from other towns, and laborers of all sorts gave their support: in salutes, nods, hands over hearts. Inara smiled when Mal's gaze landed on her once again, and she nodded right along with the rest. She'd only known the duchess for two days, having been introduced to her soon after her arrival. (And hadn't that been awkward, a hired Companion being introduced to the woman her client was in love with. Certainly far from the most awkward occurrence of her career, but a strange and sad moment all the same, even with the conversation staying strictly on the topic of revolution.) And yet, two days had been all she'd needed to witness the plight of the people and the duchess's dedication to serving them. She would give her full support however she could. She didn't think it would be necessary, though. The duchess could stand well enough on her own, and Inara was willing to bet she'd reel Mal in before long.

The duchess bowed gratefully to her people and returned their gestures of support.

"Fortunately," she said, raising her eyebrows, "this broken system also gives me free rein with that Alliance operating budget, once the duke is out of the way. My dear friends and colleagues have neglected to mention the matter of payment."

Mal turned to Inara with a "what the hell?" gesture, and she held up her hands to protest.

"Hey, don't look at me. I don't know the particulars. I simply thought your conscience and deeply held sense of right and wrong would guide you to the right decision," Inara said, blinking innocently.

"Oh, what a crock of *niú shi*," Mal grumbled, turning back to the duchess. "Payment, you said?"

"I did. Before I turn over the keys to the accounts to our new leadership, I'd be delighted to pay you double whatever the duke promised for the jobs he offered you, directly from the Alliance's coffers."

There was a beat of silence. *Got him.*

"Well then," Mal said in a jovial voice. "I'd say we have an arrangement."

The duchess and Xiùyīng looked to each other wearing matching grins of relief and joy, and a cheer went up from those assembled around the room. Inara couldn't help herself; she threw her arms around Mal's neck and squeezed tight, breathing in the scent of him in the rare moment of closeness.

"Thank you," she murmured as he lifted one arm to return her embrace.

"Well, you know," he said as he pulled away, unable to meet her eyes. "The pay is good. Get to piss off a duke. Pretty good deal all around, I'd say."

Inara hovered between the general and Mal as the meeting began to break up, unsure where her obligation lay at the moment. Xiùyīng had been recalled from her vacation, though Inara had committed to three entire days and nights. She would surely need support in the coming day as she prepared to lead her troops to revolution. And yet, Inara had her place among the crew of *Serenity*. She wasn't technically part of the crew, but most of them took some comfort from her presence. And, of course, she was far from helpless in combat. Was it truly her place, though?

"What's our plan then, sir?" Zoë asked before Inara could make her decision. "Are we just making the drop-off, or do you mean to participate in the offensive?"

Mal hooked his thumbs through his gun belt and leaned back, all cocksure ease and blustery confidence now that the decision had been made.

"Oh, I think we can lend these folks a gun, don't you, Corporal?"

"I surely do, sir."

"We'll work out the details with these fine folks here. I'm sure we all have our roles we can play."

As Shepherd Book strode over to join up with Mal, Zoë, and Simon in their planning, Inara took a step back, decision made.

She was not part of their crew, not really, and her obligation to Xiùyīng remained no matter what the duke declared. She had already crossed a boundary in inserting herself this far into crew business, and she had no doubt Mal would bring it up to spite her at some future date.

In the meantime, she simply enjoyed the triumph of the moment, and the quiet knowledge that with the crew of *Serenity* on their side, everything would turn out all right.

Probably.

Well, maybe.

As Mal was fond of saying, things didn't always go smooth when Mal and company were involved. But when their cause was righteous, things had a way of working out.

As Xiùyīng prepared to leave, planning to get messages out to their forces about the impending attack, Inara pulled her aside for a quick word.

"Can we speak?" Inara asked, one hand on Xiùyīng's arm.

Over Xiùyīng's shoulder, Inara saw the duchess take note of their closeness, a flicker of emotion crossing her face. Inara dropped her hand away, her lips quirking with barely contained triumphant glee.

"Hi," Xiùyīng said, oblivious to the whole thing. "Thank you again for this. Truly, I don't know where we'd be without you all."

"I'm sure you would have found your way," Inara said. "But I'm glad we could help all the same."

"In more ways than one," Xiùyīng said, her smile becoming more intimate. Inara glanced away, then back up to meet her eyes.

"That's what I wanted to talk about, actually. I know you said our time together was about drawing a line in the sand between past and future. About moving on."

Inara paused, not wanting to overstep. But part of her training as a Companion was in giving counsel, in nurturing the emotional and spiritual selves of her clients. In this, she saw her duty. And so, she forged on.

"I think you may be giving up too quickly," she finally said, letting her eyes drift to the duchess. "Let this battle play out. And once the dust has settled, you might find that the rubble has blocked off some paths, but created new ones as well."

Xiùyīng's expression fell. "I appreciate your hopefulness, but I'm pretty sure there's a ten-foot-thick steel wall blocking that road."

Inara shrugged delicately, her expression serenely confident. Her instincts were right on this one; she knew it. "Maybe. But is not this whole operation about bringing down walls?"

"I suppose, but I can't exactly just plonk a spaceship full of troops down inside her walls and declare victory," Xiùyīng said, and they both laughed quietly at the silly image.

"Still, though," Inara insisted, making one last play, "all this will be over one way or another in less than a day. What will it hurt to wait and see where the pieces fall at the end? At the very least, we know she'll be getting a divorce soon. And hey, perhaps if it all goes horribly, you can simply make a grand escape and run away together. The 'verse is a big place full of all kinds of possibilities."

"Now you're just being a romantic," Xiùyīng said, shaking her head ruefully.

"Maybe," Inara admitted. "Or maybe not. Just think on it. You know, when you're not busy planning the grand battle to come."

Xiùyīng sobered a bit at that. "Speaking of which, I should get to it. I need to work out some details with that gentleman friend of yours."

"Oh, believe me, he's far from being a gentleman," Inara said with a scoff.

"And yet, somehow I get the impression you like it that way," Xiùyīng said with a sly grin, a parting shot as she walked away to talk strategy with Mal. Inara wanted to protest, but it was too late.

In more ways than one, if she was honest.

Not for the first time, she wondered if this should be her last trip with *Serenity*. She had a whole mess of reasons for needing to leave… but a few very compelling reasons to stay.

Mal, as always, managed to be both.

With a sigh, Inara slipped from the room, keeping her head down. Maybe a cup of tea before battle would be just the thing.

21

Shepherd Book had struggled with a great many moments of doubt during his time with the crew of *Serenity*. The work they took on was often not of a moral variety, and their loose way with the triggers of their weapons took a toll on his faith. More than once, twice, thrice he had seriously questioned his place aboard their vessel and the moral fiber of its captain. He'd come within a hairsbreadth of leaving.

This was not one of those moments.

In this moment, Book knew: Mal would come down on the side of right. He would protect those in need, those being abused by ones in power. He could always be relied upon in such a situation, no matter how neutral he pretended to be. He tried to play the mercenary only out for profit, but everyone aboard *Serenity* knew: there were lines one didn't cross with Malcolm Reynolds. It was part of why they were all there.

Once the group assembly wound down and Mal had committed their help, he called for a crew meeting back at the guest quarters. Though Book occasionally protested at being ordered around like one of Mal's troops, in this instance, he was happy to take part. Sometimes a more moderate guiding voice was needed in these sorts of proceedings, someone to temper violent instincts and propose alternate solutions. He wasn't often listened to, but his faith demanded he try.

Besides, for once, Shepherd Book was fully on board for the mission the crew was about to undertake.

With genuine gratitude and fondness, Book approached Mother Serrano and clasped her hands in his.

"I truly appreciate the opportunity to assist your abbey through this crisis. Thank you for providing me with a physical and spiritual home for the past two days."

Mother Serrano smiled and patted his hands. "Thank you for being patient with me as I attempted to push you out. In the end, it turned out that we needed your help after all. Brother Hewson—"

She broke off, struggling to speak against the sudden surge of emotion. Book squeezed her hand and waited for it to pass.

"Before he was killed," she finally managed to say, "Brother Hewson was urging me to trust you. Said he had a good feeling about you. I suppose he was right. I should have listened."

"It wouldn't have saved him if you had. If it's any consolation, I'm certain that the townspeople will remember his kindness fondly once this is all over."

Mother Serrano wiped away a tear and nodded. "You're quite right. We'll make sure he is remembered. Now get going, Shepherd. It looks like your captain is leaving."

Book glanced over his shoulder to see that, indeed, Zoë, Mal, and Simon were making their way to the exit, led by the young woman who had escorted them in. Simon looked back and raised a hand, which Book returned with a nod.

"I suppose you're right. If all this goes well, we'll speak again before I leave the planet for good. Best of luck to you during the offensive, Mother Serrano."

"And to you, Shepherd."

Book caught up with the others as they entered the underground tunnels, where they were led quickly and quietly to the basement of the tavern and instructed to leave through a side entrance.

"We've had someone sweep your rooms for the listening devices that were planted there, and I've received word that your room is clean, Ms. Washburne," Fia said, turning to Zoë. "The other rooms have been more difficult to clear, so we recommend keeping all conversation to the one room. We've had someone posted in there to ensure no new devices are planted."

"Maybe we could use the other rooms that are still bugged to sow a little misinformation," Simon suggested.

"A good idea, Doc," Mal agreed. "Think we just might do that. Fia, thank you for the escort. We'll let you get back."

"Thank you, Captain. Good luck," Fia said, then disappeared back down into the tunnels.

If anyone thought it was odd that four random people emerged from the servants' tunnels and passed the kitchen to leave from the tavern's side entrance, then they didn't say anything. Book suspected all the employees were in on the resistance, judging by the way they very deliberately did not acknowledge the crew's presence.

Once outside, Mal started down the path toward the guest cottage, but paused as they passed by the outdoor seating area around the back of the tavern. As always, there was Jayne

Cobb, leaning back in his chair, nursing a pint of ale, and laughing with a group of soldiers.

"Jayne," Mal barked, startling the man so badly his chair fell forward onto all four legs, sloshing his drink.

"Aw, what the hell, Mal?" Jayne said, flinging spilled ale off his hand. "A waste of good drink, that is."

"Ain't my problem," Mal said. "We're leaving. Heading back to pack our things, then calling down *Serenity* for pickup ASAP. You coming with us, or have you decided to stay here and join His Grace the Duke's army?"

"Aw, man," Jayne groaned. "We was s'posed to have a whole 'nother day. Why we leaving early?"

"This ain't a discussion," Mal said. "Come with us or stay, your choice."

And with that, Mal turned his back and started walking toward the guest cottage. Shepherd Book shot a look at Jayne, hoping to convey that he believed in Jayne's ability to do the right thing. He wasn't sure he did, actually, but expressing a little belief in folks often went a long way toward them stepping up as they should. High expectations, and people often rose to meet them. Low expectations, and people always sank even lower.

Sure enough, a moment later Jayne jogged to catch up with the group, grumbling all the way.

"Why, Jayne, how nice of you to join us," Mal said. "I must admit to being a mite surprised. Way you were talking earlier, I figured you were gone for good and we'd be tossing your belongings down the ramp on our way outta here. Ain't that right, y'all?"

"I'm a bit surprised myself, sir," Zoë said, dry as ever.

"Shocked, really," Simon added.

Book frowned. "Well, I, for one, always believed you would rejoin us, Jayne. *Serenity* is your home."

"Eh, for now it is," Jayne said. "But I gotta say, the way some of those soldiers were talking about the regular folk out there beyond the walls was downright disturbing. One of 'em was a little too into the torture aspect of those Devil's Thorns. A man has limits, you know."

"I'm glad to hear you say it," Simon said with a pointed look at Jayne, who suddenly looked sheepish. Book wasn't sure what he'd missed there, but there was clearly some sort of tension between them. It had started fairly recently and had resulted in Simon and Jayne avoiding each other even more than they typically did. When they did cross paths, Jayne seemed almost... afraid of Simon, maybe. It was a strange new dynamic, one that worried Book a little, but was ultimately for the best, in all likelihood. Anything that tamed Jayne Cobb even a bit was a positive influence.

Unfortunately, not everyone had the tact to let it be.

"Oh, has some of the shine worn off your new drinking buddies?" Mal said as they crossed the threshold of the guest house and began climbing the stairs. "Could it be that Jayne Cobb is admitting I was right?"

"Don't push it, Captain," Book said gently. "We're all here and that's what matters."

Mal's expression darkened for a moment and Book expected to be berated for daring to scold the captain. Mal settled for a warning look, though, and gestured to Zoë to open the door to her room. When she did so, a servant looked up sharply from her tidying work, then relaxed upon seeing who was at the door.

"The room is still clear," she said, gathering her cleaning supplies. "But the walls are thin. Be careful, and good luck."

As soon as the door shut behind her, Mal called up Wash on *Serenity* so all could be present for the meeting.

"Wash, you copy?"

"Just been sitting here waiting to hear your dulcet tones, Captain," Wash said cheerily. "Ready for pickup?"

"Not just yet," Mal said. "Got a quick errand for you to run first. Need to you stop off somewhere on Madcap to pick up some reinforcements."

There was a brief silence over the connection, then Wash's voice returned with a hint of resigned amusement.

"I don't suppose this pickup is in a place called Thompson's Wake, is it?"

Mal blinked. "It surely is. Wanna tell me how you know that?"

"Let's just say a little bird told me we might be needed there."

"I am not a bird," River said from somewhere behind Wash. "But I can sing for you, if you'd like."

"Maybe later," Mal said. "You saying you're already there?"

"We're parked on their landing pad as we speak," Wash confirmed. As always, Book marveled at the mysteries of River Tam's mind. She was troubled, to be sure, and Book did not in any way want to minimize the struggle she endured. And yet, whatever was done to her had unlocked something in her mind that let her see connections in the universe invisible to the rest of them. It must be beautiful and terrible, Book mused, being able to see the threads of God's workings in such a way.

"Okay, well, I won't turn my nose up at a tidy bit of convenience," Mal said. "Get Kaylee up on the bridge so's we can all have a chat."

"Already here, Cap'n!" Kaylee chirped. "Hiya, everyone!"

Book saw Mal pause and blink, ever wary of an excess number of "conveniences." One was handy, but two or more was suspicious. Where Book saw the Lord's hand easing the way, Mal saw conspiracy, felt the dread of things going too smoothly, just waiting to collapse on his head. Understandable, he supposed, given Mal's history, though a certain amount of it was undoubtedly brought down on his own head through reckless action and hubris.

"Nice to hear your voice again, Kaylee," Shepherd Book said to cover Mal's moment of hesitation.

"You too, Shepherd," Kaylee said.

"Yeah, yeah, we all just can't wait to hug and squeal and hold hands again, oh boy, it's just the best," Jayne mocked. Everyone present gave him a look, with varying degrees of disgust, exasperation, and annoyance.

"Enough chatter," Mal snapped. "Here's how it is. We're leaving the job of occupying the duke's forces to the Killarney Liberation Forces. Confusion will be on their side, as to them it'll look like their own people are attacking each other. Instead, we've got three tasks we've promised to lend a hand with."

Mal ticked them off on his fingers as he listed them.

"One, we're going to take out the guards at one of the gates and open the door to let the friendly local townsfolk inside."

"With pitchforks, I assume," Simon said.

"I'm personally hoping for guns, myself, but the choice of weapon is up to them. I suppose we'll find out when we open the door. Number two, we're going to head to the armory and destroy what's left of the Devil's Thorns."

"Now, hold on a minute," Jayne said, and everyone groaned.

"What?" he protested. "Someone's gotta think about the ruttin' money, since none of you seem to give a good gorram thing about it. Those weapons are one of the most expensive things on the black market. Why are we not taking them for ourselves and reselling 'em? Would pay for an awful lot of real food and liquor."

Mal worked his jaw as he visibly struggled with not punching Jayne, and Book slid a little closer to Jayne, ready to intervene if necessary. Much as Book shared Mal's frustration at Jayne's poorly calibrated moral compass, the last thing they needed right now was a fistfight between crewmates.

"I'm gonna say this exactly one more time, so I'm gonna need you to clean your ears out and listen real close, Jayne," Mal said, his voice low and dangerous. "Those weapons are an abomination. I sincerely hope the ones sitting in that armory are the last of their kind so we can have the pleasure of eradicating them from the 'verse entirely. There is no version of these events that will ever result in those weapons ending up in the hands of some other who will use them."

Jayne scoffed. "What someone else does with it is their problem, not ours. We aren't making 'em use it. Maybe there are collectors out there. Can you imagine how much a weapons collector would pay for something this rare?"

"You saw with your own eyes the way those people were suffering. You had them at the end of your gun, had to watch the pain and horror in their eyes as you put them down. We delivered the weapons into the hands of those what caused that suffering. The fact that you can see that and still want anything other than to destroy those things for good makes me seriously question having you on my boat."

Book cleared his throat gently and spoke in an even tone to bring down the tension in the room.

"I do believe Mal is right on both counts. We share some responsibility for what happened to those people. Ensuring that it can never happen again by destroying the Devil's Thorns is the best way we can atone."

"That and helping the people harmed by the weapon," Simon said.

Zoë nodded. "Which is exactly what we'd be doing by destroying it."

"And aiding in their little coup here, of course," Wash added.

"Even a lioness requires a pack to hunt," River said. Everyone else fell quiet for a moment at that, unsure what exactly to make of the comment, until Mal once again took the reins.

"Right," he said. "Well. Our final part of the job will be to accompany the duchess and general to confront Mr. Murder himself. Here's my thought. We split into two groups. One group will open the gates and then go to support the confrontation with the duke. The other will head to the armory after it's been secured by the duchess's forces and ensure the weapon is destroyed."

"I imagine you'll be in the group paying a visit to the duke, sir?" Zoë asked, a thread of amusement in her tone.

"You bet your bullets I am. I absolutely need to see that man's face when he realizes his little empire is falling apart. I'm just tickled at the thought. Zoë, I want you with me, and I imagine Inara is like to be there at the general's side, too."

"Yeah, storming an armory with weapons blazing ain't exactly her thing," Kaylee said.

"Too right," Mal agreed, though Book imagined it went rather deeper than that. The confrontation with the duke was likely to be the safer of the two options, and Mal would always put Inara wherever was safest. Watching their dance was both sweet and infuriating. Whatever disagreement Book might have with Inara's profession, he respected her immensely and appreciated her company as the only other more spiritual member of *Serenity*'s crew. He wished her happiness, and though he wasn't sure whether she and Mal would do much more than drive each other crazy, it seemed worth a go.

"Does that mean I'm on the weapons team?" Jayne said with a gleam in his eye. Mal shut it right down.

"You are, because I expect we'll need the firepower, but I'm sending Shepherd Book and Simon along to keep an eye on you."

"What? Come on, Mal, I don't need no babysitters, and certainly not some fancy-pants doctor and a preacher who ain't even gonna be of use with a gun."

"I think you might be surprised to know just how useful I can be," Book said, leaving aside any further detail. He did not talk about his past—ever—but he was well acquainted with a gun and had no qualms about using one in self-defense.

Simon winced. "I… am not the best with a gun, as we all know. But I'm happy to go along and help however I can. Shepherd Book will make up for my terrible aim with his kneecap shots."

Book suppressed a chuckle at the memory of Simon's anguish over his non-existent kills as they defended their shuttle from Adelai Niska's forces. The boy was next to useless with a gun, but he would at least make a good backup for Jayne's conscience, should anything happen to Book.

"What about us on team Madcap up here?" Wash asked. "We're bringing in the reinforcements, but what then?"

"You need to stay with the ship, Wash, keep her running in case we need to make a quick getaway. Kaylee, River, y'all just keep your heads down—"

"I'm no gazelle," River broke in, voice serene but words insistent. "I can hunt same as you."

"River, no. You should stay on the ship, *mèi mèi*. There's no need for you to get involved in all this," Simon said, shooting Mal a look that said, "Back me up on this."

"'Fraid I'm with Simon on this one, River," Mal said. "Not that I don't think you're capable. It's only that we all know Kaylee ain't no good in a fight—no offense, Kaylee."

"Absolutely none taken, Cap'n."

"So's we need someone on board that can keep an eye on her and Wash and defend them if needed. Can you do that for me?"

"A hawk in the treetops, waiting for the slightest twitch of movement. Deadly once in motion. The mouse never sees what hits them until their entrails meet the sky."

An intensely awkward silence followed.

"Well, that was creepy as hell," Jayne said, and everyone in the room shot him a dirty look. "What? It was! Don't even lie and say it weren't."

Mal rolled his eyes and moved on.

"Thanks, River. Kaylee, you good?"

"Always happy to stay with my girl. We'll keep her ready for ya, just in case."

"Okay then," Mal said. "We'll talk some specifics here in a bit, but this whole shindig is supposed to go down right at dinner time, when the duke should be at his fancy table with his fancy wine and his fancy friends. Should be a right entertaining time. Questions?"

Simon raised his hand and spoke. "Will the specifics include how exactly we're supposed to destroy the Devil's Thorns without setting them off?"

"Oh, come now, where's the fun if I don't leave you a little creative license?" Mal said, leaning back with his thumbs looped in his gun belt. Simon gaped like a fish, as always completely unsure whether Mal was joking or not. Shepherd Book took pity on the poor boy and clapped him on the shoulder.

"Why don't you, me, and Jayne sit down and have a chat about our mission? I agree that we should have a plan a bit more detailed than 'blow it up' before we get in there."

"Oh, thank God," Simon said, then sputtered as if unsure whether that was inappropriate to say to a preacher in this context.

"Thanks be to God, indeed," Book said with a chuckle. "Though I can't imagine he made you with this sort of job in mind, I have no doubt that he will lift you up to the task."

"He better," Jayne grumbled, throwing himself on Zoë and Wash's bed with the air of a petulant child. "Pretty sure I'm gonna end up babysitting you two, not the other way around. Why do I get stuck with a doctor and a preacher on a mission to go blow something up? Can't I at least get Zoë?"

"No," Mal and Zoë said in perfect unison, then Mal continued. "Should be a cakewalk, Jayne. I have every confidence you three will get it done. Now quit your moping and get to planning."

Jayne grumbled to himself but sat up on the bed and glared up at Simon and Book.

"Just so we're clear, I'm in ruttin' command on this mission," he said, daring either of them to disagree.

Simon and Book shared an amused glance, both remembering the delightful experience of Jayne's last command. It had been so bad Simon had secretly administered a sedative to knock Jayne out so cooler heads could prevail. Jayne caught the look and his eyes narrowed.

"You best not be thinking of stabbing me with no needles, Doc," Jayne said with a glare. "You need me and Vera on this one. I ain't letting you anywhere near me with so much as a bandage."

"I'm sure that won't be necessary this time," Book said placatingly. "The job is straightforward. We should, however, work out the details ahead of time, as was said."

And with that, a doctor, a preacher, and a hired gun sat on the edge of a bed in a fancy guest room to plot how to destroy one of the worst weapons in the 'verse. It wasn't a situation Shepherd Book ever imagined he'd be in, but then, his life had taken him in many directions he'd never imagined. Or wanted.

In this instance, at least, he could be assured that his actions would fall on the side of righteousness.

22

Wash toggled the comm as he guided *Serenity* down into Kerry's atmosphere, holding her steady as they angled in toward the duke's compound.

"How are things holding up back there, Kaylee? Everything shiny?"

"S'pose so," she replied, sounding wary. "There's an awful lot of them packed in back here. We have a rough landing of any sort, could be a lot of bleeding and hollering."

"Shouldn't be any rough landings on the menu today, don't you worry your cheery head about it. We got permission and everything," Wash said, silently hoping against hope that would remain true. He and Kaylee had both been with *Serenity* long enough to know that whenever things seemed to be going smooth, that was exactly the time you had to worry. He readjusted his grip on the controls and scanned all the sensor readouts once again, but still: all normal. Nothing to panic about.

Funny how having a cargo hold packed full of armed insurgents could make one twitchy.

Wash angled for the largest continent and switched comm channels. "Kenmare traffic control, this is Firefly

Serenity, coming in for a scheduled landing to pick up our remaining crew."

There was a long pause, longer than normal, and Wash shifted in his seat. Still nothing to worry about. They were just a mite lazy down there, living in the lap of luxury and all. No need to hurry when you only had one or two vessels per day to handle. Besides, they were expected. Everything would be totally, completely—

"Firefly *Serenity*, break off your approach and return to orbit. The landing zone is hot and the landing pad is unavailable," the controller finally replied, voice rushed and tense.

"What the hell is going on?" Mal shouted over the all-crew channel. Over the shouting and gunfire in the background, Wash could barely make out Inara's reply.

"General Xiùyīng said one of the groups started the attack early," she said, her usual calm wearing thin. "The whole offensive has to start now, or those people will be slaughtered."

"*Dà xiàng bào zhà shì de lā dù zi,*" Mal swore prolifically. "All right, fine. Wash, you get that boat down here fast as you can."

Wash gave a little nervous laugh before swapping back to the crew channel to reply. "Yeah, so, slight problem there. We don't have permission to land. Traffic control told us the pad is 'unavailable,' whatever that means, and that the zone is 'hot.'"

"Oh, well, if they said no, then by all means, break off the landing before you get a slap on the wrist and a stern scolding." More swearing from Mal. "Get that gorram ship down here now, Wash! We need those reinforcements!"

Wash's jaw tightened, his face flushing with anger at Mal's jab, but he stayed the course.

"Yes, Captain. Whatever you say, Captain," he muttered under his breath. "Kaylee, gonna need you down in the engine room for this, I think."

"Heading there now," she said. "How bad is it?"

"Please hold," Wash said in his best robotic customer service voice. "Your imminent death probability report will arrive momentarily."

"You're always so comforting," Kaylee said wearily.

Hey, it wasn't Wash's fault they went charging headlong into certain doom on a weekly basis. Not like anyone asked him his opinion. He held course, waiting for the inevitable protest.

"Firefly *Serenity*, our scans show you still on approach. Break off and return to orbit or we will fire upon your craft."

"Think your scanners might be lagging behind a bit, is all," Wash said, his voice a bit higher pitched than normal, but admirably even, he thought. He was totally pulling it off. "We've already adjusted course. Maybe give it a minute and try again?"

That should confuse them for at least another twenty seconds, and *Serenity* could eat up quite a bit of sky in that time. He poured on the speed and grabbed the intercom for a quick announcement.

"Your attention please, passengers. Please brace yourselves for a potentially rough landing. Maybe crouch on the ground or something, and definitely stow any sharp objects or weaponry you might be holding. Everyone check on your neighbor. Safety compliance is caring."

Wash hoped desperately that the nice, friendly insurgents filling the cargo hold would listen and put away their guns. The last thing they needed was a bunch of holes punched in *Serenity*'s hull. And, of course, he imagined it would put quite a damper on their little revolution if they arrived with half the reinforcements bleeding out.

"They know how to lie still in the tall grass before a pounce," River said from behind him, making Wash nearly leap out of his skin. *Serenity* bucked under his hands, and he quickly wrestled her back under control.

"*Āiyā!* River, you scared the pants off me!"

"The hunt begins once the pack is reunited," River said.

That was almost downright clear, compared to River's usual speech. Wash hummed his agreement, keeping a sharp eye on the sensors.

"Working on reuniting the pack right now," he said. "Do me a favor and strap yourself in, please. I can concentrate so much better when I'm not worried about delicate fleshy bodies flying all over the cabin during hard maneuvers."

To his surprise, River complied right away.

"It's okay. You're a leaf on the wind. But I'll do it if it makes your brain feel safer," she said, clicking the straps into place and flicking switches at the captain's station like she co-piloted the ship all the time. That was the last attention Wash could pay her, though, as they began their approach to the compound. The comm channel opened once again, the voice on the other end sounding increasingly harried.

"Firefly *Serenity*, our sensors still show you on approach. This is your final warning. Turn back or we will be forced to open fire. The landing pad is currently a combat zone. You must turn back before—"

The crew channel crackled with gunfire and shouting, drowning out the rest of the warning.

"Wash, where the hell are our gorram reinforcements?"

Mal shouted, followed by three gunshots that sounded worryingly close to the comm. "I'm gonna find whoever jumped the gun on this attack and strangle them with their own bootlaces, I swear to—"

"Sir, on your six!" Zoë's voice shouted from somewhere nearby, and Wash's heart leapt into his throat.

The comm cut off, leaving the cabin in terrible silence for all of two seconds before traffic control decided that one more warning was in order.

"Firefly *Serenity*, we are firing in three… two…"

"Sorry, control, Captain's orders!" Wash called back, then put *Serenity* into a hard dive toward the compound. "Kaylee, I'm gonna need as much as you can give me from the RCS and docking thrusters in about thirty seconds here."

"Gee, thanks for the warning," Kaylee said, no doubt rushing to make the appropriate adjustments. She was a wizard in that engine room, making *Serenity* purr and sing and dance on tiptoes the way no one else could.

As the bullets started flying, he could only hope it would be enough.

Wash let himself sink into the flow of *Serenity*'s movements, feeling her every slip and twist in the wind, making microscopic adjustments when possible and larger corrections when needed. Bullets whizzed past, but he handled *Serenity* like a needle threading a complex stitch pattern, hardly blinking in the process, floating between the gaps in the firing pattern.

The gun was a model that favored rapid fire over outright power, though, peppering the sky around them with projectiles and making a hit almost inevitable. A few bullets pinged off the hull harmlessly, but a hollow punching sound finally damaged his calm.

"Kaylee? What was that?" he asked, not much able to spare a glance at *Serenity*'s diagnostic report at the moment.

"It's not bad!" Kaylee called back. "Well, not very bad. We've got a hole in the port side fuel line, but the leak is pretty slow."

"Don't need much longer anyway," Wash said as the duke's estate rushed toward them way too quickly, more bullets flying at them from within. The gun was far too close to the landing pad for them to make a direct approach. But if Kaylee could give them the juice, he had a wild idea that just might work.

"Okay, you've got all I can give," Kaylee called, and Wash smiled.

"Hold on to something!"

Sometimes a pilot had to be a leaf.

Other times, they had to be a drunk jackrabbit.

With a manly yell full of motivation and strength and definitely not terror, Wash hauled back on the controls, pulling *Serenity*'s nose up, up, up until she was as level to the ground as she could get, hitting the RCS and docking thrusters as hard as he could to slow them down. Time slowed as he strained against the yoke, watching the compound rushing toward them, the insurgents outside the gate, flashes of explosions in all directions… and a clear patch that opened up right outside the estate wall.

"Wash, baby, looks like you're coming down outside the wall," Zoë said, trying to keep her voice kind and even and not at all panicky. "We really need those troops inside."

"Trust me," was all he could get out before he cut the main engine entirely and hit the landing thrusters at maximum, and wow they had a helluva kick. Kaylee had done good work. *Serenity*'s momentum combined with the sudden push from the thrusters to bounce the ship straight up into the air… and right over the wall onto the landing pad.

Well, approximately on the landing pad.

In the vicinity, at least.

Her tail end was probably touching it.

"Did you just bounce my ship over that wall?" Mal asked, disbelieving.

"Sure did," Wash replied, quickly looking everything over to see how badly the ship was screaming at him. She was not happy, to be sure, but she was in one piece and able to deliver on her promise, relatively sheltered by the warehouse buildings surrounding the platform.

"We've got additional friendlies incoming to keep the area clear and provide cover fire for the reinforcements," Zoë said. "Very creative flying, baby. Be careful."

"You too," he said, then shifted over to the ship intercom as he flicked switches to secure their landing.

"This is your captain speaking," Wash said. "Apologies for the rough landing. We've set down inside the compound and the exit ramp should be descending… now."

He felt and heard the familiar mechanical hum of the ramp opening, hydraulics pushing down the thousand-pound ramp all the way to the ground outside.

Except the sound cut off suddenly with a shuddering screech that must have been horrific to the troops standing in the cargo bay if Wash heard it all the way up in the bridge.

River and Wash looked at each other with wide eyes, then winced as the screeching stopped.

Well, that didn't sound right.

"*Tài kōng suǒ yǒu de xíng qiú dōu sāi jìn wǒ de pì gǔ,*" Wash swore, throwing off his restraints and sprinting to the cargo bay, River right on his heels. "Kaylee?"

"Hydraulics system musta got hit on our way down. Diagnostics report says the ramp is stuck but it's giving a generic error. It's gonna be a minute."

Wash skidded onto the catwalk above the troops gathered in the bay and saw that, indeed, the ramp had stopped at three-quarters down. Once in a while it made a strained whirring sound, like it was trying to finish lowering, before the system coughed and gave up. Wash groaned. To successfully get the ship where it needed to be, then not be able to actually let anyone off the boat?

"Wash, the area is secure," Mal's voice shouted over the comm. "Bring on the cavalry."

Wash gave a nervous laugh. "Yeah, we're working on that. There's been a slight issue. Please hold."

Wash looked across the sea of armed strangers packing the hold and wracked his brain for a solution. There were other ways out, of course, but it would take a lot of splitting up and leading strangers through their ship, which Mal would not be wild about. Nor Wash himself, honestly. He rubbed his hands together, then cupped them around his mouth to amplify his voice.

"Okay, um, attention insurgent fighters?" he called out. Those closest to him turned to listen, and word eventually filtered through the group until those at the front were paying attention too. Wash swallowed nervously, his chest heaving with his breaths.

"You're the captain right now, Captain," River said, looking up at him with big, solemn eyes. "Lead."

He took another deep breath and nodded, feeling the rush of power that came with those words. He never got to be in charge on this boat, never got to flex any sort of authority, not with Mal around. And most of the time, that was fine. People who made big decisions also got in the biggest trouble, and got the most pushback. He preferred to be a more easygoing sort. Pilot the ship, make people laugh, have a good time. It was only when Mal felt the need to swing his *zhàn dǒu de yī kuài ròu* around that Wash started to chafe.

But right now, leadership was needed, and he was it.

"We're working on assessing the problem with the ramp, but it could be a while," Wash called out across the cargo bay. "Those of you nearest the front, can you squeeze out through the sides? Maybe boost each other up? Get a nice little pyramid going?"

Those at the front conferred for a moment, then Wash saw two on either side of the ramp pop up and leap out through the gap between the ship's hull and the stuck ramp.

"Nice! Okay, about ten of you in the back can follow me to one of the emergency exits. And…"

Wash trailed off and looked over at River, assessing whether he could trust her with a similar task. She seemed to be in a good headspace right now, and she looked back at him with sharp intelligence and clarity in her eyes.

"I've got this, Captain," she said, then turned back to the

crowd. "I can take ten more to the starboard side shuttle and leave from the ramp there. Follow me."

She pointed at one soldier on the end, who charged up the steps to follow her. Nine others fell in line and followed, so Wash did the same thing on the other side.

"Kaylee, any updates on the ramp? We've got folks moving, but there's still a big crowd waiting to get out."

"I'm sorry, Wash," she said, dejected. She always took it so hard when *Serenity* was down and out. "'Fraid it's well and truly humped. Our girl can't do much else without some serious one-on-one time. I don't think the damage is bad, but it has to be fixed at the point of mechanical failure, which is going to involve me strapped to the outer hull hanging from the stabilizer—"

"Which is not the best idea in a firefight, I get you," Wash said, cursing under his breath. "You done your best, Kaylee. Thanks. Once we've unloaded our passengers here, River and I will give you cover so you can work on that fuel line. If nothing else, we need to be ready to get the hell outta Dodge in a hurry. Long as we stay in atmo, the ramp won't be too much of a problem."

Wash cut down a side hallway, then down a ladder, and finally came to a door with a bright red handle marked EMERGENCY ONLY in both English and Mandarin. For thankfully the first time in his tenure as *Serenity*'s pilot, he hauled back on the door lever and kicked it twice until it popped out, exposing a straight six-foot drop down to the ground.

"All yours," Wash said, pressing himself against the side of the hallway so each person could squeeze past. "Good luck! Shoot good and stuff!"

Wash slammed the hatch shut behind them and booked it back to the hold, where River was already leading a second group into the spare shuttle. All the rest were clumped up at the front, scrambling for their turn to be vaulted out the gap. There were only about fifteen left, though, so once a few more had gone through Wash whistled to get the attention of the last stragglers.

"Come on out this way!" he called. "Ain't no one around to give you a leg up once you've boosted everyone else."

If Wash's logic hadn't convinced them, the hail of bullets that pinged off the partially lowered ramp did the trick.

"Wash, the enemy is converging on your position," Mal called over the comm. "They've figured out the source of the reinforcements and they're gunning for *Serenity*."

"Yep, we definitely noticed!" Wash said as he turned to lead the remaining troops to the emergency exit. "I'm getting the last of the cavalry out the emergency exit right now, but then me an' Kaylee gotta patch a very minor bullet hole in the fuel line before we can hit sky again."

"You letting people shoot my ship?" Mal shouted, quickly followed by the report of his pistol. "I've got Jayne, Book, and Simon on the way to help."

"No offense, sir, but for once I certainly hope Jayne is the only help we need."

"Don't you worry, the preacher and doctor are coming armed."

A pause, then:

"I wouldn't stand anywhere in front of Simon, though, if I'm honest."

"Sage advice, Captain. How's my wife?"

"Alive and kicking, hon," she replied, barely sounding winded. She was definitely in her element. Wash would be much more in his element later, once the fighting had died down and the business of reaffirming life was in order. He would crack jokes, and laugh, and take his wife into his arms and hold her until the next morning, until it sunk in that she was okay. That they still had each other and could carry on with their chosen family.

"See you soon, love," he said, then cut off the comm before Mal could make a smart remark in return. He refused to be made to feel lesser for openly loving his wife and worrying about her. He may not be a gun-toting alpha male, but he was a damn good husband who knew how to tell a woman he loved her. Mal could take a leaf out of his book, honestly.

With that boost of confidence, Wash kicked open the hatch to let the final batch of soldiers out, then switched back to the ship intercom as they streamed past him.

"River, Kaylee, updates?"

"The pack is on the hunt," River said.

"And I'm just about done getting together what I need to fix the fuel line," Kaylee added. "I'm just gonna slap a quick patch on it, just enough that we can make it a few miles in case of a quick getaway."

"That's all we need for now. If our new buddies have a good day, then we'll be able to park right here and take our time, make all the repairs we need."

"Ain't that just the dream," Kaylee said with a sigh.

"No one shooting at us, money in our pockets, time enough to relax and tend to the ship while eating great food… yeah, sounds like a dream. Meet you both at the port side stern emergency hatch in a minute?" he asked as he yanked the door shut behind the last of the troops.

"On my way," Kaylee said. "River, did you seal up the shuttle good?"

"They can knock, but they can't come in. It's not allowed," River replied, which was about as clear as River ever got.

Wash did a quick mental calculation and decided he had time to make a quick pit stop before they charged out into danger. He made a quick run for it down the main hallway and stopped off at his and Zoë's quarters, heading straight for his bedside table. He pulled the top drawer open, and amid secret snacks, unopened contraception packages, a half-drunk bottle of cheap celebratory rice wine from their last anniversary, and other miscellany from a life in space, there sat a single small pistol. Zoë insisted he keep it within reach while he slept, just in case the ship were ever boarded. Just in case of Reavers. Wash tried to tell her the gun wouldn't do much good, unless the invaders were scared off by its very presence. His ability to actually hit anything with it was incredibly limited.

And yet, here he was, gun in hand, ready to go point it at some folk. Guess she was right after all.

With that, he checked the chamber just like Zoë had taught him, then ran back to meet River and Kaylee with his finger safely away from the trigger.

"You know, I never thought I'd say this," Wash said as he arrived back at the emergency hatch to find the other two already there. "But I really hope Jayne Cobb is waiting for us on the other side of that door."

23

Jayne shifted impatiently as he and Book waited near *Serenity*'s stuck boarding ramp, crouched for cover and armed to the teeth, watching the stream of reinforcements leaving the ship. Simon was not armed to the teeth, but he did stand next to them with a gun in his hand, which was still a step up from the usual.

Frankly, Jayne wouldn't have trusted him with anything more and was wary about even the dinky little pistol in the doctor's hand. Not only did he not want to be shot in the ass by accident, but he and the doc weren't exactly on the best of terms, and once the fighting was over he didn't want Simon getting any ideas in his head over how to use that weapon. The preacher would protect him, most likely. Unless the preacher found out how he'd sold out Simon and River back on Ariel. Then maybe even a holy man would feel justified in a little light shooting.

"Where the ruttin' hell are they?" Jayne wondered aloud, watching the progress of the battle through the sight of his gun. The insurgents had cleared the area around the landing pad as Zoë had promised, and they were doing a solid job of pushing the duke's loyalists back beyond the loading dock and warehouses. It was a messy fight, though, and Jayne was glad not to be in the thick of it. With half the duke's forces defecting and joining the duchess, it was hard to tell friend from foe. Most had tried to get out of uniform and into plainclothes before battle, but those who were on duty at the time of the attack still wore uniforms. The best they'd been able to do was throw off their uniform jackets and slip on a bright orange armband, same as the plainclothes folks wore. It helped somewhat, but there was still a lot of confusion and hesitation, which never made for a good situation when it came to shooting.

Yet another reason why Simon Tam with a gun was a terrible idea.

Behind them, *Serenity*'s emergency hatch popped open with a clang. Jayne whirled around, gun at the ready, but it was only Wash who dropped down to the ground, a dinky-looking pistol like Simon's in one hand. He held it like he expected it to bite him, which, once again, didn't bode well. Jayne supposed the actual defending and shooting would be up to him and him alone. Probably for the best.

Kaylee came next with a small satchel of tools slung over one shoulder, looking nervous as all hell. Girl wasn't made for combat situations, only for getting super friendly with engines and posh doctors. River, on the other hand… when she dropped down behind Kaylee, she landed with perfect gracefulness, but in a way that reminded Jayne more of a predator than a dancer. He'd already been cut up by her the one time and was not happy to see a gun in her hand.

"Who decided it was a good idea to give the girl a gun?" he growled, stalking toward her with half a mind to snatch it away. Right up until she raised the gun and pointed it at him. Jayne's eyes went wide and he stumbled back a step.

"Now wait a second—"

She pulled the trigger.

Jayne dropped to the ground, one hand clutching Vera and the other over his head, like that would stop a bullet somehow. But the pain never came. Was he in shock? Was it the adrenaline? It would start hurting any second now…

But then the laughter reached through his panic. He uncovered his head and looked up to find River giggling at him.

"I wasn't shooting at you," she said in the same voice she used to call her brother a dummy. "They were about to pounce."

Jayne's brows knitted in confusion, but when he took in the paled and shocked faces of the others, he spun around. One of the duke's soldiers had apparently broken through the defense screen and decided to sneak up and play hero. Now, he was on the ground in a pool of his own blood, which was leaking from a neat, perfect hole directly between his eyes.

"Laughing in the middle of a gorram gunfight, the hell is wrong with you, girl?" he snapped as he got to his feet. "Doc, you better control your crazy sister. Get that gun away from her afore she hurts someone on the wrong side."

"She did just save your life," Simon said, but he looked just as wary as Jayne about his sister and the gun. Jayne supposed it must be downright disturbing to see your baby sister killing someone for the first time, and doing it well.

"You know, you're right. 'Bout time we found some kinda use for her. She can start pulling her weight around here," Jayne said, scanning for anyone else taking too much note of their group.

"Um, not to make light of the situation or nothing, but every second we stand here bickering is more fuel leaking out of *Serenity*," Kaylee said, her voice small but certain. Jayne shot her a glance—she didn't even look surprised like the rest of them. Considering her usual shock at any act of violence and her friendship with River... well, it made a man wonder if she'd seen such bloody work from River before.

"Let's get moving, then," Jayne said. Someone needed to be in charge, and it was absolutely going to be him. "I'll take point. Preacher, with me. River and Doc, cover our backs. Wash... I guess just keep an eye out and try not to shoot yourself in the foot."

"Gee, thanks," Wash said, but he looked relieved all the same. Man wasn't a fighter, and there weren't no point in treating him like one. Together, they moved as a pack around *Serenity*'s aft, putting the ship between them and the worst of the fighting. Jayne held up a fist and paused before they passed under the reactor manifold, peeking around to look for trouble. And he found it.

A pack of three soldiers was lurking on the other side, inspecting the fuel leak and discussing how to make it worse without blowing themselves up. Jayne swapped out Vera for his pistol, less likely to set off the leaking fuel and blow the whole ship, and sighted down the barrel—then hesitated.

McElroy and Ashana. He didn't recognize the third person, but two of them were people he'd been drinking with frequently over the past two days. He'd gotten to know them rather well in that time, swapping stories and jokes and spilled drinks. They weren't bad folk, not the kinds of people who were getting off on the use of them torture weapons. Just decent people, making a living, enjoying the cushy gig they'd landed and milking it for all it was worth.

Jayne thought it over for two whole seconds.

"Stay here," he growled to the others. Then he stepped out into the open, weapon still at the ready but slightly lowered. A risk. He knew he could likely take at least one of them out before the others got him, and hell, maybe River could even get the others. But he couldn't just straight out kill these two in cold blood without giving them a chance first.

"McElroy. Ashana," he called to them. As they whirled around, he kept walking sideways, away from the ship, drawing their gaze with him.

"Jayne?" McElroy said, not pointing his weapon at Jayne yet, but not *not* pointing it at him either. "What's with all those insurgents pouring outta your ship here?"

Jayne shrugged. "The captain has apparently decided he's on their side. I don't much care either way. Ain't nothing to do with me. But I do care about y'all messing with our ship there."

"Bit of a fuel leak," the third member of their squad said, a dangerous glint in his eyes. "Wouldn't take much for the whole thing to go up."

Ashana rolled her eyes at that. "Take your pyro hard-on elsewhere, you creepy *xiōng měng de kuáng rén*. Jayne, I'd appreciate it if you lowered that weapon."

"And I'd appreciate it if you all lowered yours," he said in return. "Better or worse, *Serenity*'s my home, and I won't let you torch her."

"You're outgunned, Jayne," McElroy said. "No point in this."

"It looks that way, don't it?" Jayne said, letting his seriousness show. "But trust me, there's things you ain't seeing. You're the ones who are massively outgunned right now, and it ain't gonna go well for you."

Jayne blew out a breath to steady his pulse. He really, really did not want to kill these people. He would if he had to, to defend his home, but he hadn't felt this conflicted over pulling a trigger in... hell, he couldn't even remember.

"Like I said," he continued. "I don't give a damn what happens here today. I like you two. Your friend there, I dunno, he seems weird. But you two are good folk. Let's just let this be, all right?"

McElroy and Ashana looked at each other and silently conferred for a moment, but Ashana shook her head, turning back to Jayne.

"Sorry, Jayne," she said with real regret on her face. "I wish things could go that way, but after all the stories you told us, I'm afraid we know exactly how dangerous you are. We can't let you be running around with Vera, blowing holes in all our comrades. Get your weapons on the ground and your hands in the air. Please."

Damn, he'd bragged too much. His own reputation was blowing this whole situation out of proportion. He shook his head, mentally calculating the shots it would take to bring all three of them down... when suddenly four shots cracked the air. McElroy and Ashana dropped, but their creepy third stayed standing, wide-eyed and surprised. Before he could recover, Jayne raised his gun and fired, taking him out with a clean shot in the chest. Didn't care none for what happened to him. McElroy and Ashana, though... He rushed forward to kick their guns out of reach as they writhed on the ground, groaning in pain.

They'd both been hit by perfect shots in the knee.

The others all came running up, still on guard with their weapons out. Kaylee went straight to work on the fuel line, while Simon stowed his gun and slid a bag of supplies off his shoulder. He set about performing some basic triage to make sure McElroy and Ashana were stable, which filled Jayne with a warm kind of appreciation he didn't often feel for Simon.

"Thanks for not killing them," Jayne said to River as they all took up defensive positions around Simon and Kaylee.

"Shepherd Book told me a kneecap would suffice," she replied. Jayne raised an eyebrow at Shepherd Book, who did not comment on the fact that he, too, had just blown the kneecap off a soldier.

"Hey, how do you know it weren't me or Simon what made that shot?" Wash protested. "We got guns, too!"

Everyone turned to look at him in silence.

"I mean, it could have been a lucky shot?" he added weakly.

"Y'know, I do think I heard four shots," Jayne said, eyeing Wash. "What exactly were you and the doc aiming at?"

Simon's ears went pink but he didn't turn around. Wash rubbed the back of his head with an awkward laugh.

"Their target was the third soldier," Book said evenly, no judgment in his tone. "I thought it best to assign them the target that was farthest from *Serenity*, and the one you wouldn't mind being accidentally killed if their aim was off."

"No worries there," Jayne grumbled. "Them two apparently couldn't hit the broad side of a barn."

"We knew you could pick up the slack if it came down to it," Book said with a pat on Jayne's shoulder.

"Okay, that's it!" Kaylee chirped from *Serenity*'s side. "All patched up. I mean, temporarily. I wouldn't take her into the black or nothing. This is strictly an atmo-only fix. And a… brief hop to the next town over sorta fix. More of a—"

"We get it," Jayne said, his tolerance for cheerfulness at a minimum with the constant sound of gunfire in the background. A hundred meters past *Serenity*'s bow, the duke's forces were regaining ground, pushing the insurgents back toward the landing pad. Not good.

"Wash, Kaylee, get back inside and hunker down," he said, taking a knee and peering at the action through Vera's scope. "Doc, honestly, you should too, you're useless with that gun."

Simon glared over his shoulder at Jayne as he finished up field dressing McElroy's wound and moved on to Ashana. "So you can conveniently lose Shepherd Book and do exactly what the captain told you not to? No, I think I'll stick with being your backup conscience, thanks."

Jayne huffed an annoyed sigh. "Your funeral, I guess. River, you're coming with us. You're a hell of a shot, could use you."

"No," Simon, Book, and Kaylee all said simultaneously.

"I can help," River said.

Everyone opened their mouths to argue at once, but Wash beat them to it.

"But then who will protect me and Kaylee?" he said, holding his gun like he was afraid it would bite him.

River leveled him with a frank stare that clearly said, "I know what you're doing," but she sighed and slumped her shoulders.

"Fine, I'll be your guard dog."

"Go on, then," Jayne said, then fired two quick rounds that sent a forklift up in flames, taking two of the duke's soldiers with it. "We got a job to do. Wash, take their guns with you. Wrap it up, Doc."

"Literally doing that right now," Simon said, winding a dressing around Ashana's bleeding knee. "You'll both be fine. If I give you something for the pain, do you promise not to do anything stupid?"

"I promise to do nothing at all, because I have a bullet in my knee," McElroy ground out, his head thrown back against the dirt in pain.

Ashana shook her head at his theatrics. "Gimme the pills, Doc. I ain't gonna do nothing but lay here."

Her eyes shifted to Jayne and she managed a half-smile, half-grimace. "I don't blame you. We're good."

"I blame you. We're not good," McElroy said, but Ashana punched him in the arm and he shut up.

Simon stood, rubbing sanitizer over his hands. "This probably goes without saying, but don't try to tough it out just because the pain pills make you feel good. You do actually need to get the bullet removed."

"Think I'll keep it, actually," McElroy said. "Think I'll name it George."

Ashana rolled her eyes. "Go do whatever it is you're planning, Jayne. We won't be following, obviously."

Jayne nodded, working his jaw as he tried to figure out what to say. It wasn't every day your friends shot your other friends as you went to attack their employer.

Eventually, Jayne settled on another nod. Nothing much else to be said, really.

Besides, he had some weapons to steal. Or, uh, destroy.

…or steal.

24

Simon wasn't sure he'd ever get used to being shot at. It was miraculous, truly, how the human brain could adapt to things with enough practice. He could literally open up a human being, poke around in their organs with knives, and not even blink at the blood. But the second a gunshot cracked somewhere near him, his nervous system lit up like the Capital City skyline on Osiris.

Of course, there wasn't a single safe place in the 'verse for Simon and River other than aboard *Serenity*, so he supposed he'd have to get used to it. Especially since River was apparently an excellent shot and wanted to "help." The thought terrified him, honestly, but that was a problem for another day.

Today's problem was plenty. Today's problem was a wide-open area between the overturned Mule currently providing Simon, Jayne, and Book some measure of cover and the armory they were supposed to be infiltrating. That area was adorned with well-laid stone paths, decorative streetlights, dainty flower beds, and a growing collection of bleeding soldiers. A fierce skirmish between the duke's troops and the insurgent forces had been raging since before their arrival, and it showed no signs of stopping. There was no crossing the gap without earning a whole lot of bloody holes in the process.

"Can we just… I don't know, shoot some of them? Thin their numbers?" Simon asked, wincing even as the words left his mouth. He sounded like an ignorant, combat-inexperienced Core worlder. Which, of course, he was, but he liked to think of himself as a little bit more worldly these days. Jayne snorted a laugh, as expected, but answered his question anyway.

"The second we start picking people off it'll give away our position and they'll pile up on us. If we had some way to talk to the folks on our side, that'd be one thing, but…"

Shepherd Book pulled out his comm.

"We may not be able to talk to them, but we aren't totally alone, at least." He keyed the comm to the crew frequency. "Captain, this is Book. We're on our way to the armory, but they've got us blocked off. Are there any reinforcements available?"

A pause, then Mal's voice replied.

"We're on our way to the palace from the gates. Might be we could swing by and lend a hand."

"That'd be shiny," Jayne said. "Once you start shooting, we can start shooting."

"Sounds like a plan. We'll try to get some high ground," Mal said, then closed the channel. Barely two minutes later, several new shots rained down on the duke's soldiers from the direction of a residential area bordering the battlefield. Chaos erupted as everyone on both sides scrambled to find the location of the new shooters.

"That's our cue," Book said, keeping his pistol lowered as Jayne added his own fire to Mal's and Zoë's. Simon supposed this didn't count as self-defense to Book, since no one was directly attacking them. For his own part, Simon kept his pistol firmly pointed away from any living target. He knew his own strengths and weaknesses well enough to know there wasn't a chance in hell of him intentionally hitting a foe—and plenty of chance that he'd hit a friendly by accident. Originally, he'd been assigned to this job purely to keep Jayne honest and treat him or Book if they sustained an injury. But he had other skills to bring to the table.

Over the course of his medical training, he'd picked up some strong chemistry skills. And when it came to destroying something that couldn't be blown up, sometimes a chemist was exactly what you needed. That, and a surgeon's steady hands. Simon was tailor made for this assignment.

"We've got a path," Jayne said, snapping him out of his observation of the fight. "Let's move."

"Thanks for the help, Mal and Zoë," Book said over the comm, ever polite.

"No problem, preacher man," Zoë replied. "We're on our way to our main target."

"Likewise," Simon said, clutching his bag to him. In among his medical supplies were a series of vials that very much needed to not be spilled or shaken too much. Though it was unsettling to carry them around, it was actually more comfortable for him than the gun. He thought of Mal, all casually heroic with his pistol in one hand and his hair blowing in the breeze, and could not believe how far he felt from that image. He had his own role, though, and he would play it. *Serenity* was home now, and he'd make sure he did everything in his power to earn his and River's place. And their safety. He trusted Mal when he said they were part of the crew now, but others might take a little more convincing.

With the skirmish mostly broken up and the last remaining fighters occupied, Jayne beckoned for Simon and Book to get ready to follow him. At his signal, they sprinted across the clearing toward the armory, weaving between small ornamental trees that stood in little manicured and mulched rings. Wasn't much for cover, but better than nothing, Simon assumed. On either side of the armory entrance, two uniformed guards lay slumped with bullet holes in important places. Presumably that was what had started the fighting in the courtyard, their reinforcements coming to support and then avenge them.

"Hey, uh, Simon, Book, Jayne," Wash's voice said over the comm. "Caught some radio chatter. Sounds like you might have some more fun heading your way."

"*Zhēn dǎo méi*," Jayne grumbled. "Mal?"

"We're too far along to break off now," Mal said. "'Fraid you're on your own. I'll check with the general to see if she can spare anyone, but assume the worst and go with it."

Well, if that weren't the *Serenity* motto, Simon wasn't sure what was.

"I mean, this is an armory," Simon said. "In theory it's pretty well reinforced. Can't we close it up and hunker down? We only need a few minutes."

Jayne visibly wrestled with what should have been a very simple decision, which had Simon and Book exchanging a meaningful glance. The only reason they'd need more time was if they were planning to do more than just destroy the Devil's Thorns. They both needed to watch Jayne closely.

"Don't see we have much of a choice," Jayne finally said as they reached the armory doors. He went in first, leading with the muzzle of his rifle and doing a sweep of the first room while Simon and Book stood in the doorway facing out.

"Clear," Jayne called back. Simon and Book ducked inside, barring the door behind them and turning to follow Jayne.

The armory was essentially a giant warehouse divided into quadrants. A section at the back near two large bay doors held massive industrial racks of small vehicles, both ground and airborne. Another section was walled off with thick transparent panels that Simon assumed were bullet- and explosion-proof, given that the area was devoted to shelves of ammunition: crates labeled with grenades, rockets, bombs, landmines, bullets of varying calibers, and so on. The third was home to all things that shot that ammunition: racks and racks of standard-issue pistols, rifles, and shoulder-mounted launchers among others. A subsection within that area housed larger weapons that required stationary mounts and vehicle transport. The final area was for things that protected a person from getting killed, rather than the supplies for doing the killing. Armor, helmets, shields, and more, all arranged by size.

Simon, Jayne, and Book walked to the center of the complex from the main entrance and spun in a circle, taking it all in. The quiet inside was eerie after the cacophony of the battle, made all the creepier by the racks upon racks of deadly instruments. Somehow, Simon had thought the location of the Devil's Thorns would be obvious. Something so expensive and lethal and heavily restricted would be guarded, locked up, or at the very least stored in a brightly colored crate that said VERY DANGEROUS ILLEGAL SUPERWEAPON, DO NOT TOUCH.

As it was, most of the crates had some kind of warning label on them, as most of the things in this building were designed to explode in some fashion or another. A disturbing thought, now that Simon was actually standing among it all.

"So, any ideas?" he asked, looking to Book. For whatever reason, the shepherd seemed to know a lot about the art of violence and war, though he was reluctant to trot that knowledge out unless it were desperately needed to keep folks safe. Simon hoped this would be one of those times.

Book looked around at the four quadrants and tapped his chin with a thumb. "I would expect them to be stored with the ammunition. You agree, Jayne?"

"Don't know why it'd be anywhere else," he agreed. "It's a thing that explodes, so you'd think it'd be with the other explodey things."

That decided, Simon led the way toward the single door leading into the ammunition area, unshouldering his pack. Before they'd parted ways, Mal had given him a digital lock popper, along with a quick tutorial that had made Simon finally feel like a real criminal of the sort that belonged on *Serenity*. Something in Mal's eyes had said the same thing. This wasn't like the job on Ariel, where the whole point of the heist he'd planned was to get a scan of River's brain. All he'd had to do was pretend to be a doctor—not exactly a stretch—and tell the others what to steal. They'd done all the actual thieving. Even now, he wasn't stealing anything or seeking any profit, only destroying a weapon that shouldn't exist to begin with.

He affixed the lock popper to the digital security system and watched the red numbers spin through endless combinations, and it took that whole time for Simon to finally put his finger on what was different. It was that Mal had trusted him with a critical part of the mission. Two critical parts, actually: both destroying the weapon and keeping watch over Jayne. It showed that Simon wasn't just part of the crew in name, not just because of circumstance, and not even just because it was useful to have a doctor around. He could contribute to their work. He wasn't entirely sure how he should feel about that, but what he *did* feel was a strange sort of pride and warmth. Belonging.

This was definitely not where he'd seen his life going. But he couldn't say he was disappointed.

With a near-silent click, the door to the ammunition wing popped open, the numbers flashing blue with the correct combination. Simon pulled the door open and slipped in first before Jayne could rush through, immediately scanning the shelves for something that looked new, out of place, or… extra dangerous? He paused in between two shelves and sighed, running a hand through his hair. He truly had no idea what he was looking for.

"I guess we just start reading labels?" he called to the others.

"Woulda been so much easier to just blow up the whole building," Jayne grumbled from the next aisle over. Simon eyed him between the gaps in the shelves, watching as he pocketed a few grenades and other odds and ends, but nothing that seemed out of the ordinary.

"Your pockets can't be that deep," Simon said, just to let Jayne know he saw what he was doing. "Hope no one shoots you in the leg and blows the whole thing clean off. Hard to fix, you know: wouldn't be much I could do about that."

"You could let me store them in your little fanny pack instead," Jayne sneered.

Simon almost rose to that bait but stopped himself.

"Mm, nah, I think I'd rather not have any limbs blown off either, thanks."

He'd meant what he'd said to Jayne on Bellerophon, when he'd confronted him about his treachery during the hospital heist on Ariel. There needed to be trust between them, if they were going to be crew members. But there was trust, and then there was *trust*. Mal clearly trusted Jayne enough to have him aboard *Serenity*, but not enough to do the job that needed doing without supervision. Simon trusted Jayne on a daily basis not to simply wake up and decide to place a call to the feds, but he absolutely would be watching his every move until the Devil's Thorns were destroyed.

"Gentlemen, I think I've found it," Shepherd Book called out from a few rows over. Simon and Jayne locked eyes through the shelves, then went to meet Book, subtly jockeying for position. They found the shepherd standing beside a set of three crates that were stacked on the floor rather than in a cataloged place on the shelves.

"Seems about right," Simon said, studying them. They were, indeed, the same type of crate that had sat in *Serenity*'s hold during their journey to Kerry, but that wasn't saying much—they were very generic sealed crates with no external labeling or distinguishing features. Considering most everything else in the armory was labeled with the appropriate warnings, though, it did seem promising.

"Guess there's only one way to find out," Jayne said, and he unceremoniously lifted the lid off the top crate. Simon and

Book both winced and flinched back, which put a smirk on Jayne's face. Nothing exploded, though, so Simon took a few steps forward and peered inside.

Yep. That was it. Devil's Thorns. They matched Mal's description exactly. Not quite grenades, not quite rockets, but of a size to be fired from that sort of launcher. Seams ran over the surface of each projectile, showing all the places it would crack open after firing to release its deadly, torturous spores. They were bright and gleaming, clean and unmarred, with nothing at all to show on the outside that they were one of the most strictly outlawed weapons in the 'verse. Jayne and Shepherd Book each took one side of the top crate and lifted, setting it down on the floor, then repeated it with the second crate so that all three sat directly on the concrete.

Simon blew out a breath, then set his pack on a nearby shelf and began unloading small vials of chemicals. Once he got to the bottom of the bag, he withdrew three ventilator masks and handed one each to Jayne and Book.

"One of the stages of this solution will give off a noxious gas. It should dissipate after only a minute or so, but it'll burn your lungs from the inside out if you breathe it in."

Jayne rushed to put his mask on like the gas was coming for him right then and there.

"Why didn't you just mix it ahead of time?" he said, his voice muffled and echoing in the mask.

Simon took his time securing his own mask before he answered. "Because the solution is very volatile. It wouldn't take too kindly to being sloshed around as we ran from being shot at. Or being shot, for that matter. If it leaked, it'd burn a hole through the bag and probably me, too. If it—"

"Okay, okay, I get the point," Jayne said, stalking to the end of the row to take up a guarding position, scanning for intruders.

Simon looked up to make sure Book's mask was secure too before he began his work. He carefully poured one clear liquid into the acid-proof container he'd packed for the job, then added a few drops of a viscous pink substance that reacted instantly. The mixture sizzled and spat, and the aforementioned gas began to waft out. Simon picked up the pace, working quickly. He'd never made this compound before, but his research told him that time was of the essence, critical to maintaining the potency of the acid and to keep it from bubbling over and taking his hand off at the wrist. He added careful measures of two other chemicals before the liquid could get too out of control, and the whole substance calmed down to a simmer, then stillness.

Done. In theory. With slow, careful movements, Simon took a small handful of screws out of his pocket, given to him by Kaylee, all of which were made of the same metal as the weapons. He dug around in his bag for some long surgical tweezers, then used them to pick one up and ever so slowly inch it toward the mixture until it was nearly touching. Once it was as low as he could get it without breaking the surface, he dropped it, then yanked his hand back. The mixture roiled around the screw for about ten seconds, then began to eat away at it, melting it into a pile of goo.

It worked.

"Won't the crate melt, too?" Book asked.

"No. Well, not right away," Simon said. "The crates are coated on the inside with a barrier that will slow the acid way down. The weapons themselves will be long destroyed before the acid ever eats through the bottom or side."

"And we'll be gone, I hope," Jayne grumbled. "I ain't getting no torture spikes in me."

"We'll be long gone," Simon assured him. At least, that was his understanding of the acid, the crates, and the weapons. He could always be wrong, but probably best to keep that to himself. "Shepherd, why don't you stand back, just in case? You too, Jayne. The both of you can head back out to the entrance. No need for all of us to die horribly if this goes wrong."

"Don't gotta tell me twice," Jayne said, and walked away without another word. Shepherd Book stepped forward instead, placing his hands on the lid of the crate.

"I think I'll stay, if you don't mind," he said. "It'll be safer for both of us if you pour and I get the lid back on as quickly as possible, yes?"

A small bit of the tension in Simon's chest unwound, and he smiled appreciatively.

"If you're sure. Whenever you're ready."

Shepherd Book nodded, pausing to center himself, then lifting the lid off the crate as slowly as possible. Simon blew out a long, slow breath as he looked down at the neat rows of carefully packed devices, arranged two layers deep and isolated from the sides of the crate by shock-absorbing material. They were so brightly polished, so perfectly formed, and they had caused such suffering. Had forced him to euthanize patients out on the battlefield and witness the haunted look in Mal's eyes as he'd led them in the effort. He'd known intellectually that the war was still wound through every fiber of Mal's and Zoë's beings, but witnessing the way the Devil's Thorns had brought it all to the surface in such a real and visceral way had shaken Simon. It had also brought him a new respect for both of them—and, as their doctor, a new concern. He'd have to make a point of talking to them both about their mental health once this was all over.

Simon pulled on a set of elbow-high insulated gloves and gently lifted the container of acid. He was thankful all over again for the steadiness of his hands that had allowed him to train as a surgeon, and that now prevented him from shaking and spilling a highly corrosive substance all over himself. As he lowered the container over the crate, he had a moment of sheer panic that surged in his throat and shoved his heart into a frantic rhythm against his ribcage.

Every sense he possessed screamed at him to get farther away from the deadly devices, to hold the container higher and back off, but his logical nature won out. He needed to be as close as possible to prevent splashing that would injure Book—or himself. He needed to keep his center of gravity near the crate to stay balanced. He needed to tip the container ever… so… slowly…

He poured the acid over each row of devices, moving as quickly as he dared once the liquid was pouring. It spread over the surface of the top layer, then quickly dripped onto the bottom layer, occasionally soaking into the shock absorbers on the sides. As soon as the container was empty, Simon backed out of the way so Book could fit the lid back on top with quick, efficient movements. He flipped the latches that held the lid tight to the side of the crate, and then they both backed away, waiting. Waiting.

After a long, tense moment, a muffled *pop* echoed inside the crate, followed by a hail of tiny metallic pinging sounds. Simon and Book both backed away from the crate, eyes never leaving it, waiting for something to go wrong.

"Maybe we should at least move to the next aisle?" Book suggested.

Simon nodded, nearly laughing with the hysterical tension of the moment.

"Probably wise, yeah."

He set the container down on the shelf and jogged around the corner, crouching behind a large stack of crates on the bottom shelf. At the other end of the aisle, Book did the same, and they locked eyes, listening intently. Another pop, then another, until the crate clanged and jangled with the horrific clamor of death contained.

Then, the noises began to die away. One last *pop*, a rain of pings… and it fell silent.

"I counted eighteen pops," Book said. "That should be all of them."

Simon blew out a breath.

"How sure are you? Sure enough to open the crate?"

Book hesitated.

"Maybe let's give it a minute."

"Just in case," Simon agreed.

When a minute elapsed with no further sounds, they both crept into the next aisle, cautiously approaching the crate as if expecting it to pounce at them. Once they'd dawdled as much as was reasonable, Shepherd Book made the move. He flipped the latch on one side, waited, then flipped the rest and ever so carefully lifted the lid away.

Inside was a melted and fused mess of metal. The perfect shining orbs were completely gone, replaced by a twisted sculpture of half-disintegrated husks. A rain of tiny glittering projectiles covered every surface, the actual delivery mechanism for the nanobots and the paralytic agent. Simon reached in with the tweezers, holding his breath, and tried to pick up a few.

They were all fused to the surface. Simon's shoulders slumped in relief.

"It worked," he said, then stood up straight. "Let's do the other two. If there's any extra, we'll hit them again just to be sure."

"Sounds like a plan, Doctor," Book said. "While you're mixing this batch, I think I'll just go make sure Jayne hasn't stolen more than he can safely carry."

Simon rolled his eyes. "Probably a good idea. Maybe remind him that once this is all over, this will be the duchess's armory, and it's not a good look to steal from your employer?"

"Let him have his moment of faux triumph. It'll make the lesson sink in deeper in the end," Book said with a chuckle, and he walked away.

Simon turned back to his chemicals and rubbed his gloved hands together.

"Okay then. More highly corrosive acid, coming right up."

25

Mal pulled his head back behind cover just in time to miss the stream of bullets determined to riddle it full of holes. So far, the battle to take the duke's compound had been far more exciting than he would have liked, and he was ready to be done. First the entire platoon that had jumped the gun, kicking the whole thing off early. Then the forces from the other towns that they'd let in through the gates had nearly trampled them on their way in, then nearly shot them in their excitement to get to work. Now, they were cleaning up the last of the skirmish that had broken out in front of the armory, cutting off Jayne, Simon, and Book from doing their jobs. They were behind schedule, and far too many things were going wrong.

Not that he ever really expected things to go smooth. Not on his watch.

He leaned out with his Liberty Hammer at the ready, fired off two quick shots that both hit their marks, then returned to his crouch behind the foundation of a very fancy front porch.

"Zoë? How's it looking over there?" he called over the comm. Zoë was perched on a low rooftop just above him, picking off the last few stragglers in the courtyard outside the armory.

"They're in, sir," she said. She came sliding down the roof, caught the edge with both hands, and lowered herself down next to him. "Recommend we get back to our own objective ASAP."

"Too right," Mal agreed. "Can't keep our benefactor waiting."

They darted between buildings, dodging fire where it came and returning it where necessary, until they came to the general's private residence. A quick knock at a side door and a wave at the peephole got them admitted, and they ran to the staircase leading down to the servants' tunnels below the compound. They'd briefly thought about storming the palace from the front—or at least, Mal had, until Zoë had called him on his theatrics—but ultimately they decided that entering via the tunnels was both the safest and most likely to succeed. Meaning, the strategy least likely to get them immediately killed.

As they ran through the tunnels, they passed armed members of the Killarney Liberation Forces at every junction and door, all of whom saluted as they passed. Mostly they were the folks less suited for combat—servants, a few nobles, that dancer friend of River's. Folks who could hold a weapon and threaten someone, but wouldn't necessarily be good in a real fight. It was safer down here, but they could also do some good. The comm in Mal's pocket crackled, then buzzed with Simon's voice.

"It's done," he said. "All three crates have been completely destroyed."

Mal blew out a breath, and one small piece of the tension in his chest fell away.

"Thank you, Doc. Job well done. You three get yourselves back to *Serenity* in case this goes pear-shaped. We'll be in touch."

"Roger that," Simon replied, and Mal snorted. Fancy doctor trying to sound all military-like. Though Mal wouldn't mind Simon actually obeying orders and showing a little respect more often. Maybe this mission would have a positive influence on him.

"You heard that?" he asked Zoë.

"Sure did, sir," she replied. "Like music."

"Certainly is."

And weren't that just the best thing about having Zoë Washburne around? She was a top-rate fighter and a competent and trustworthy first mate, but when it came down to it, what they really had was history. The sort of shorthand communication and baseline understanding between them that made everything else easier. As soon as they'd seen the Devil's Thorns in action, there'd never been a doubt in his mind that Zoë was feeling all the same awfulness that was turning his stomach and clouding his mind. There were things they'd shared that no one else on the crew would ever understand. Horrors. And he'd known right from the start that he'd have Zoë by his side when he confronted the duke. She needed it like he needed it, to see the man who'd ordered the use of the weapon brought low. It probably would have been the better strategy to send her to the armory instead of Jayne, but it was never an option. She was always going to be his second.

The strategy called for making as little noise as possible on the way in, so as soon as they approached the door leading up into the palace, he silenced the comm. Near the door stood a small contingent of insurgent forces, all armed to the teeth and gathered in a ring around the duchess and Inara. The general was with them, walking from person to person and speaking to each in a low voice. Bits of black hair were falling loose from her tight bun, and a still-bleeding cut on one cheek had been hastily bandaged, but whatever scrapes she'd been in had done nothing to dampen her fire. She nodded to Mal and Zoë as they approached, then rejoined Inara and the duchess at the center of the group. Mal frowned.

"Inara, you sure you wanna be here?" he asked, knowing even as the words left his mouth that they were pointless. "Anyone not strictly needed or armed should be sheltering."

"I'm here to be a neutral observer to the transfer of power," she said, her expression darkening as it always did whenever Mal tried to block her from anything, no matter how necessary or good for her safety and well-being. "And, as always, my business is none of yours."

Mal pursed his lips, a thousand arguments rising to mind, but he fought them back and shot her a tight smile instead.

"As you wish, Ambassador," he said, turning back to the general. "Who's coming with us for the initial incursion?"

About a dozen hands went up, leaving a half-dozen in gold-trimmed uniforms remaining.

"The duchess's personal guard will remain with us," the general said. "You'll be taking Alpha squad for the incursion into the palace. Once you have the duke secured, we'll escort the duchess to meet him. Minetti?"

A woman stepped forward from the group, offering him a salute.

"Sir, I'm Sergeant Minetti, Alpha squad leader. We've received word that the duke is taking his breakfast in the receiving hall rather than the dining hall, so I recommend skipping the kitchen entrance and heading straight for the central hallway."

"Thank you, Minetti, good work. Me and Zoë are on point. We're heading straight to the receiving hall to end this thing, no pit stops. We have a diversion going outside, so the majority of his forces should be occupied elsewhere. This should be nearly bloodless, but be prepared for anything. Good?"

A chorus of murmured replies acknowledged the plan, so Mal turned to Zoë to receive her final ready check, then tossed a salute to the general and the duchess.

"Hopefully ten minutes, no more," he said.

The duchess inclined her head, regal to the last. "We'll be awaiting word from our forces. Thank you again for your help, Captain Reynolds."

Mal searched for a quip that could encompass his full reasoning for doing this. That as much as he hated getting involved in other people's business, he also couldn't stand by and watch while some wannabe king tried to arrange the world for his convenience. Abusing his people, threatening their liberty, destroying their land, and denying them the basic services they needed to have a decent life—no, there was no world in which Malcolm Reynolds could have stood by and watched that happen, even without the Devil's Thorns in the picture. But it was too much to express in one quick phrase, tossed out with a casual confidence bordering on arrogance.

He settled for a nod, then began the climb up the stairs to the duke's palace.

The palace was quiet inside, and Mal couldn't decide if that was a good thing or a bad thing.

Once they reached the main level, Mal cracked the stairwell door open and paused to listen, trying to gauge direction for what little combat sounds he could hear. All seemed to be coming from outside, bleeding through the floor-to-ceiling windows that flanked the main entrance. He eased the door open to get a visual assessment, slow and quiet, and began to lean out to take a look—until a bullet splintered the frame directly next to his ear. He jerked backward, his heart jackhammering away with the adrenaline of the near miss.

"*Wǒ de mā!* That is happening way too often today," he said. "I only spotted two."

"Let's rush, sir," Zoë said, cocking her Mare's Leg. "Don't much like being bottlenecked up here."

"Yeah, they won't be shooting no fish in this barrel. Let's go," he called back, then dove out of the doorway and kept low. The crack of Zoë's weapon was impossibly loud in the opulently appointed hallways of the palace, every surface flat and reflective. Mal added his own to it. There were the two guards he had originally spotted at the far end of the hall, dressed in the same style of uniform as the duchess's personal guards, but edged in silver instead of gold. The duke's personal guards. Perfect. If they could take them out before ever getting to the duke, that would make things infinitely easier. Both quickly fell to the combined fire of Zoë and the rest of the Killarney Liberation Forces, but that left at least four more somewhere in the palace.

Then Mal's left arm exploded in burning hot pain as the unfortunately familiar sledgehammer feeling of being shot slammed into his shoulder.

"*Tā mā de!*" he swore, spinning to look behind them as he fell to one knee.

Well, there were the rest of the duke's guards.

"Behind!" he called out, but too late. Gunfire took out three more of their force before they could scatter and react. Zoë managed to wedge herself behind a fancy polished wooden piece of cabinetry, which surely had some kind of name Mal had never encountered, and leaned out with her Mare's Leg to fire again and again. She managed to hit one of the guards square in the chest and clipped another before they concentrated fire on her hiding place, blowing splinters and chunks off the front corner of the cabinet.

Zoë made herself as small as possible as her cover shrank, her knees drawn tight up to her chest and her arms over her head. Even still, the toes of her boots were sticking out. She needed help. A member of Alpha squad leapt out from cover and fired twice, the crack of her rifle clear above the smaller arms. One of her bullets found a home in the chest of the guard blasting away at Zoë's cover.

The other missed.

Its intended target returned fire.

The squad member's momentum carried her across the hall, and she collapsed next to Mal with a cry of pain, her weapon clattering to the floor. He glanced down for a split-second evaluation… and saw the scattered rain of arterial blood soak into his trousers as it spurted from her leg in time with her pulse.

Not good.

Instinct kicked in. Mal holstered his gun and ripped the orange armband from his own arm, pressing it down over the wound as hard as he dared with his uninjured arm. The wounded woman cried out, her face going pale.

"Medic!" he barked. "Do we have a medic in this squad?"

He should have checked before they charged in. Stupid mistake. He must be getting old.

"Stay with me, you'll be okay," he murmured to the woman, then raised his voice back to a shout. "*Mǎ shàng!* Where is that medic?"

A young man ran in a crouch across the hallway with a small satchel on his back, landing on his knees in front of Mal. His eyes skipped back and forth between the bleeding hole in Mal's shoulder and the injured soldier beneath him, clearly unused to real combat action or triage under pressure. Probably took a Cortex course on field dressing and, in an operation as slapdash as this, that had qualified him to carry the med pack.

"Take care of her first," Mal snapped, a hand pressed over his own bleeding wound. "Better patch that up quick or she'll bleed out right here."

The kid went wide-eyed, but nodded all the same, rifling through the pack with shaking hands until he came up with a tourniquet and a pressure bandage. Mal watched just long enough to ensure the young medic actually knew what he was doing well enough to save the soldier's life, then drew his weapon again and leaned out to assess the situation. Reinforcements had been called, but the fighting was winding down. One of the duke's guards leaned out to take a shot, but Mal caught him low in the chest with a shot from his Liberty Hammer. Someone should tell these people that shiny trim on a uniform was a really stupid idea. Made for much easier targeting. Prodding fingers at his aching shoulder drew him back behind cover and he shook the kid off.

"Think it was just a graze. Slap a bandage on it and we'll call it good for now."

"Captain, I really think—" the kid started, but Mal cut him off.

"It's fine. I've got my own doctor back aboard my ship. Unless you tell me this little mosquito bite is life-threatening, I'm moving on the second this hall is cleared."

"Mosquito bite" was perhaps making a bit too light of it—his shoulder did, in fact, hurt like hell and was soaking his shirt with blood, but not at a rate that seemed dangerous. The poor kid looked like he wanted to argue, but did as ordered, digging through the pack for a sterile bandage he could apply to the area. Mal glanced down at the fallen soldier beside him to see her passed out, but no longer spurting blood or soaking her pant leg with it. For all his inexperience, the young medic had probably saved her life. As he returned with a bandage for Mal's shoulder, Mal caught his eye and gave him a nod.

"Good work, kid. You saved a life today. Make sure this gets called in so someone can get her to the hospital as soon as the day is won."

The kid hummed an acknowledgement, focusing on his work, but eventually looking up at Mal with serious eyes.

"You think we're going to win, then? You think this'll work?"

Mal grinned. "Soldier, this day's already won. Time's just working to catch up now. You think a force as mighty and righteous as we could go down in defeat?"

The light that brought to the kid's eyes was worth all of what it cost Mal to say those words. He knew, had learned the hard way, that righteousness never guaranteed victory. That he'd said similar words to a dozen young soldiers just like him, on battlefields that had ended the day soaked in blood. The young medic didn't need to know that, though. He finished up on Mal's shoulder, flashed him a wan smile, then moved on to tend other minor injuries from the fight.

"Hallway is clear, sir," Zoë said, stepping over a fallen painting riddled with bullet holes. She narrowed her eyes at his bandaged shoulder. "You good?"

"Good enough," he replied. "Let's go pay the duke a visit. No guns ablazing yet. Man's a coward. Shouldn't take much to make him back down."

Zoë nodded. "The people here deserve to be the ones to bring him his justice."

"Ain't it so," he agreed.

Mal checked in with the squad leader, who broke the remaining force in half, leaving part behind to guard the hallway and stairwell entrance, with the other half trailing after Mal and Zoë.

As they approached the grand double doors of the receiving hall, Mal slowed, holding up a hand to the troops behind.

"You all stay out here and keep this entrance clear for the duchess," Mal ordered. "I don't want no one getting trigger happy and popping one in the duke before Her Grace has the chance to make her appearance, hear?"

The squad leader looked like she wanted to argue, but held her tongue.

"We'll be right outside," she said. "Shout if you need us."

"If I'm hollering, please do burst on in and come to our rescue," Mal said. "Good work today."

The squad leader's shoulders straightened at that, and she went about the business of stationing her people around the doors and the last stretch of hallway.

"Step aside, sir. I'll knock," Zoë said.

She clutched her Mare's Leg in both hands and brought the butt down hard on the knob, knocking it clean off.

"Pretty sure I heard them say 'come in.' Didn't you?" Mal said.

"Surely did, sir. Let's do this."

26

Mal threw open the double doors to the receiving hall with enough force that they slammed back against the wall. Inside, the small handful of nobles who were taking breakfast with the duke started so hard that their heavy, expensive silverware clanked and shrieked against their fine china plates. They were all seated at a round table on the far side away from the picture windows, which had heavy curtains drawn over them (likely fireproof and rated to contain broken glass).

The duke, upon seeing their approach, scooted his chair back from the table and turned sideways in it to address them. His face was cool and calm, as if totally unruffled by the faint sounds of explosions and gunfire coming from outside his walls. His eyes, though, were hard as steel and just as cold.

"Captain Reynolds, forgive me, but this is hardly the time to be negotiating business. Or perhaps you've come to lecture me about morality once again? In case you failed to notice, the insurgent forces are making a rather steady go of it this time, so I'm afraid I'll have to ask you to leave."

Mal smiled the kind of smile that tended to get him shot at and hooked the thumb of his free hand through his belt.

"Forgive the intrusion, Your Grace. We just got word from our distributor that there was a problem with the cargo we delivered."

"Oh really," the duke deadpanned. "And what might that be?"

"So unfortunate, really. Seems it got delivered to a lying, murdering *hún dàn* by mistake. We've taken the liberty of correcting the error," Mal said, pointing his gun at the duke. "And yes, there are many hard feelings."

Most of the noble guests at his table gasped, scooting back in their chairs or leaping to their feet. All but four of the women, who drew pistols from their skirts and pointed them at their spouses or the duke, as was appropriate. Zoë cocked her gun and leveled it at one nobleman who looked about ready to make a run for it.

"Have a seat," she said, nodding to his chair. The man slowly eased back down with his hands raised. The duke rolled his eyes.

"So, what, you've taken the cargo back and will just resell it to another buyer? And keep my money, no doubt. Petty thieves."

Ooh, that one smarted. Mal had a thing about being called a petty thief. He ignored the bait, though, eager to see the look on the duke's face.

"And let the Devil's Thorns go to some other sick *wáng bā dàn* who would use them again? Hell and also no, Your Grace. We poured acid inside each and every crate and made real good and sure that every single device was destroyed."

The duke paled.

"Do you—do you have any idea how much that cargo was worth? How much I paid for it?"

"Not near as much as the people you used it on," Zoë snarled. The duke's eyes flicked to her, then right back to Mal as he opened his mouth to vent his outrage. Mal, having known Zoë as long as he had, could feel the change in the air that came with the breaking of Zoë's fury.

Zoë stalked right up to the duke and cocked her gun, pointing it straight at his forehead.

"No," she snarled. "Keep your eyes right here. You will hear me. You will acknowledge the words *I* am saying. Don't you dare look back to the captain when I'm talking to you. You don't need to hear my words coming out of his mouth to take them seriously. Let me assure you—"

She pressed the muzzle of her gun harder into his forehead.

"I am serious enough for the both of us."

The duke's eyes narrowed, but he didn't move a muscle, staring coldly back into Zoë's eyes.

"You are lucky, *Tarmon*," she said emphasizing the use of his given name over his title. "You are so very lucky that I am not the one bringing you justice today. Whatever your people choose to do to you, I would most certainly have done worse."

A chill ran down Mal's spine. He hadn't seen this side of Zoë since their last days on Hera, while they were still holed up in Serenity Valley even after the surrender had officially ended the war.

"Then just do it," the duke hissed. "If you're so brave and tough, woman, why don't you kill me yourself? Right here, right now?"

Mal whistled. "Hooo, damn, you have absolutely no self-preservation instinct, do you? I would *not* tempt her."

Just then, a bout of quiet laughter came from the hallway as a messenger servant ran through the door.

"Your Grace, I'm sorry to interrupt, but air traffic control said the Firefly just landed and it was carrying a load of insurgent forces. If you see any of the—"

The kid slowed, then stopped as he took in the scene of Zoë with the barrel of her gun pressed against the duke's forehead. He started walking backward, slowly at first, pointing back toward the door.

"Ah. I see you've already heard. Well, never mind then, I'll just…"

And he sprinted out of the receiving hall. The laughter in the hall doubled in volume. They must have let the poor kid in on a lark. It did, at least, serve to bank the fire in Zoë's eyes. She took three slow steps back, her aim never wavering.

"Your life is not mine to claim. If it were, your brains would already be dripping into your very fancy omelet," she said. "But I do hope I'm around to watch when they take you down."

The duke heaved a sigh.

"Well, Reynolds, Ms. Washburne, you have me. This was all very dramatic. Congratulations. Now what?" the duke asked, spreading his hands and putting on an expectant look.

Mal grinned in anticipation.

"Now that we know you're absolutely no threat at all, we introduce you to the one who'll be running this sorry joint once your ass is in jail. She should be here any second, I think—ah, perfect timing!"

The duchess's personal guard led the way in with General Li at the front, her service pistol drawn and her eyes hard. They stayed in tight formation, concealing the other members of their party until they gauged the safety of the situation. The duke's mouth pressed into a hard line, his eyes blazing with fury.

"General Li," he spat. "I should have known. Colonel Blenner was supposed to—"

"Colonel Blenner has been taken into custody," the general interrupted. "I'm told he'll probably survive. He tried to play at defecting, but you should really choose your pawns better. He's never been anything other than your utterly transparent puppet."

The duke's lip curled into a snarl. "I should have had you removed the second I took office. I tried to respect my father's appointments, but now see where it's gotten me? I told him a woman had no place leading an army, but—"

Every gun in the room trained on the duke, the wave of fury nearly a physical sensation, and Zoë took another threatening step forward.

General Li shook her head. "I won't deny I've played a significant role, but I never could have done this alone. I am a leader of soldiers, but what this place really needs is a leader of hearts and minds."

And with that, the general stepped aside, along with the two guards flanking her, revealing the duchess Jīn Mèngyáo, with Inara standing behind her and to her left. The duchess's fine gown of golden silk swirled as she strode forward, her hair swept up in a twist that fully exposed her confident composure and frank gaze.

Mal and Zoë locked eyes, and he nodded to her to take the lead. Her lips twisted in amusement as she turned back to the duke.

"Tarmon Farranfore, may I introduce to you the Duchess Jīn Mèngyáo, leader of the Killarney Liberation Forces, and the person who's going to drag your sorry ass through the streets."

The duke's sarcastic, biting front finally collapsed into red-faced rage.

"You traitorous bitch," he snarled, launching himself out of his chair. Zoë cut him off with a blast from her Mare's Leg, straight over his head and into the fancy artwork on the wall behind him. Several of the nobles seated at the table shrieked, and one threw himself under the table on his hands and knees. The duke stumbled comically, feeling his head and looking at his hands as if searching for blood. The guards, Mal, Inara, and Zoë all chuckled at his panic, which only made the duke turn redder.

"You never did anything!" he shouted at the duchess. "You only ever sat in your corner with your ladies, drinking tea and painting pretty pictures. When did you ever have the chance to plot a coup?"

The duchess smiled, delicately pretty and sharp as razor wire.

"I was gone all the time, husband. You just never cared to notice. And that right there is what brought about your downfall."

She stalked forward, looking every inch the lioness River had proclaimed her to be.

"You never could see me as a real threat. Or see me at all, for that matter, nor any of the other women at court."

She paused when she was nearly nose to nose with the duke, then reached down to pick up his cup of tea.

"What you call drinking tea and painting pictures," she said, meeting his eyes over the rim, "we called plotting a revolution."

She took a sip of his tea and smirked.

"Guards, please arrest this man on charges of dereliction of duty, human rights abuses, and possession of a Class IV restricted weapon of war. Find the coldest, darkest cell in the compound and leave him there until his trial date."

She shrugged delicately as the guards came forward to seize the duke's arms and wrest them behind his back.

"It could be a while, though. New government to organize, elections to hold, people to feed, medical aid to arrange, new judges to appoint to the courts… so much to do, really. If you hadn't been so neglectful in your duties, perhaps we could have dealt with this more quickly. Alas."

And with that, she turned her back on the duke. The guards took that as their cue to haul him away as the duchess addressed the nobles remaining at the table.

"Latoya, thank you for the critical role you and your agents played here today. You four are free to go," she said to an older Black woman who sat at the duke's breakfast table polishing the gun she'd drawn from her skirts earlier. The other three ladies with guns—her agents, apparently—flocked to her side as she stood and nodded to her other tablemates.

"A pleasure," she said to them, in a way that made it clear it was absolutely not. Mal had never heard a middle finger so clearly communicated via voice alone. A pale man next to Latoya began to stand as well, but the duchess stopped him with a gesture.

"Oh, no, William, you're going to stay right here. You don't get to coast on your wife's dress train anymore. The rest of you seated here, I hope you enjoy your exile. I expect you gone from this estate in six hours."

One of the women still seated at the table sputtered in disbelief.

"But—but where are we supposed to go?"

The duchess smiled.

"Lady Charlotte, I am delighted to say that it is not my problem. Go to one of the other continents, leave the planet, whatever you wish. I honestly, truly and deeply, do not care."

Outside the walls of the palace, the explosions and gunfire slowly died away, replaced by cheers.

"Ah, I see the parade has begun," the duchess said. "Captain Reynolds, Ms. Washburne, Ms. Serra, would you care to watch the former duke be marched through the streets to his new home?"

Mal, Zoë, and Inara shared a look.

"Let me call in the rest of the crew," Mal said. "I think they'll all want to see this."

And, with that decided, the duchess strode to General Li, threaded her arm around the woman's elbow, and left to join the procession with her personal guard in tow.

Mal looked around at the shellshocked nobles and grinned.

"I think that went well, don't you?"

27

Inara sat on the low couch in her shuttle, preparing tea to chase away the morning's brain fog. There had been quite the party the previous night, and all of *Serenity*'s crew were rather the worse for wear. Not just from the party, of course, but from the battle and subsequent cleanup.

The fighting had ceased quite early in the morning, with the duke's parade of shame taking place not long after breakfast time. A few souls who worked night shifts and slept with ear plugs or noise machines had miraculously managed to slumber through the proceedings and had woken up to a very different world. The rest of the day had been devoted to tending the wounded, cleaning up the debris, and repairing the damage from the fighting. The last of the duke's loyalists had to be rounded up, and the duchess and general spent much of the day sorting out the fanatics from the ones who could deal with the new state of affairs. Messages were sent to all the towns and villages of Killarney, inviting them to send delegates to a new Killarney Congress that would begin meeting the following week to decide on a new system of governance. By the time evening rolled around, everyone had been desperately in need of a hot meal and a stiff drink. The duchess, anticipating this, had arranged for food and drink for everyone. Not just the nobles and the people inside Kenmare's walls, but everyone.

The weather had thankfully cooperated, so she'd had servants and kitchen staff prepping food and setting up long serving tables outside for the better part of the afternoon. Once night fell, the duchess ordered the work to cease and everyone to eat and drink their fill. The gates were thrown open, the townsfolk invited, and the musicians hit their first chords. It had turned into a massive party that went well into the night and the wee hours of the morning. A real "barn burner," Mal had called it, well into his cups.

There had been mourning, tears, toasting the dead, toasting the living, and ultimately celebration of their victory. The dancers had danced, but for themselves and their compatriots, not because they were ordered to by the duke to entertain his guests. River joined them, of course, smiling ear to ear as she whirled and performed complicated steps right alongside her friend. The people of Kenmare, Dunloe, and the rest of the Killarney continent opened up in a whole new way that really went to show just how bleak things had gotten for many in the territory.

The crew of *Serenity*, too, were able to take the evening to relax and celebrate. Zoë and Wash sat with their arms wrapped around each other swaying to the music and eventually disappearing back to the guest cottage. Jayne had reconnected with some of his soldier buddies who had either fought for the duchess or said their penance, and managed to draw Mal into the conversation too. Kaylee had spent the first part of the evening on the impromptu dance floor with some of the friends she'd made during the first two days, wearing a glorious green dress and laughing with a dark-skinned girl with a brilliant smile. Before long, though, she'd dragged Simon out with her to teach him some dances that he most certainly hadn't learned in Osiris high society.

And Inara had, as often happened, felt like a bit of an outsider. It was even more pronounced this time, though, as Xiùyīng and Mèngyáo laughed and toasted and engaged with their people well into the night, taking the time to hear concerns even as they sipped wine and drifted ever closer, hands brushing and heads bent close. It had been sweet to see, and it warmed Inara's spirit to know that Xiùyīng's strong and dedicated heart would be well cared for.

And yet, Inara had chosen to leave the party early alongside Shepherd Book, the two of them returning to *Serenity* for evening prayers and solitude before sleep. It wasn't that she didn't enjoy a good party, whether fancy ball or informal get-together, but her status as a Companion often left others too awed or intimidated to interact with her. And, with the rest of *Serenity*'s crew occupied, Inara had simply sat back and enjoyed a quiet drink with Book, watching everyone drink and cheer and whirl around before finally excusing herself.

That morning, Inara had briefly ventured into *Serenity*'s kitchen in search of a light breakfast to find a surprisingly chipper Jayne, a monosyllabic Mal, a cheerfully twirling River, and a Simon barely managing to navigate through eyes squinted against a pounding headache. Everyone else, Jayne informed her, was still sleeping off the previous night's festivities. And so, she'd taken her meal back to her shuttle for a quiet morning of meditation and reading. A lighthearted novel sounded like just the thing with a hot cup of tea. Though she typically didn't perform any sort of tea ceremony when drinking by herself, she did feel a certain sort of reverence every time she prepared a pot, watching the leaves uncurl and release their flavors into the steaming hot water.

She was fully engrossed in the meditative process when a knock came at her shuttle door. A flash of irritation bloomed in her before she even had a chance to see who it was, as these days it always seemed to be Mal being obnoxious. But then, if it were him, he wouldn't have knocked. Perhaps Kaylee or River had come to pay her a visit. She pulled aside the curtain, opened the door, and found Xiùyīng standing there.

"Oh!" Inara said, unable to master her surprise quickly enough. "Please, come in. I wasn't expecting you."

"Well, I didn't exactly give you any notice, did I?" Xiùyīng said, striding in and looking around with her hands in her pockets. "Is it okay for me to be here? I know I'm technically not your client anymore, so I don't want to intrude."

Inara gestured to the couch and the tea set and moved to retake her seat. "Please, join me for tea. You are never intruding. Besides, I think the events of the past few days go a bit beyond the usual Companion and client arrangement."

"Yeah, about that," Xiùyīng said, rubbing the back of her neck awkwardly. "Are you going to blacklist me in the Companion database for dragging you into a coup?"

Inara shrugged. "Everyone gets one free pass for coups against violent, bigoted men. Next coup, though, you're on your own!"

They laughed together as Xiùyīng sat and took the offered cup of tea, sipping gingerly. "And to think, all this began with a cup of tea."

"People underestimate its power," Inara agreed, wrapping her hands around her cup to enjoy the warmth it radiated. "How are things this morning? No unrest? All is well?"

"Just hangovers all around, it seems," Xiùyīng said, then sipped her tea. "How about the crew of *Serenity*? Is everyone well?"

"About the same," Inara said with a laugh. "Quite a few hangovers, and I'm surprised the snoring isn't vibrating the whole ship."

Xiùyīng smiled. "It was fun watching your friends enjoying themselves. There are quite a few sweet romances aboard, aren't there?"

"Yes, Zoë and Wash are an unlikely pair, but they fit together better than any couple I've met. They balance. It's quite fascinating," Inara said. "And sweet Kaylee and Simon are taking their time figuring each other out, but they'll get there. Sooner rather than later, I think."

"And what about you and your captain?" Xiùyīng asked.

Inara cursed inwardly. Xiùyīng's incredible perceptiveness and insight were a big part of what made her a great leader that soldiers wanted to follow. Having her Companion's facade seen straight through so easily was mildly unnerving, though.

"There's nothing there," Inara said, though she knew Xiùyīng would spot the lie in an instant. She quickly covered it over with a difficult truth that she knew would veer the conversation elsewhere. "Besides... I think my journey with *Serenity* is coming to an end soon. It's time for me to move on."

"Oh no, why?" Xiùyīng asked, her brow crinkled in concern. Her face showed real sadness at the prospect, true enough that Inara had to turn away before her own mask could slip. She busied herself with the tea while she came up with a suitably vague answer.

"I just don't think it's right for me anymore. I need some space from… that life."

"From Captain Reynolds," Xiùyīng amended.

"He's infuriating," Inara snapped, a little more harshly than intended, then mastered herself once again. She took a slow breath through her nose, then continued. "My time with *Serenity* has brought me wonderful friends and a firsthand knowledge of the 'verse that I couldn't have gotten anywhere else, and I will always be grateful for it. But I think the best thing for my health and well-being right now is to be in one place, rather than hopping around from planet to planet, some of which don't even have any decent client opportunities."

She looked past the tied-back silk curtains to the front viewport of the shuttle, where she could see the bustle of post-battle cleanup and repairs.

"I think it's time for a change," she said with some finality. Xiùyīng tried to catch her eye, but Inara stared resolutely out the window, her thoughts a churning mess.

"Well, fine. I'll let it go, but not before I throw some words from your own mouth right back at you," Xiùyīng said. "I think you might be giving up too easily. You never know what new paths might be created once the dust has settled."

Inara seized upon the opportunity like a life raft.

"Oh, so are you finally going to tell me what you really came here to talk about?" she said with a lightly teasing tone.

Xiùyīng looked away, blushing and caught out. "There's nothing to tell. Yet. But... I think you may have been right. There may be a new path to walk after all."

Inara sipped her tea, letting the pleasure of the good news suffuse her spirit. Xiùyīng deserved happiness. So did the duchess, for that matter. To see something genuinely good come from all this was a balm to Inara's aching heart. There was one thing she had to ask, though. It was self-indulgent, maybe even unprofessional, but in this unique case she allowed herself the question.

"You don't regret our time together, do you? Now that you know you don't necessarily have to get over your feelings?"

Xiùyīng's cheeks flushed, and she looked away, smiling. "No. Not at all. How could I regret such an experience? And, if I'm honest, it had been so long since I'd been... with anyone. I needed it. Me, just the human being, independent of the coup and Mèngyáo and all that. I needed to reconnect and do something for myself."

She paused, then her ears went red to match her cheeks. "Besides, if things with Mèngyáo and I ever do reach that point... well, I'll be grateful to have had some recent practice."

Inara laughed, loud and genuine, like she would with a friend and not just a client. She put her tea down before she could slosh it everywhere and covered her mouth to contain her mirth.

"Oh, *bǎo bèi*, you have nothing to worry about in that department," she said, patting Xiùyīng's knee.

They finished their tea, making light conversation, until Xiùyīng took her comm from her pocket and glanced down at it with a sigh.

"Duty calls," she said, setting down her teacup and standing. "One last time, then: thank you. Truly, Inara, I am grateful to you for your visit, your guidance, and your assistance. I do hope we'll meet again someday."

"As do I," Inara replied. "I hope you'll keep in touch and let me know how things get on with Mèngyáo."

"I most certainly will," Xiùyīng said.

And with that, she took her leave. Inara poured herself another cup of tea and stood, holding the cup up to her nose to inhale its floral aroma as she stared out the shuttle viewport. Everywhere she looked there were people chatting, carrying takeout bags of food, and starting in on the next round of repairs. Things were already improving, a new energy and hope suffusing the air, and it had only been twenty-four hours. Inara was willing to bet there'd be an understated but joyous wedding here in a year's time. She only hoped she'd earned herself an invite and would be around to attend.

Killarney would be a very different place by then. A better place. She looked forward to seeing it flourish.

28

Mal hissed as Simon pulled back the bandage on his shoulder, exposing his wound to the cool air of *Serenity*'s infirmary. He'd removed the bullet the previous morning (not a graze after all, oops), but insisted on checking it and replacing the bandage every eight to twelve hours.

"What do you think, Doc, will I live? Can I keep the arm?" Mal said, blinking up at Simon with feigned worry. Simon rolled his eyes and dabbed the wound with an antiseptic wipe.

"I still reserve the right to amputate later on," he said in a semi-distracted tone as he worked. "But for now, I suppose you can keep it."

Mal gritted his teeth against the stinging pain of the antiseptic but turned it into a grin.

"Oh, good. It's my second favorite arm, would be a shame to lose it. You're a miracle worker, Doc."

"Wonders never cease," Simon replied, pulling back to grab a fresh dressing. Once it was securely taped down, Simon stepped back and handed Mal his shirt, fixing him with an intent gaze as he dressed.

"I still have one thing I'm curious about. You said you told the field medic it was just a graze. Why didn't you just let them treat it more thoroughly on the spot?"

Mal shrugged with his good shoulder as he struggled to get his shirt pulled up over the injured one. Simon leaned forward to help, which Mal was quietly grateful for but never would have asked.

"What, and deny you the fun of getting to use your hard-earned schooling?" Mal said, starting in on the bottom buttons. "I could tell it wasn't that serious, and it weren't my gun arm, so I could do without it for the bit of threatening and monologuing the day called for."

Simon crossed his arms and leveled a stare at him. "But you risked infection and further damage in the process."

A fussy way of saying, "That answer isn't good enough, try again." Mal worked his jaw and nodded, thinking of how to phrase it so a man like Simon would understand.

"You never know when a battle's going to turn," he said finally. "I could have waited another few minutes and gotten treated, but those few minutes could have cost us the duke. Reinforcements could have come and smuggled him out of the palace, or another wave of guards could have hit us."

Mal hit the middle buttons of his shirt and strongly contemplated just leaving the rest of it open like a hero from one of Kaylee's romance novels. Doing anything with his injured arm beyond letting it hang there was a non-starter, now that the adrenaline of battle wasn't there to cover up the stiffness and pain. He kept talking to cover up his momentary struggle.

"Besides, that kid was totally green. I appreciate his work

and all, but calling him a field medic is generous. Why risk his shaky hands when I have my very own doctor right here on the boat? Top three percent of his class, if I remember correct, real genius type."

Simon's cheeks flushed, and he stepped forward to finish up Mal's buttons, which conveniently hid his eyes.

"Yes, well, in the future if it comes up again, I hope you'll choose immediate treatment over me getting to have a little fun in the infirmary," Simon murmured. He finished the buttons, then turned to clean up his tools and wash his hands. "You're free to go, Captain. We lifting off soon?"

"Soon as I check in with everyone, make sure everything's shiny," Mal said, hopping down off the table. "Thanks for the doctoring, Doctor."

"My pleasure. Try not to get shot for a few days."

"No promises," Mal called over his shoulder as he walked out of the infirmary, heading for the galley. He had a sneaking suspicion he would find most of the crew either there or in the cargo bay, all clustered together. They had a way of congregating after a job had kept them split for a while, a need to check in with each other and ensure all limbs were accounted for and all sanity was intact.

He arrived in the galley and found the instant coffee sitting out and a kettle of recently boiled water, but no crew. He made himself a quick cup, then hesitated, wrestling with his better impulses.

They lost, of course. He passed through the doorway off the galley that led to the shuttle airlock and nearly ran into General Xiùyīng leaving Inara's shuttle.

"Oh, hello, General!" he said in his loudest, most jovial

voice, which would certainly bring Inara running. "Didn't know we could expect a visit from you today."

"Forgive me, Captain," Xiùyīng said. "I know you're leaving shortly, I hope I haven't held you up. I just wanted to say a quick goodbye. Thank you again for your assistance. Kenmare and Killarney as a whole won't soon forget you and your crew."

"Happy to help, General. And, of course, very happy to have gotten paid for it too. Think we might even take a day off at our next stop."

"It would be well-deserved rest. Safe travels, Captain," Xiùyīng said with a casual salute, then turned to head down the gangway that would lead out into the cargo bay and to the boarding ramp. He watched her go, hearing the faint laughter of the crew echoing up from the cargo bay. That would be his next stop. But since he was here…

"Hello, Mal," Inara said from the airlock doorway. She leaned one shoulder against the wall, her hands wrapped around a steaming cup of tea, and looked up at him with a no-bull sort of expression. "I suppose you were planning on barging into my shuttle unannounced once again?"

"Now, what gives you that impression?" he asked, sipping his coffee with an air of innocence. "I was simply heading from the galley down to the cargo bay where, if my ears do not deceive me, the rest of my crew is having a dandy good time without me. Then, much to my surprise, I discovered we had a visitor aboard. Did you clear that with me and I'm just having a forgetful sort of morning?"

Inara scowled. "Zoë let her in, if you must know."

"Ah. Well, I s'pose that's okay, then."

He let the silence hang between them and sipped his coffee, watching Inara from the corner of his eye. He'd hardly seen her over the past few days, and it made something settle inside him to have her around again, even when she was glaring at him.

"You sad to be leaving?" he asked. She met his eyes briefly, then her gaze slid away, back to the cup of tea in her hands.

"It was a nice enough place, once the murderous misogynist was unseated and all."

"Yeah. Good people," Mal agreed. "Except for the obvious, of course."

Another beat of not quite awkward silence, then Mal gave voice to the question that had been eating at him since he'd first learned of the duchess's and general's roles in the insurgency.

"I'm surprised you got so involved. I thought you were supposed to stay out of the politics of your clients. What would House Madrassa think of you assisting with a coup?"

Inara's mouth twisted into a disappointed frown. He did manage to bring that out in her an awful lot.

"I'm not apolitical, Mal," she said, and he laughed.

"Oh, I know that. Supporting unification and all. Wouldn't have thought you'd be behind the plight of those people down there, given that."

A troubled look passed over her face, but she shook her head and moved past it.

"I know you see every conflict in the 'verse as a metaphor for the Unification War, Mal, but not everyone does. Every situation has its own nuance and context." She took a slow breath through her nose and blew it back out again, keeping that perfect unshakeable cool that Mal so wanted to break through. "I couldn't sit by and watch that horrible excuse for a duke restrict and abuse people simply for not being men, or wreck that strange and beautiful land he'd been given stewardship of. I got to know Xiùyīng quite well in our short time—"

"I bet you did," Mal couldn't resist interjecting. Inara sighed and continued without missing a beat.

"—and, by extension, the duchess. The coup attempt was going to happen regardless. I was in a position to save lives and support what I saw as the right side of the conflict."

She paused, staring resolutely forward without so much as a glance in Mal's direction.

"I've been wrong in the past. This time, I knew it would be right. No matter what the house would say."

Mal sensed a whole iceberg beneath that small statement, but let it rest. What Inara did and how she threaded the needle of her morality was ultimately none of his business. Much as he sometimes wished it were. They were too close to breaching that veil that always separated them, keeping them strictly in their roles as captain and tenant. And so, as he always did in this situation, Mal pulled back. Inara was the only thing in the 'verse that had ever made him retreat.

"Well then. We're fixing to leave shortly. Might wanna secure your shuttle for takeoff."

"Will do. And thank you," she replied.

The "thank you" was for more than the simple courtesy of updating her on their itinerary, but since neither of them was capable of engaging in a real discussion with emotions and everything, they let it stand alone. Inara gave him a faint smile, then turned and strode back into her shuttle, slipping without a sound between the silks that covered the doorway.

Mal stared after her for a beat until another burst of laughter and shouting from the cargo bay freed him from his hypnosis. He continued down the gangway until he emerged onto the catwalk above the cargo bay, hoping he'd find the rest of the crew there. Sure enough, Kaylee, River, Jayne, and Book had set up the folding table again and had their heads bent over the board game that had so bedeviled Jayne a few days ago. Zoë stood at the opposite end of the catwalk, looking down on the scene and calling down occasional advice. She cradled a mug in her hand, probably the same instant coffee Mal sipped. No doubt she'd been the one to leave the coffee out on the counter in the first place. She was notorious for it. Mal leaned on the railing a few feet away from Zoë and gave her a nod.

"Who's winning?" he called down to the group at the table.

"Remains to be seen," Book replied, studying the game board intently.

Jayne scowled. "Yeah, so he says as he mops the floor with the rest of us. I don't know about this preacher man, Mal. He's a cutthroat *hún dàn*, don't let him fool you."

"Oh, stop," Kaylee said, swatting Jayne on the arm. "Shepherd Book is a kind sort, and he just happens to have a sharp mind for gaming, don't you, Shepherd?"

"He also read the game manual cover to cover last night," River said, serenely reaching out to move her piece across the board.

"Now how did you—no, you know what, I'd rather not know," Book said, shaking his head and covering his eyes in mild embarrassment. "Let it be a lesson. A bit of time studying a good book can make a world of difference."

"You know, I do believe he means that to be a biblical sort of suggestion," Mal said to Zoë.

"You always were the sharpest knife in the block, sir."

Mal turned more fully toward her, careful not to move his injured shoulder too much. "Hey, now, I detect some hurtful sarcasm in them there words. I'll have you know I'm captain of a ship. Might show a bit of respect."

Zoë rolled her eyes. "Of course, sir. My deepest apologies."

Mal let the chatter below wash over him for a moment before speaking again.

"How you doing after that little encounter yesterday? Things got pretty heated with the duke."

On the outside, hardly anything changed in Zoë's expression. Mal could read the shift in her body language loud and clear, though.

"In my dreams, I pull the trigger," she said finally.

Mal hummed an acknowledgement. In his dreams, he would have let her.

"You happy about that?" he asked.

"The reality or the dream? Either way… not sure."

"Remind me never to cross you, Zoë."

"Yes, sir," she replied. The set of her shoulders told him the topic was closed. She'd be fine, though. The same dark creature ate away at her insides sometimes that he battled on the regular, but they had *Serenity*. They had their crew. And they'd have each other's backs, always. That would do.

"Think that husband of yours is ready to go?" he asked.

Zoë's lips turned up at the mere mention of Wash.

"Just waiting for you to give the order, sir."

"Thought he didn't like taking orders."

"Not from you," she said with a grin, and Mal winced, rubbing at his forehead as if he could physically erase the thought from his brain.

"Yeah, yeah, okay, great. Hey, folks!" he shouted down to the group below. "We're hitting atmo in five, pack it in!"

"Aw, come on, Mal," Jayne protested. "I was about to win this one!"

Shepherd Book shook his head and mouthed, "No he wasn't," from over Jayne's shoulder. Kaylee and River laughed as they began putting pieces back in the box.

"We got this, Kaylee, you go ahead," Shepherd Book said, taking the game board from her hands.

"Thanks, Shepherd," she said, then sprinted up the gangway to the main deck, heading for the engine room. "Reporting for duty, Cap'n!"

"Good girl, Kaylee," Mal called after her, then pulled out his comm.

"Wash, take us home," he said.

"You got it, Mal," came the reply.

They hadn't decided on a destination yet, but there was time to figure it out. For now, Mal needed to feel the wide-open 'verse around him. No fences or walls or borders, just endless stars in every direction. *Serenity* rumbled to life under their feet, ready to carry them back into the black.

Wherever they went, new jobs and new trouble would most certainly await.

ACKNOWLEDGMENTS

I still can't believe I'm actually in the 'verse. It's been a wild whirlwind of a year, capped off by this dream of an opportunity, and I'm so grateful to everyone who made it happen.

Eric Smith: My agent and the one holding the rope that keeps me from diving straight off that cliff. Thanks for reeling me in and creating opportunities for me. Also for inadvertently introducing me to Bluey.

At Titan Books: To Cat Camacho, thank you for having me on this project, for your eagle-eyed editing, and for laughing at my jokes. It was tons of fun to nerd out over these characters with you. Thanks also to the rest of the team at Titan making this into a book-shaped thing: Natasha MacKenzie for the cover, Sam Matthews for copy editing. I know there are many others I'll never hear about at both Titan and 20th Century Television, and to all of you, I hope you know your work is appreciated.

To Lisen, Dave, and all my other Browncoat friends over the years: Thanks for constantly bringing up that time I played a Companion in the *Serenity* RPG, many late nights playing the *Firefly* tabletop games, and cosplaying the crew with me. Please burn your photographic evidence, I made a terrible Mal.

Miscellaneous thanks: To Jamie, Leigh, Steph, Stephanie, and Mike R. for being great writing buddies and generally keeping me sane with your support and friendship. To my mom for helping me brainstorm this plot. To Kelly and Christy Jane for your excitement and all you bring to the bookish community. And, as always and ever: to my partner N for unending support, and to my toddler for bringing so much joy and taking good naps so I could get this written. Love you both to the ends of the 'verse.

ABOUT THE AUTHOR

M. K. England grew up on the Space Coast of Florida watching shuttle launches from the backyard. These days, they call rural Virginia home, where there are many more cows but a tragic lack of rockets. In between marathon writing sessions, MK can be found drowning in fandom, rolling critical hits at the gaming table, digging in the garden, or feeding their video game addiction. They probably love Star Wars more than you do. MK is the author of *The Disasters*, *Spellhacker* and other forthcoming novels. Follow them at www.mkengland.com.